Return to Atlantis

J.M. Dover

EVIL ALTER EGO PRESS

www.evilalteregopress.com

Evil Alter Ego Press

www.evilalteregopress.com

Published by Evil Alter Ego Press, 869 Citadel Drive NW, Calgary, AB T3G 4B8, Canada

Return to Atlantis, Copyright © 2020 by JM Dover.

Edited by Jeffrey A. Hite and Renee Bennett.

Cover by Jeff Minkevics, copyright © 2020 by Jeff Minkevics.

Interior design and layout by Michell Plested.

All rights reserved. Without limiting the rights under copyright reserved above, no part of this publication may be reproduced, stored in or introduced into a retrieval system, or transmitted in any form or by any means (electronic, mechanical, photocopying, recording or otherwise), without the prior written permission of both the copyright owner and the publisher of the book.

Publisher's note: This book is a work of fiction. Names, characters, places, and incidents either are the products of the author's imagination or are used fictitiously, and any resemblance to actual persons living or dead, events, or locales is entirely coincidental.

Print version set in Cambria; titles in Cambria, byline in Cambria.

Published in Canada

Library and Archives Canada Cataloguing in Publication

Dover, J.M., 1960-, author

Finding Atlantis / J.M. Dover.

Electronic monograph issued in EPUB and print format.

ISBN 978-1-988361-20-8 (pbk.).
ISBN 978-1-988361-21-5 (epub).

For Dan, with all my love always.

Chapter One

Adam stood with his classmates waiting for the tour of the Egyptian Exhibit to begin. He watched as a shimmer appeared between the stone pillars forming the doorway to the Temple of Dendur in New York City's Metropolitan Museum of Art; it rippled like the air above hot pavement on a summer's day. When he glanced around the crowded area, no one else seemed to notice what was happening.

He turned his gaze back to the gate. He never stepped into the gate, he never reached out to it. One moment he was staring at the ancient doorway in the museum and the next moment he stared up at another ancient structure.

The wide marble stairs before him led up to a building with tall columns across the front and down the sides supporting a flat roof with an imposing dome rising behind.

The Temple of Nethuns. In Atlantis.

This can't be happening again. "Why am I here this time?" he asked, not expecting an answer.

Two years ago, Adam had been transported to Atlantis through an underwater portal and he landed next to a gate at the edge of the fabled city. This time, through what must have been a portal inside the museum, he had arrived at the bottom of the stairs leading up to the temple in Atlantis.

On his last visit he had been part of a trio with Orri and Tya. Together they had saved Atlantis from destruction, and right after that he had been sent back to Earth. Adam had desperately wanted to return to the ancient city, the only place he felt normal. He used everything he'd learned about his powers trying get back, but nothing worked. It was as if Atlantis had abandoned him because he wasn't needed anymore. Out of frustration, Adam vowed he would never go back to the Lost City again.

Just when he had finally shaken the feeling fate ruled his life, he was back in this world where fate and prophecies controlled everything.

He wished he could hate this strange place existing in the thirteenth dimension, but it wasn't as simple as that. In Atlantis, he could do amazing things with his unusual powers drawn from the natural world. This place had shown him he wasn't weird, he could handle challenges and be strong. Because of that, he had a special place in his heart for this wondrous, destiny-controlled land.

He glanced down to see the tunic and loose pants everyone in Atlantis wore. The clothes he'd worn in New York had disappeared. Based on what he experienced last time, the change in outfit meant Atlantis needed him again. He knew he couldn't go back now, even if he wanted to. Turning away from the stairs, he gazed down the wide cobblestone boulevard leading away to the temple.

Normally the street would be busy with people going about their daily tasks, but now it looked like a ghost town. Crumbling two and three storey sandstone buildings lined both sides of the road. These buildings hadn't been falling down the last time he was here. He checked the horizon for the black cloud of dark energy that threatened Atlantis before. The sky showed no signs of the darkness. What was going on? Heaviness filled him like he'd swallowed a rock.

Putting his hand on his chest he touched something solid and cool hanging from a chain. His crystal skull pendant was back. His fingers wrapped around the crystal and a warmth filled his chest. The little skull helped him to focus and control his energy and he knew how to use it. *I need to figure out what I must do to save Atlantis this time.*

"You're back."

Adam heard the familiar voice with its normal sarcastic tone. He knew, before he turned around, that it was Orri. How weird

Orri was the first to greet him, just like last time. "I guess I am." Adam shrugged. "Were you just hanging around waiting for me to show up?"

The older boy stood staring down at him from the top of the steps that led up to the temple entrance. "I have more important things to do than that."

Same old Orri, he wouldn't help me unless he had to. No way Adam would admit he didn't know what was going on. "If you don't know then I better go find Noor." Adam sprinted up the steps.

When he reached the top, Orri's grey eyes examined his face. They glanced down at his body and back up again. He saw surprise in the other boy's face because he wasn't the skinny kid from two years ago. Adam smiled at the fact his eyes were now level with Orri's.

"I'm coming with you." The second Orri made the statement the stones beneath their feet shuddered. Adam lost his footing and fell down hard on the pavement. Orri landed next to him.

"Is it happening again?" Adam shouted over the sound of stones grinding against each other. On his last visit, Atlantis had been torn apart with tremors and earthquakes caused by the dark energy.

Orri didn't respond, he just stared down the boulevard. Adam followed his gaze and could see the road rolling in waves. A young girl stumbled into the street. She turned and stared at them with wide eyes. A large gargoyle on the roof above her teetered precariously.

"Watch out!" Adam shouted, but the noise obscured his words. She glanced left and right, appearing unsure of which way to run.

Orri still looked down the street.

This is why I'm here. I'm supposed to save her! Adam jumped up. His stance wide and his arms out, he shifted his weight like a surfer on the ocean until he found his balance. Rooting his feet into the ground, a familiar sensation, like a gentle surge of electric current, flowed into them. The warm vibration moved in waves, up his legs, through his body, and into his head. Adam focused all the feelings swirling in him into the small skull resting on his chest.

The carving on the roof rocked harder.

Trying to remember how to move objects he focused on the effigy. Before he could do anything, it tipped over the edge of the building.

"Run," Adam screamed as he attempted to deflect the falling chunk of sandstone.

The gyrations of the street caused the girl to lose her balance and fall to her knees.

Adam's hands shook with the effort he poured into them. Why can't I move it?

A second before hitting the ground, the stone shifted to the left. Landing with a sickening crunch it cracked down the middle. The gargoyle's grinning face split in half.

One side of the carving trapped the girl's leg.

A sick feeling rose in Adam's throat and he swallowed hard. "We have to help her."

"No," Orri shouted and scrambled to his feet. "It's too late. We have to leave. Now!" He grabbed Adam's arm and pulled him toward the temple entrance.

Adam yanked against Orri's grip. With his strength equal to Orri's, the pair stood locked in place. They had to do something. What was wrong with Orri? A tightness squeezed Adam's chest, the Orri he knew wouldn't act this way.

"You don't understand." Orri jerked his arm.

A cold breeze crawled up the back of Adam's neck. Glancing over his shoulder at the street where the girl lay, he watched a black void open underneath the gargoyle and the girl. In an instant, both disappeared into the cavernous hole. The mouth of the chasm widened and gobbled up the street like a hungry animal.

What was happening?

Silence gushed from the hole. The dark nothingness dragged at Adam. He could feel the blackness winning the battle to suck his body into its gaping mouth.

Orri's grip tightened and he pulled harder on Adam's arm. Seconds ticked by, each one an eternity, as Adam faced being eaten by the hole or being torn in half by Orri.

He couldn't breathe. The muscles in his chest and arms threatened to separate from his skeleton. A scream blocked his throat.

The hole snapped shut, taking the silence with it.

Adam heard himself groan as he crumpled to the pavement. He gulped for air, hiccupping to pull oxygen into his starving lungs. "What... what was that?" Adam felt as shaky as his voice.

"The tremors come with black holes now," said Orri. "We did all we could."

"We?"

"I added my energy to yours."

Orri helped me. He remembered how the older boy had become part of the trio with him and Tya.

"Together we shifted the carving," Orri continued. "But it doesn't matter, she was in the wrong place at the wrong time." He shook his head.

Tightness gripped Adam's chest again. "Is there any way to save her?"

"I wish there was, but the black hole sucked her into another universe." He made the statement as if this was a known fact and an ordinary occurrence, but something in Orri's eyes told Adam he was scared too.

"She's dead?" Adam's voice shook.

"It's not likely she survived the gravitational pull."

Adam leaned toward him. "What if that was you?"

"It could have been you, too," Orri shot back. Then his eyes widened, and he shook his head again. "There's nothing we can do," he said in a softer voice.

Adam stared at him, but the older boy shifted his gaze. "There's something I can do. I'm going to find Noor." Adam intended to jump to his feet and stomp away from Orri. Instead, he wobbled as he stood up and almost fell on the first step.

"Always Adam the hero," Orri commented. "Don't you think we've tried? We haven't been sitting on our butts waiting for you to show up."

Adam clenched his fists and imagined how satisfying a jab at the older boy's jaw would be.

A crowd of people streamed out of the temple. An old man leaned on a twisted wooden staff as he led the group toward them. His long white hair flowed into his white tunic, and the skin on his face looked like the bark of an ancient tree.

Chapter Two

Adam knew Noor was old, even by Atlantean standards, but he had never looked so ancient.

Despite all the wrinkles, Noor's eyes still twinkled with youthful exuberance. "I wondered when you would be back." His voice sounded the same too.

Then Noor's words sank in. *He didn't know I was coming.*

Noor turned to the people gathered at the entrance to the temple and raised his staff. The murmur of conversation stilled. "The danger has passed. You can go back to your homes." The mumble of the crowd filled the air again as they flowed down the steps. Noor, Orri and Adam stood at the top watching them go.

"Orri, find Alima and tell her to come to my office," said Noor.

"Is there anything else you need me to do?"

"Not at the moment, I will let you know when the council is meeting."

Orri nodded and trotted down the steps with no argument.

Orri helping Noor? This keeps getting stranger and stranger. Adam noticed his eyes were almost level with Noor's. The aging mentor stood taller than most even with his rounded back. Being as tall as Orri had felt good but being almost as tall as Noor only highlighted the changes since he left Atlantis. It left Adam feeling uneasy.

The creases on Noor's face deepened when he smiled. The warmth in his mentor's gaze prompted Adam to ask, "Do you know why I'm here?"

"Let us talk somewhere more private." Noor gestured toward the temple and they walked between the columns into the foyer.

In the middle of the foyer sat a life-sized golden statue of six winged horses pulling a chariot. Inside the chariot stood a tall, muscular figure of a man holding a trident. Adam had always thought the man looked like a younger Noor. Adam pointed at the statue. "He looks a lot like you."

Noor chuckled deep in his throat. "That's because he is me. Many years ago, on Earth they mistakenly called me Nethuns, the god of the sea. Although I do not come from the sea and I am not a god, I never corrected them. The statue was a gift from Earth to Atlantis and I have had to live with my mistake for a very long time."

Adam smirked. "Are you kidding me?"

"No, I am not." Noor raised an eyebrow. "But that is a story for another day, we have more critical things to talk about."

Adam glanced over his shoulder at the statue. Wow. He turned and saw Noor's wrinkled face again. No one would mistake him for a god now.

As they walked through the temple in silence, Adam's mind swirled with questions. Why was he here? What did he need to do? Would it be just like last time? And after his mission here was complete would he be unceremoniously dumped back on Earth?

He knew he could trust Noor, so he would listen to what his mentor had to say, do what he must do, and go home.

They turned down a hallway where a painted ceiling curved high above their heads. A web of cracks marred the painted blue sky and fluffy white clouds. Fissures covered the marble floor and walls too. Those weren't here before. The Atlantis Adam remembered had been ancient but well taken care of. "Why aren't you fixing the cracks?"

Noor sighed. "As soon as we repair them, they come back. We just leave them now."

A chill ran down Adam's spine. They weren't even attempting to fight the dark energy. He was about to question why when Noor opened a carved wooden door halfway down the hall. Pushing it open wider, he motioned for Adam to enter.

Across the room a large window overlooked the city, flooding the grey stone room with light. Noor's office remained as Adam remembered it, but the view of Atlantis had changed. He could see most of the buildings were falling down in the section of the city closest to the temple. Bricks and debris littered the roads. Another chill shook his body.

Noor gazed out the window. His shoulders sagged even more, and he shook his head.

Noor loved this city. How could he watch it crumble? "There must be something we can do."

Noor gestured toward two worn, comfortable chairs facing each other. "Please sit down and I will explain."

Seeing the chairs, Adam recalled his conversations with Noor in this room. During one conversation, his mentor had admitted to being his grandfather. Adam had refused to believe him and called him a liar. Raising his eyes to Noor's face, he saw the old man remembered too. The corner of Noor's mouth lifted slightly. The small gesture recalled the forgiveness Adam had also found that day.

Once they were settled Noor continued "The dark energy returned some time ago."

"Why wasn't I brought back when it started?" All the muscles in Adam's body tightened and he grabbed the arms of the chair.

"You know time is different in Atlantis." Noor frowned at him as if he expected better of him.

Warmth flooded Adam's cheeks. He couldn't argue with that. He knew Atlantis existed in the thirteenth dimension, and time didn't move the same way it did on Earth. Two years on Earth might be one year here or it might be three years.

"Time in Atlantis is not in alignment with Earth's. I cannot give you a sequence of events that will make sense to you." Noor's eyes focused on him.

Adam dropped his gaze to his lap to avoid his mentor's stare.

"The dark energy has grown. Now we can't repair the damage caused by the tremors. If we repair something it just happens again. This is why I believe time loops are happening as well as the tremors and black holes."

Adam nodded as if he understood, but the truth was he was more confused than before Noor had started talking. This time loop thing was crazy. How could he save Atlantis if time could reset? He would just end up having to save it again. "Do you know how dark energy is causing time loops?"

"Time loops are a result of time folding back on itself and resetting the present to a different place in time. We have not determined how dark energy and time loops are related." Noor rubbed his chin. "Perhaps your arrival before a destructive event will give us more information and help solve the mystery."

"Did I cause that girl to die?" Adam swallowed hard.

"A girl died?" Noor placed a hand on his knee.

Adam saw the girl lying on the pavement and his stomach rolled. Banishing the image from his mind, he told Noor what happened.

"I am sorry you witnessed that." Noor looked deep into his eyes. "I believe the girl would have died anyway. That was not your fault. You were brought here because Atlantis needs you now."

"Why didn't you know when I was coming?" Adam asked.

"We have no current prophecies to tell us that information." Noor leaned toward Adam. "It might help if I knew which portal you used to enter Atlantis?"

"I was standing with my class in the Egyptian exhibit at the Metropolitan Museum of Art."

Noor frowned. "The museum in New York City?"

"Yes."

A frown deepened the creases on Noor's face. "I did not know an open portal existed there…"

Adam interrupted Noor. "Is how I entered Atlantis important?"

"It might be. You wouldn't be able to come to Atlantis unless the time was right. When we have a prophecy, it will show us what to do now that you are here."

Adam sighed. He should have known Noor would believe in a prophecy showing them the way to save Atlantis.

A clap of thunder reverberated around the room. Adam stared up to see a large clear crystal skull hanging above their heads. It glowed with a chilling, icy blue light.

Noor focused on the crystal skull. "Hello, old friend."

The skull didn't reply to Noor's greeting, but he obviously thought it was the thirteenth skull. Blue flames wreathed the skull's face. Adam thought the skull's grin mocked him.

Can you hear me? Adam reached out with his mind to connect with the thirteenth skull like he used to. It didn't respond to him either.

In the blue glow emitted from the skull, Noor sat with his eyes closed and his fingers linked across his belly. A slight smile played across his lips as if he enjoyed what he felt from the skull. Adam could sense the energy flowing from the skull too, and it wasn't pleasant at all. He shivered.

Something was wrong. Very wrong.

Adam peered at the skull. The thirteenth skull was a part of a trio just like him, Orri and Tya used to be. The skull sat on a crystal hand and the two pieces were locked together with a flat, oval shaped ruby keystone. Adam, Orri and Tya had fought Adrian Zador, an evil businessman from Earth, for the keystone but he had escaped with it. Without the third piece, they had relied on the power of the great crystal to protect the city, but it was clear the temporary solution wasn't working anymore.

Adam's breath caught in his throat when he noticed this skull has no slot for the keystone to fit into. This was definitely not the thirteenth skull.

Another crack of thunder filled the office and the skull disappeared.

Noor opened his eyes. "That felt good. He always knows when I need an energy boost."

What was going on? How could Noor think that? "The skull gave you an energy boost?"

"My connection with the thirteenth skull has strengthened in the last little while. My age is catching up with me and I depend on him more now." His face brightened with a smile.

Adam had to consciously stop his mouth from falling open. How could he tell Noor, his wise mentor, that he had been fooled by a fake skull?

"It is getting late." Noor stood up. "Once Alima gets here, I will call a council meeting so we can discuss what to do now. You should get something to eat and then meet us in the council room."

Adam rose to his feet. His mind overflowed with even more questions.

Chapter Three

Adam stared at the cracked floor tiles beyond his feet as he moved away from Noor's door. The thoughts rolled through his brain in unison with his steps.

The skull Noor thought was the thirteenth skull was bigger than the real thirteenth skull. Adam had felt the cold energy the skull emitted, it was not warm like Noor believed, and it had no slot for the keystone. He knew without a doubt that it was not the thirteenth skull. The question was, how could Noor be fooled by that skull?

Noor had a powerful connection to the thirteenth skull. He believed it kept him alive.

The thirteenth skull with the crystal hand and the ruby keystone was vital in uniting all the counselor's skulls to create the powerful force needed to move Atlantis. Adam swallowed the sickness rising in his throat. Atlantis couldn't be moved to safety without that unified energy.

I have to figure out what's going on. But I don't even know where to start. Despair crept into his heart. He was so deep in thought that he didn't even hear the footsteps behind him.

"I am so glad you came."

Startled, Adam swiveled and gazed into the big grey eyes staring up at him. Unlike Noor, her wrinkled face hadn't changed at all and she still wore her hair in a long grey braid hanging over one shoulder. "Alima! It's good to see you!" Perhaps she knew what was going on. The heavy weight on his shoulders lifted just a little.

She reached out and squeezed his arm. "I was not sure you would hear my call."

"You brought me here?" Adam's words echoed in the empty hall. Last time, a prophecy had caused his arrival.

"Lower your voice. This is not a good place to talk. Come with me."

"But Alima..."

She held up her hand. "Not here." Her tone was so uncommonly sharp that Adam fell silent. He followed her through the maze of hallways within the temple. At the end of a corridor Alima opened a thick silver-colored metal door. If he remembered correctly, this was near Raine's lab.

The floor, walls and ceiling of the room were white marble, so white the room seemed to glow. A row of beds sat against the wall across from the door. They looked like the beds found inside any modern hospital on Earth, except for one difference.

Mounted on the wall at the head of each bed was a life-sized, marbled green crystal skull with several thick wires sticking out of both sides. The skulls didn't surprise Adam. He knew crystals performed many functions in Atlantis. They were adaptable and user friendly when you had the skills to work with them.

Adam had never been here before, but he knew without being told that this was Alima's infirmary. He found it slightly odd that both Raine and Alima had doors that looked the same.

Alima sat behind a small desk on one side of the room and gestured for Adam to take the chair across from her.

He sat. "Why did you bring me back to Atlantis?"

She leaned forward with wide eyes. "Because you must save it."

"How am I supposed to do that?"

Alima's steely grey eyes bored into him. "Your destiny will unfold, and you will find a way. I brought you here, and I am the one that will give you a way to go home when your task is complete."

Her words trapped him. She could hold him here the way he had been held here before. "This time I will make my own destiny." Adam jumped up to leave.

"Sit down!"

The command buckled Adam's knees, and he sank back onto the chair.

"I wish I could make it easier for you," she said reaching for his hand.

He pulled back and crossed his arms over his chest.

Her eyebrows lifted a little, but she continued in the same quiet tone. "In time, if you learn to trust your dreams, you will know what you need to do."

Dreams. Alima knew about dreams, she was a dream caster too. He'd forgotten the visions, showing him vital information that helped save Atlantis on his last visit.

Dreams. He remembered a recurring vision he had had over the last couple of years at home. The trio, him, Tya and Orri, standing in the middle of the Plaza of Athena next to the octagon-shaped altar covered with carvings. On top of the octagon table, glistening in the bright light, the 13th skull nestled in the palm of the crystal hand with the ruby red keystone in a slot between the two pieces locking them together. The council and the people of Atlantis were crowded around them, cheering. He'd had the dream so many times he believed it showed the true future.

A heavy cold feeling settled over Adam. Just before he returned to Atlantis new images had fractured his sleep instead. The impressions he had tried to forget came flooding back. Broken shelves and shattered skulls scattered about. A blast of white light shooting out of his outstretched hand. Orri's dust-covered face with tear tracks down each cheek. The terrifying snapshots had left him shaking and sweating.

Stupid, he thought. I should have known the visions were a warning. If he knew what was coming, maybe he could prevent the dark images from happening.

Alima interrupted his thoughts. "My visions tell me only you can save Atlantis."

Her words wrapped iron bars around his chest. "I can't do it by myself!"

"You are a dream channeller too, your dreams can show you the way." Alima stood up. "That is all I can tell you for now. Noor is calling me, so I must go to him."

But both dreams couldn't be true.

She gazed at him. "For now, it is best if this stays between you and me. There are council members who would not agree with you being here if they knew I brought you back."

Adam nodded.

In the hallway outside the infirmary he watched Alima walk away from him. As soon as she was out of sight he realized he hadn't told her about the thirteenth skull.

It hadn't been intentional, but Adam knew because of her close friendship with Noor she would tell him about the impostor skull, and he wasn't sure that was a good idea. He had to figure out what was going on. Noor thought the skull gave him much needed energy boosts. Even if the skull was fake Noor relied on it.

Adam rubbed his chin. The stolen keystone. The missing skull. Alima's insistence he had to save Atlantis—alone. Instead of learning how he could rescue Atlantis and go home, every piece of information he received put another nail in the door to his escape.

He wasn't convinced he could save Atlantis alone; even if he had to, he needed more information. Only one person could help him now: Tya. She had been his friend and without her he wouldn't have been able to accomplish what he had on his first visit to Atlantis. She would know what to do and he knew where she might be.

Adam walked down several hallways that twisted and turned in different directions. Some were wider with a variety of doors, and others had no doors, just plain grey floors and walls that seemed to go on forever. The temple still appeared much larger on the inside than it looked from the outside. But now, cracked tiles and fallen stones littered most of the corridors. Dust coated the floors, and when he stepped into it small puffs rose and tickled his nose.

With no one in the empty corridors to help him, he luckily only made a couple of wrong turns before he found his way to a door guarded by a big bear of a man. Horatio's immense size would have been terrifying except for the huge grin he had on his face.

"Hello, Horatio." Adam just got the words out before the man's massive arms lifted him and smashed his face into his substantial belly. Adam could smell cookies in the fabric of the dark blue tunic pressed up against his nose and he remembered the treats Horatio had given him and Tya. Unable to reach his arms around the big body, Adam patted the side of the man's stomach with his palms. Still Horatio didn't release him. Unable to breathe, he tried a little push. When that didn't work, he pushed harder.

"Oh, sorry." Horatio stepped back and squeezed Adam's shoulder. "I'm so… so very glad you're back, young Adam."

"It's good to see you too." Horatio continued to grin at him without saying anything. Adam shuffled his feet in the awkward silence. "Is she in there?"

"Of course." Horatio leaned down to open the door, handing Adam a cookie as he passed through. Adam had always wondered, where do the cookies come from? Maybe one day he would ask Horatio.

The door closed behind him and he stood in another hallway that led to the main doors of the library, finishing the cookie in two bites as he walked.

The library in Atlantis held all the knowledge they had collected over thousands of years. The information stored there was irreplaceable. The council worried it could be stolen or destroyed. So they guarded it, not only with Horatio but with safety systems created by using energy. Adam knew this place had better security than a vault full of priceless jewelry on Earth.

The uproar from other side of the double gold doors at the end of the hallway assaulted his ears. He paused and used his skull pendant to pull a soothing wave of energy into his body and up to his head. By protecting himself this way the sound became a low buzzing instead of an ear-piercing blast. As he continued down the hallway, the noise only got a little louder. The sounds came from the crystal skulls in the library, not people. Adam and

Noor shared this unusual talent. They could hear crystal skulls without touching them like most people had to. This made the library challenging because they could hear all the skulls talking at once and without the control Noor had taught him the resulting din would become overwhelming.

Reaching the end of the hallway Adam pushed the big gold doors open. As far as he could see the great hall had rows and rows of shelves reaching up to the high ceiling. The shelves held crystal skulls in many colors and sizes. These were the books and computers of Atlantis.

Adam drew a deep breath. The library smelled like the air outside after a rain shower, nothing like the musty book smell of a library on Earth. Tya, he knew, would be at her favorite table in the middle of the library. He headed there. Sure enough, there she was engrossed in what the skull in front of her was saying.

Skulls littered the surface of the table. Tya's long red hair fell like a curtain obscuring her face. Her hand moved from one skull to another as she listened intently to what they were telling her. She was so focused on her studies she didn't hear Adam's approach

Still the same, he mused. As he watched her, she tucked her hair behind her ear revealing the side of her face where he could see her chewing her lip, a sign she was deep in thought.

As he gazed at the freckles on Tya's cheek, a thought tickled his mind. Something about Tya had changed. Not just the physical differences that made a lot of girls he knew so distracting in the last couple of years, but something else. Now that he saw her, he knew he'd missed her.

"Black holes are the ultimate energy generators, but they evaporate over time." This from the larger green skull sitting to her left. "For more information on these theories refer to Skull 17, shelf 19 in aisle 111."

Tya touched an alien-looking yellow skull in front of her. "The radiation that is predicted to be released from black holes reduces the mass and energy of the black holes and is known as black hole evaporation."

"Hello?"

"Adam!" She jumped up and wrapped her arms around him, pulling him into a tight hug. "You're here!"

He stood rigid in Tya's embrace. The hair on the top of her head tickled his nose and smelled like wildflowers on a summer day. His heart raced, and heat flooded his body. He clenched his hands to stop them from encircling Tya's slim waist. He was torn between enjoying Tya's hug and pulling away.

Tya stepped back abruptly. The space between them was as awkward as the closeness of a moment ago. She wrapped her arms across her body and a rosy flush covered her freckles. "I'm glad you came back," she said in a quiet voice.

Her bright cheeks looked as warm as Adam's face felt. "It's, um-mm, good to be back." He stuck his hands in his pockets. "I mean...if things were better it would be good to be here." His eyes scanned this older Tya. The loose tunic she wore didn't quite cover up her curves. Get a grip, she's your friend, he told himself.

Tya raised her eyes to meet his. "That's why I begged the thirteenth skull to bring you back." Her face flushed even more. "We need the power of three, you, me and Orri, to fix what's happening."

Adam wanted to tell her it was Alima who brought him back, but the words caught in his throat. Instead he said, "The skull with the flames? The one Noor talks to?"

Tya nodded.

"It isn't the thirteenth skull." The skull had Tya fooled too.

Tya frowned at him. "How do you know?"

Adam remembered that look. Tya, the know-it-all, convinced he didn't have any idea what he was talking about. "I've seen the skull. It has no place for the keystone to fit into, that's how I know."

"No, you can't be right." Tya shook her head. "I would have noticed, and Noor believes it's the thirteenth skull."

"I know he does." Adam's voice softened. "Are you sure you saw a slot for the keystone?"

Tya sank into her chair. After taking a deep breath she peered up at him. "I never thought to look for it. The skull felt so right to me."

"That's what Noor said too. For me, the energy from the fake skull is cold and..." Adam struggled for the word. "The only way I can describe it is evil."

Tya tilted her head to one side. "Okay, if you're right, then where is the thirteenth skull?"

"That's what we need to figure out." Adam sat down across from her. "If we can find it, maybe we can fix what's wrong."

"Well, I know where the answer is." Tya gestured to the surrounding shelves. "It's always here, and with Caileen's help I'm sure we can get the answers we need."

Adam leaned forward. "Someone on the council must have switched the skulls. We don't know who we can trust."

"You're judging Caileen based on her father's actions. She's my friend and I trust her."

"I didn't say she's not a good person, I'm saying we should keep it between you, me and Orri."

"Caileen should be part of the group. She knows the library better than I do, and definitely better than you do." Tya's eyes narrowed.

Adam shook his head in disbelief. His dislike of the library was well-known, and Tya using it against him was a cruel blow. "That's not fair."

"You don't understand what's happening." Tya stood up and put her hands on her hips. "You left Atlantis."

Again, Tya's words punched deep into Adam's gut. He hadn't abandoned Atlantis. He'd tried to come back. His attempts to find a way back to Atlantis flashed through his mind. He'd gone snorkeling in the ocean where his family vacationed too many times to count but he couldn't find the gate leading to the fabled land. He'd worked on grounding himself and pulling energy into his body. The vibrations were there but no matter how hard he tried he couldn't make them powerful enough to allow him to travel between dimensions. He'd even convinced his mom to buy him a small crystal skull. That attempt had been the most discouraging of all. Adam could connect with the sensations within the little skull. But the crystal never held his energy long enough to use it to travel back to the one place where he felt normal. He hadn't rejected Atlantis, Atlantis had discarded him.

His breath caught in his throat and his eyes burned. Afraid Tya would see how much she'd hurt him, he turned and kicked his chair out of his way. As he stormed down the aisle, he forced himself not to look back. I'm supposed to do this alone. I don't need anyone else. *Especially her!*

Adam shoved his hands in his pockets and strode through the temple with his eyes focused on the floor beyond his feet. Standing at the entrance he gazed down at the main boulevard of Atlantis. The pounding of his heart began to slow, and his thoughts traitorously remembered the Tya who had coached him when he materialized inside a stone wall. And the Tya who had fought by his side when they battled Adrian Zador. He recognized she'd been his only real friend in Atlantis. The thought caused the anger to flow out of him like air leaving a deflating balloon, the weight of being on his own sat heavy on his aching chest.

He jogged down the steps to the temple. Maybe walking would clear his head. His feet led him to the Plaza of Athena. This was where the trio had received their skull pendants and where his triumphant dream took place. Adam reached up and rubbed the little skull hanging on his chest. The marble columns that used to surround the plaza were chunks of stone scattered across the tiled patio. In the center, the octagon-shaped alter lay split in half. His shoulders sagged. The dream about the trio saving the day couldn't be true.

What do I do now? The impostor skull had fooled Noor. And he couldn't talk to anyone about his conversation with Alima.

He could go to Raine, but the gruff scientist would want proof. Adam didn't know if he would be able to show Raine the skull, and he couldn't be sure that Raine wouldn't tell Noor.

The only person left to talk to was Orri. The same Orri who hadn't welcomed him with open arms. Nope. Orri wasn't an option.

I will save Atlantis. By myself, like Alima said.

A lot had happened, and Adam knew he needed to go to the council room.

The plaza plunged into darkness and he remembered Noor's comment on the interesting sense of timing the Time Crystal had. When you least expected it, the crystal would turn day into night. He chuckled, and the ironic snort echoed around the square. The light change reinforced the feeling he had to figure out what to do...and soon.

Chapter Four

A light tap on James McKenzie's door interrupted his thoughts. Samantha, his assistant, opened the floor-to-ceiling glass panel and stuck her head in. "Adrian would like to see you in his office when you have a moment."

"I'll be right there," James answered.

The door silently closed. He watched through the glass walls of his fish-bowl office as the slim young woman walked back to her desk. The archaeologist sat in his spacious, modern office on the west side of Manhattan looking down at Central Park. This space existed in a completely different world than the cramped site office at the Drumdrye archaeological site in northern Scotland where he had worked two years ago.

James had been reluctant to work with Adrian Zador. He didn't trust him at all back then, sometimes he still didn't, but the businessman had a vision to save the world. Adrian believed he could grow enough food to feed everyone on the planet. If he could find Atlantis and study their advanced technology, no one on Earth would ever go hungry again. It was this vision that had convinced James to work for Adrian again.

"You wanted to see me," James asked opening the door to Adrian's office.

"Close the door and have a seat," Adrian said.

James had gotten used to Adrian's direct, unemotional approach. The businessman had no use for courtesies. Adrian pressed a button and the glass walls became opaque.

James wished he could do this in his office, but this was an option only the boss had.

"I've just spoken with my contact." Adrian never revealed who this mysterious person was, but the information he had received from them had led to several useful leads in the search for Atlantis.

"We need another artifact for the crystal skull to work," continued Adrian.

"What artifact and where is it?" James asked.

Adrian leaned back in his chair. Something akin to a smile uncharacteristically skittered across his lips. "You don't need to know anything other than the artifact is in Atlantis."

Was he joking? A cold shiver ran down James' back. This was one of those times when he wasn't sure he could trust the man sitting across from him. "But we don't know where Atlantis is."

"With all the research I've paid for you to do, I think you should be able to figure that out." This time the corners of Adrian's lips did curve up, but the smile didn't reach the rest of his face.

An icy lump formed in the pit of James' belly.

Chapter Five

Noor sat with twelve empty chairs at the round stone table in the middle of the council chamber. The ceiling soared high above him. Ribs of stone radiated from a round opening in the roof and flowed in graceful curves down to the floor. This room had seen so many pivotal decisions made by the council. What would they decide tonight?

He had not slept well last night. To be truthful, he had not slept well for a long time. Maybe that was why he felt so old. He took a deep breath in and let it out slowly. The energy in the room reminded him of the strength of Atlantis. The city had endured so much through the centuries. Atlantis would survive this latest danger. It had to.

Noor trusted the prophecies; they provided valuable guidance for him so he could lead the council. If only he had listened to the prophecies and not left Atlantis all those years ago. But he had needed time on Earth, away from the responsibilities that weighed on him. He knew, without a doubt, that his selfishness had contributed to the problems they now faced. But if he had stayed in Atlantis, he would not have found love. He would not have had a daughter or a grandson. Adam, his grandson, the child who had been prophesied to save Atlantis last time.

He sighed. He could not change the past, but he would do better in the future. I must fix this. I will fix this. He repeated the mantra in his head, willing it to be true.

He nodded to each of the council members as they entered the chamber. The councillors who returned his nod he could count on to support him, the rest had him clasping his hands tightly under the table. Some chatted quietly waiting for the meeting to begin. Thuan and Andros both sat with arms crossed over their chests glaring at him. No surprise there. Both thought Noor had lost his ability to be a strong leader.

Alima gracefully lowered herself onto the seat beside him. She squeezed his forearm and smiled. Raine sat down on his other side. Placing his elbows on the table, Raine stared at a spot in front of him. Noor wondered why his friend was behaving so strangely.

Caileen, Tya and Orri arrived, followed a few moments later by Adam. The boy slumped onto the only empty chair between Tya and Orri and turned his back to Tya. Interesting, thought Noor. Adam and Tya were as thick as thieves the first time Adam was brought to Atlantis. Perhaps he would have to talk to Adam to find out if there was a problem, because he was sure the three of them would be needed to save Atlantis this time, too. No time to worry about that now.

Noor rose to his feet and the room quieted. "You know why we are here. Adam has returned to Atlantis, and as Alima predicted another black hole appeared. The black hole caused the death of a young girl despite the efforts of Adam and Orri to save her."

Several councilors gasped.

Noor continued, knowing he had their attention. "Now that Adam has returned, we must decide how to save Atlantis."

The room erupted in argument. "Maybe black holes are caused by travel between Earth and Atlantis. That's what the boy did! We should send him back to where he came from," yelled Thuan.

Noor frowned at him. Whatever position Noor took Thuan would be the other side.

"Maybe it's been Adam all along," said Caileen in a timid voice.

Caileen had only been on the council since her father had been punished for his actions. It was not like her to express an opinion in a meeting. Noor glanced around the table, by the looks on other faces at the table he wasn't the only one who thought Caileen's reaction was unlike her.

"Noor is right. Adam is here to save Atlantis," stated Alima.

"Send him home! We don't need him." Andros slapped his hand on the table and glared at Alima.

"We need the power of three. The boy must stay," Croston countered. "And sending him home will cause another black hole."

"How many black holes will he cause if he stays?" Andros fired back with a smug look on his face.

Noor knew he must stop the division within the council, but before he could say a word a voice resonated through the chamber.

The trio's power must not be
Alone each will come to see
Then they can become free
And Dunphora all shall be.

Noor smiled as he gazed up at the large crystal skull looming above their heads. At last, a prophecy to follow. Complete with bad poetry as usual.

"You heard what the prophecy said. He is not a part of the three. We don't need him." Caileen's voice was stronger this time.

"The prophecy makes no sense." Raine stood and the glow from the skull added a blue shine to his bald head. "The message isn't clear enough to show us the way. How will 'they become free'?"

Adam jumped to his feet with his hands fisted at his side. "I know I must save Atlantis on my own, but none of you can tell me how to do that." He turned to leave.

Noor could see how the prophecy pressured Adam, and he reacted the same way he did the last time.

Before Noor could stop Adam from leaving the skull thundered, *"Adam, Son of Earth."*

Then another skull, identical to the first, appeared. Noor clutched the edge of the table with both hands. In his memory, there had never been two thirteenth skulls.

The same voice filled the chamber again.

The power together must be there
Or Dunphora are found nowhere
Saving Atlantis they will share
And energy will come to bear.

Noor's legs wobbled so much he had to sit down. What was happening? There had never been two prophecies either.

Is the Creator testing my ability to lead? Noor wondered.

He watched the skulls float side by side above him. They cast no shadow on the surface of the table. Blue flames wreathed around the sides of their faces, and if he didn't know any better, he'd think they were laughing at him. Reaching out with his mind he hoped to connect with his skull, the thirteenth skull. Are you there? I need your help.

Silence answered him, and a heavy weight pressed on Noor's chest.

"You see what I mean." Raine gestured at the skulls. "This makes no sense. How can we follow both prophecies?"

"This shows us that Noor must lead us. He will find the answer," Alima's gentle voice carried clearly throughout the room."

Thuan pointed at Noor. "It's clear he doesn't know what is going on."

Noor opened his mouth, but no words came out. So many thoughts swirled in his head but overriding all was the knowledge it could be the decisions he made that had caused this catastrophe. What if he no longer had the strength to lead Atlantis? His heart raced.

Raine glanced at Noor before pounding the table. "This proves it is time for the council to lead. Following the prophecies has brought us to this state of confusion. We can do better than this. Ignore the prophecies and restore balance in our world."

"Well said," Thuan agreed.

Adam stood and left the council chamber without looking back.

Although Noor wondered what had caused Adam to leave, he didn't have enough time to stop him. Recently, certain council members had been insisting it was time to move away from the prophecies. What had happened today only reinforced the division.

Alima's hand gripped Noor's arm.

A warm glow infused his body giving him a burst of energy. "Listen to me!" All eyes turned to him, and Noor worked to keep his lips from curving up. I still have some control, he thought.

He gestured to the two skulls hanging in the air and projected his voice. "The thirteenth skull is my skull." The words reverberated in the room. I have their attention now.

"One of those skulls is mine. The other one is a test to try our strength as a council." Noor's voice boomed. "We are losing focus. Forget about our differences of opinion. We must concentrate all our effort on stopping the dark energy. If we stop the dark energy, we save Atlantis!" He raised his arms. "I will work with Caileen and Tya to discover why there are two skulls and two prophecies. Atlantis is in peril, so we do not have much time. We must work together, all that matters now is saving our beloved home and the people of Atlantis."

Chapter Six

Give me a break, thought Adam. It was bad enough to have one prophecy last time, but now there are two fake skulls and two probably fake prophecies. Where did they come from? And what was he supposed to do? Adam stared up at the statue of Noor as the god Nethuns. Nothing made sense, and the gold statue offered no answers. He'd have to figure out the stupid prophecies on his own.

After a moment of consideration, Adam slipped around the side of the effigy. He examined the white wall blocking his way, then ran his hands over the smooth surface until he found the marble tile with a small chip on one corner. When he pressed on the marred block, the wall slid silently open. Glowing crystal sconces shone a soft light on the treads of the spiral staircase.

Adam ran up the stairs and stepped out onto the flat roof above the foyer of the temple. He was glad it was dark. During the day you could look out over Atlantis all the way to the edge of the city. Still he wasn't going to take any chances, so he slid down against the side of the domed roof as far away from the edge as he could get. No one would think to look for him up here.

Adam hugged his bent legs to his chest, rested his chin on top of his knees, and hunched his shoulders.

Hearing someone running up the stairs, Adam turned. Orri stepped onto the roof. Great, just what I need. Orri telling me he doesn't want me here.

Adam scrambled to his feet. "How did you find me?"

"I know you better than you think I do." Orri smiled.

Adam opened his mouth to disagree.

Orri continued. "If I wanted to escape, I would go to the place where everyone would think I was least likely to be." He raised an eyebrow. "Because you're afraid of heights that means you would go to the roof."

"If you came here to tell me you don't need my help, I already figured that out."

"That's not what I'm here for."

Adam crossed his arms and leaned back against the domed roof. "Let's hear it."

"Haven't we got past that?" Orri looked at him with calm grey eyes. "Come on, we worked together when you were here last time."

"What about yesterday?"

Orri rubbed the back of his neck. "Yeah, I can see how you got the wrong impression." He pressed his lips together. "Remember when you thought no one was listening to you?"

Adam nodded.

"Well, that's how I feel. Something is very wrong. Noor's changed, and I can't explain how. I tried talking to Raine, but he's mad about something and doesn't want to listen to me. Then I tried Alima. She believes Noor will still be able to do what he needs to when the time comes."

Can I trust him? Adam thought.

Orri laughed. "I can tell by the look on your face you don't believe me."

Adam moved away from the domed roof. "Give me one reason why I should trust you?"

"'Cause we both want to save Atlantis."

"True," agreed Adam. "But this time the prophecy says we have to do it alone."

"The other prophecy says we have to work together," said Orri.

"But which prophecy..."

"Is real," Orri finished.

Adam rubbed his finger across his bottom lip. "Where do the prophecies come from?"

"They are given to us by the Creator."

"Who is the Creator?"

"The Creator is the one who made us."

"That sounds like our God. Do you pray to the Creator?"

"I'm not sure what that is?"

"Prayer is when you ask someone who's not there to do something for you."

A crease formed between Orri's eyebrows. "You know that makes no sense, Earth boy? We don't ask, we're told."

"Then why not just tell us what to do," Adam asked. "Why all the silly riddles?"

"That's the way it is." Orri paused. "Is that why you question the prophecies?"

Adam nodded.

Orri's eyes widened as he stared at Adam. "Maybe that's why you're here. Atlantis needs you because you question what we accept."

His heart skipped a beat, Orri's words made sense, and Orri supported him. Some of the tension flowed out of Adam's body. "I will do everything I can to save Atlantis."

Adam watched Orri's shoulders relax. "We need to help Noor."

Noor wasn't leading because he didn't know he was connecting with a fake skull. And now there were two fake skulls. Only he and Tya knew that. "Noor doesn't know that both skulls are fakes."

Orri's eyes narrowed. "How do you know that?"

"Do you remember how the thirteenth skull has a slot for the keystone to lock into? Those skulls don't," said Adam.

Orri nodded. "Now you mention it, I can see it. Maybe that's why Noor seemed confused. I thought he was just getting old."

Orri understood what was going on and he believed him. Adam's jaw relaxed. "When did Noor's confusion start?"

"About the same time as the black holes began."

"We need to figure out where those fake skulls came from," said Adam. "And how the thirteenth skull got replaced?"

"Someone on the council must have done it. No one else would have access to the thirteenth skull," said Orri.

"I agree and we can't go to anyone on the council for help because we don't know who to trust." Adam didn't want to admit to his argument with Tya.

"If we work together, we can figure this out," Orri replied.

"I don't trust you either."

"That makes two of us." A smile tugged at the corner of Orri's mouth.

"And the first time you try to kill me we're done."

Orri laughed. "Deal."

"I'm not sure how we're going to find out who took the thirteenth skull." Orri walked over to the railing and looked over the city. "The answer is here. In Atlantis." His voice was quiet and thoughtful.

Something about Orri was different. It was in the way he carried himself and the way he talked. Adam hated to admit it but Orri had grown up in the last two years, or five years, or whatever time it had been in Atlantis.

Orri continued to gaze down at the city. Fear caused a cold sweat to trickle down Adam's back. I'm not going over to the railing.

Orri turned to Adam. "We have to save Atlantis this time, not just protect her temporarily until a permanent solution can be found." His voice cracked, and he pressed his lips together. "I don't want to die." He stared at Adam with wide, sad eyes.

The consequences of not being able to save Atlantis hit Adam hard enough to take his breath away. If he failed to save the city everyone living here would die. He gazed back speechless. He took a step toward Orri and the view of the city behind the older boy filled his vision. He stopped.

Orri held up his hands. "Sorry. I forgot you don't like the railing. I'm not trying to scare you, really I'm not."

Adam shrugged, hoping to appear nonchalant.

Orri walked toward him with his cool grey eyes focused on Adam's face. "You've made it clear you don't trust me. And I don't entirely trust you. But we have worked together in the past. And the truth is, since the tremors and black holes started, I've tried to figure out what to do on my own. Nothing has worked." Orri let out a long breath. "I need your help to figure out what has to be done. Will you help me?"

Adam nodded.

"Come on, we need to get some sleep," said Orri as he turned toward the stairs.

Chapter Seven

Noor sat at the council table long after the room cleared. He ran his hand over the cool marble surface of the table, its solidness grounded him. They had made many decisions about the future of Atlantis in this room.

He had deliberately misled the council about the thirteenth skull. Although he believed one of the skulls was the thirteenth skull, he had no idea which one it was. He had always followed the prophecies but this time only one prophecy could be the right one. Again, he didn't know which one that was.

It doesn't matter, he told himself. Now that Adam had returned to Atlantis there are thirteen members on the council again and we have the right number to move Atlantis to safety. All we need is the keystone.

My time on Earth all those years ago must be the reason we are facing the effects of dark energy again. It is necessary I retrieve the keystone from Adrian Zador to correct the rifts I made in the fabric of time.

Noor didn't see any point in waiting for the council to meet again when he could get the piece needed to move Atlantis. The conclusion eased the tight feeling in his chest.

Just before they had punished Cavan for attempting to take control of the council, he discovered the lost vaults underneath the library. A vault for each location where the city had once existed. Inside some vaults were portals to Earth.

Adam had revealed the Metropolitan Museum of Art in New York City contained a gateway between Atlantis and Earth. Noor had visited New York during his time on Earth, he knew where the museum was. And through his past research on Adrian he knew Zador's New York office was a few blocks down 5th Avenue from the museum.

Noor knew his inter-dimensional travel had likely started the problems in Atlantis, but his trip to Earth was unavoidable. Noor would not make the same mistakes as he did the last time he went to Earth. He would use the gate, keep the time spent on Earth short, and have contact with as few people as possible. This was the only way to save his beloved home, he told himself.

Exhaustion flowed through Noor in a crashing wave. He needed to rest. At first light tomorrow, he would go to Earth. His age might slow him down but that wouldn't prevent him from completing this mission. With one last rub of the council table, Noor stood up and headed for his room.

The next morning, Noor nodded at Horatio as he walked past. Once inside the library, he walked between the rows of skulls heading to the portal. He took a deep breath, and clean air filled his lungs. When he let the breath go a sense of peace flooded his body.

In the back corner of the library he stopped in front of a blank wall and pushed on several bricks before a hidden door swung silently open revealing a narrow set of stairs plunging into darkness. Creating a glowing light ball, he set it above his head. The circle of light was bright enough for him to navigate the dark staircase.

Every time Atlantis moved, sections of artifacts were lost in the move. There were layers of these hidden treasures that went as far back as the Egyptian era where Noor headed now.

When he reached the bottom tread, the glow from the light ball revealed a jumble of artifacts, crystal skulls, and pieces of granite carvings piled on the floor. It reminded Noor of Raine's lab. A musty, uninhabited smell filled his nostrils.

Noor picked his way through the relics to a white stone wall with a row of symbols carved at eye level. Cavan had also discovered a scroll with the entrance codes to this part of the library. As a good librarian, Cavan had detailed records of all his research making access to the vault easy for Noor. He touched a few characters in quick succession and then paused for a moment trying to remember the next sequence. Tapping several more marks, he hoped his memory was correct. The wall vanished, and Noor let out a breath he didn't know he'd been holding.

In front of him stood the entrance to the Temple of Dendur, bathed in golden light from several large crystals hanging from the high ceiling. Noor flicked his wrist and his light ball vanished. Sitting in the middle of the marble floor the stone portal had two massive square pillars on either side of the doorway, and high above his head a scroll shaped stone topped the lintel. With the information Adam shared, he now knew the gateway's twin sat in the Metropolitan Museum of Art in New York City.

Cavan's notes also told Noor the Temple on Earth originally sat on the banks of the Nile. In the Earth year 1968, Egypt gave it to the United States in recognition of their help to save Egyptian monuments threatened by the rising waters of the Nile.

Although it had not been used for many centuries, Noor believed now it was a stable hole between dimensions. Once he was on the other side, he would have enough time to track down Adrian Zador and get the keystone back. He wouldn't be on Earth more than an Earth hour, and that would minimize any damage he would cause in Atlantis.

Noor centered the energy within his body and stepped through the portal. His heart skipped a beat, and he stood on the other side of the gateway in the museum. Luck was on his side, no one was in the room when he stepped through.

His hands smoothed down the dark business suit his robes had transformed into, and he adjusted the tie that felt like a noose around his neck.

Striding out of the Egyptian exhibit he moved into a large room filled with people. The marble floor and the huge stone arches reminded him of home. Noise echoed off the hard stone surfaces, and it sounded similar to all the skulls in the library of Atlantis talking at once. A stream of people moved toward tall marble columns at one side of the room. Noor followed them and a couple of minutes later he stood on the pavement beside 5th Avenue.

The warm spring air, the traffic on one side, and Central Park on the other brought back memories of his time on Earth. There was nothing like the energy of a busy city. It filled him with the certainty his mission would be successful.

He turned right and walked down the busy sidewalk toward Farscope Foundation's offices. Noor entered the revolving glass door of the building. After making an unplanned circuit within the rotating entrance, he exited into the two-story foyer. The huge glass wall above the door filled the space with light. He shook his head. He must remember the quirks of navigating Earth's technology to avoid looking like a fool.

Noor, cloaked in a shield of energy, stepped up to the security station. He announced to the guard, "I'm Nathan Atilan, a business associate of Adrian's." Because of the shield the guard saw someone he recognized, and he let Noor in without question.

He got in an elevator and pushed the button for the top floor. Noor stepped out on the top floor where Adrian's office was located. With his energy shield in place, he walked up to the marble reception desk.

"I have an appointment with Adrian," he said to the pretty young woman sitting there hoping his confidence would get him in to see Zador.

"He isn't here," she said as she tapped on a rectangular glass screen. "That's strange. I see nothing on his schedule." She shook her head. "I'm sorry, but he's not expected back in the office until tomorrow. I will let him know you were here, what is your name?"

Noor's heart sank and his knees weakened. His ill-conceived plan fell apart with the young woman's words.

"No need to bother him. I will contact him later." Noor tried to force his mouth into a smile. "Thank you," he mumbled and turned back to the elevators.

Noor exited the building and stood on the sidewalk for a moment before turning back to the museum. It was a gamble

Adrian Zador would be in his office. How could he be so senseless? His shoulders slumped. He couldn't stay until tomorrow because the risk of damage to the space-time continuum was too great. He had no choice but to leave without the keystone.

Ten minutes later Noor climbed the steps to the museum's entrance. Noor pushed on the handle and the door didn't budge. He tried pulling, and still nothing moved. His stomach flipped over. He rattled the door praying for it to open. What was going on?

Then he saw the hours the museum was open and knew he hadn't accounted for the way time worked on Earth. Pull yourself together old man, he chastised himself. The museum had closed, and another part of his plan had gone wrong.

He leaned against the locked door of the museum, fighting to stop his knees from buckling. I'm just a foolish old man. He gazed across the avenue at Central Park. Atlantis wouldn't be at the brink of destruction if one meeting with Adrian Zador could solve the city's problems.

Returning to Atlantis using an open portal was important, or he might cause another earthquake or black hole. But how to get to the portal?

A moment later a chuckle bubbled out of Noor's mouth. A woman walking by frowned at him and moved quickly away. The answer was simple, he could transport himself to the gate inside the museum. It wasn't crossing dimensions, and the only cost was using the last of his diminished energy. He would have to rest when he got back to Atlantis before he could use energy again.

A short time later Noor was back in Atlantis. He remembered how he had judged Adam for being reckless the last time the boy was in Atlantis. Now the one acting rash was him.

Chapter Eight

Adam awoke before Orri. A lot had happened, and he needed some time to clear his head. He dressed quietly, left the room, and wandered in the general direction of the temple steps.

Sitting at the top of the stairs he gazed at the city spread out at his feet.

The crystal skulls were fake, then the prophecies were probably fake too. Finding the real thirteenth skull was the only way to figure out what was really going on. The answer was simple and logical: before they could help Noor, they had to find the real thirteenth skull.

Unfortunately, while the answer was simple, the solution was not that easy. Adam didn't know where to find the real skull. What he did know was where the fake ones could be contacted. He turned toward the council room. The promise he'd made to Orri stopped him from taking another step. With a sigh, he swiveled toward their room knowing he had to include Orri.

Adam burst into the room he shared with Orri. "We have to find out where the thirteenth skull is."

Orri sat up in bed and rubbed his eyes. "How are we going to do that?"

Adam sat on the edge of his bed and popped a piece of pancha into his mouth. He savored the taste of French toast with maple syrup. "I used to talk to the thirteenth skull. Maybe I can try to talk to it again."

Orri's eyes narrowed. "The thirteenth skull is Noor's skull. I thought only Noor could communicate with it."

Adam held up his palm. "Don't you remember I had a connection with the thirteenth skull. It would show me things. That's how I figured out we needed to go to Machu Picchu the last time I was here."

Orri nodded. "Yeah, I'd forgotten about that, but if that's true then why haven't you tried to talk to it already?"

"Because I've been a little busy," Adam snapped. The truth was, he should have thought of it sooner, but he'd been in Atlantis less than a day and a lot had happened.

Orri sighed. "It's pretty bad when we have done nothing yet and we're frustrated with each other." He took another breath. "You have awesome skills. Can you try to contact the skull now?"

The words 'awesome skills' sucked all the anger out of Adam. He stared at this new mature version of Orri, and a crack formed in his shield of mistrust.

Adam looked around the messy room. Something told him they should go to the place where the thirteenth skull usually made an appearance. "Let's go to the council room. That's the last place I saw the real skull. I think I'll have a better connection to it there."

They walked side by side through the temple to the arched doorway of the council room. The ceiling soared above the round stone table and the thirteen empty chairs. Light poured in from the opening in the center of the roof, and Adam's spine tingled.

He stepped into the room and Orri followed. The doors to the council room were always open but something told Adam it would be best if they weren't interrupted. "Let's close the doors," he said.

Orri nodded, and they both closed the heavy oak doors.

In the quietness their ragged breathing wrapped around them. The bright room did nothing to quell the quiver running through Adam. He glanced at Orri and caught the older boy frowning at him.

What if I can't do this? Adam closed his eyes to avoid the skepticism he saw on Orri's face. If you focus you can do it, he told himself. Focus.

In his mind, Adam formed a picture of the life-sized clear crystal skull, the thirteenth skull. He could see rainbows radiating from it and feel the warm energy from the skull flow into his body. Where are you? Can you talk to me?

The rainbows died and the glow from the skull faded. His mind went blank.

No! I need you. Come back!

Adam opened his eyes, to see a crystal skull hanging in the air above them. The ice blue glow emitting from it made the hair on the back of his neck stand up.

Adam glanced at Orri. "The energy from the skull is all wrong. That's the replacement skull."

"I can't feel any energy." Orri tilted his head. "But you're right, it doesn't have a slot for the keystone to fit into."

Adam returned his attention to the impostor skull. "I know you can hear me." Adam shook his fist at the skull. "Talk to me."

"Who brought you here?" Orri yelled.

With a sudden jolt, the skull dropped to just above the boys' heads. A blue flame shot out of its eyes aimed directly at them. The heat from the flame seared Adam's face, and his hands flew up in unison with Orri's. They backed away from it. Adam had no idea how he could connect with this hostile replacement.

"I think we're getting somewhere," muttered Orri.

"Yeah, closer to getting killed."

"Let's link our energy and ask who brought it here again," Orri whispered.

"What good would that do?"

"We're more powerful together. Remember?"

Adam wasn't sure he'd ever get used to this cooperative version of Orri.

Without waiting for Adam to argue further Orri grabbed his hand and his energy flowed through their linked fingers. It moved into Adam's body, rooting his feet to the floor. A warmth grew within him. He responded to the power surging through him and deepened the link with Orri. Together they were powerful. Together they were strong. Together they asked, "Who brought you here?"

A second skull appeared next to the first one. Ice blue flames writhed from the eye sockets of both skulls forming a wall of flame. Neither skull spoke.

A shape formed in the flames. Adam leaned in. The wall of blue flame rose higher in front of him, blocking his view. His skin prickled from the heat. He ignored it and moved even nearer. He was close to getting answers. He could feel it. Through the blaze the scene became clear. Someone setting the skulls on a table in the library. The figure turned, and he saw Caileen.

How did she get the skulls? Long fingers of flame reached out and Adam felt his face blister. He cried out, unable to move. The heat seared into him until his world went dark.

A soothing cool breeze washed over Adam. Groaning, he pried his eyes open. Orri stood above him moving his hands as if he conducted an orchestra. "What are you doing?"

"I'm healing you. Alima taught me some basic first aid. She said I had talent." Orri stopped the waving movements and stepped back with his hands on his hips. "This is the first time I've had a real patient. I think she might be right. You look pretty good."

Adam rolled his eyes and touched his face. His skin was cool and felt unmarred. "Thank you." He pushed himself to his feet, and brushed off his tunic, not sure how he would tell Orri what he saw.

"Why did the skulls attack?" Orri raised his eyebrows.

"I saw something." Orri and Caileen were friends, maybe more than friends. Whatever their relationship status, Orri was not going to like what he had to say.

"What did you see?" Orri prompted.

"It was Caileen. She had the replacement skulls in the library." Adam pressed his lips together, he believed what the skulls had shown him. "I think she's somehow involved in the disappearance of the thirteenth skull." He tensed waiting for Orri's reaction.

"You're sure you saw Caileen?"

Adam nodded. "I know she's your friend…"

Orri held up his hand to stop him. "I believe you."

"You do?" Maybe, just maybe, Adam could learn to trust him.

"Caileen is still my friend, but she's changed since the black holes started." Orri slumped into a chair. "I never thought she would do anything like this. She was so angry at the way her father endangered Atlantis." Orri glanced up at Adam. "Someone must have made her do this, the way Cavan made me do those things. We have to talk to her."

Chapter Nine

Caileen stared unseeing out her office window. When her father, Cavan, had an office in this wing of the temple he used the room with no window. Caileen now suspected he feared someone could spy on him if he had a window.

She hadn't been afraid of spies until now. Recently she'd turned her sleek marble desk so it sat sideways in the space, the door on her right, the window on her left. That way no one could sneak up on her. She wondered again if maybe her father had been right in his choice of rooms.

She rubbed her temples in a failed attempt to stop the headache forming there. What have I done? She thought. Not long after the council banned her father from the library a woman named Maggie began communicating with her. It seemed innocent enough until Maggie revealed her boss was Adrian Zador. Then Caileen realized the slick businessman had tricked her too. He'd needed someone on the inside of Atlantis. He had played on her love for her father and he had duped her.

That knowledge sat as a cold lump in her stomach. She couldn't focus, she'd lost her appetite, and she ended every day with a headache. Caileen had no idea how to fix this and she was reluctant to confide in anyone, even Tya.

Movement beyond the columned stone arches framing the passageway to her office caught her eye. Orri and Adam were headed this way. Standing, she quickly grabbed a couple of skulls off the shelves and placed them on the desk. She sat down again trying to look busy.

Caileen heard the tap on the door frame and turned knowing she would see Orri standing there. She plastered what she hoped was a happy smile on her face. "Hi. What are you doing here?"

Orri stepped into the office with eyebrows lowered. Adam followed with his gaze less ominous and the corner of his mouth even lifted for a second.

"Hi, Adam," said Caileen. "What a surprise to see you both in the library." Her voice sounded false to her ears and she couldn't imagine how it must sound to them. "Please sit down." She gestured to the plain marble chairs on the other side of her desk.

Adam sat. Orri continued to stand, rubbing the back of his neck.

Caileen held her breath. If Orri was rubbing his neck, this couldn't be good news. Orri's cool grey eyes focused on her. She fidgeted and hugged her arms across her body.

"Did you replace the thirteenth skull with a fake?" Orri's words came out with clipped precision.

Caileen almost laughed. That was her Orri. Don't sugar coat it. Just say it like it is.

Orri's eyes narrowed.

She rubbed her temple where a headache pounded. How had they figured out her lie so quickly? The pain in her head increased when she thought about admitting to the truth. "I don't know how to explain it." Caileen's cheeks burned, and she lowered her gaze. "I was trying to do the right thing."

"Answer the question," Orri growled.

She raised her eyes. "Yes, I did it!" There she'd said it, but it didn't make her feel any better. Her gut twisted.

Orri placed his hands on the back of the chair and leaned in. "Why? Why would you do that? Didn't you learn anything from what your father did to Atlantis, what he did to me?" He shook his head and pushed away from the chair to pace.

Caileen watched her friendship with Orri wither as she gazed at his angry face. A sob escaped her dry lips followed by another, and another. She couldn't stop the flood. Her arms curled onto the desk and her head collapsed on top of them.

Footsteps walked around the desk and a tentative hand patted her shoulder. "It's okay. It's okay," said Adam, his discomfort unmistakable.

Get it together. You look like an idiot, she thought. Caileen sat up and pulled a cloth out of the pocket of her tunic. She wiped her face and blew her nose. Stuffing the cloth back in her pocket she watched Orri's face. I am an idiot.

"I'm sorry," she croaked, unable to think of anything else to say to take the disappointed look away.

He sat down, and Adam moved to sit beside him. Orri gazed at her. His eyes always showed his emotions; right now, they were a soft grey filled with sadness. "How did it happen?" He finally wanted to hear her side of the story.

"I was cleaning out my father's office after he was removed from council." Her voice cracked, and she swallowed the lump in her throat. "There was a gold colored crystal skull in the center of his desk. Its place on the desk made it look like it was important to him. I put my hand on it, but it held no information. I kept it because it was a piece of him."

Caileen brushed a tear from her cheek. "One day a light flashed in the skull's eye sockets and when I touched the skull a woman said she was an archeologist and she had found a golden skull in an ancient dig in northern Scotland. She believed the skulls were twins designed to allow communication between them."

"Okay, so what happened?" Orri leaned back and crossed his arms over his chest.

"I was lonely after my father left the library. You and Tya were busy, and I didn't have anyone to talk to." She confessed that in the beginning the woman, who introduced herself as Maggie, just listened to her. She commiserated with her about her problems. The questions began slowly, seemingly harmless. She was curious about the library and how the crystal skulls worked. Caileen answered her questions without any hesitation. Maggie's interest and amazement led her to brag about the home she loved. She proudly told her about the council and the thirteen skulls.

Maggie said the company she worked for, Farscope Foundation, was doing ground breaking work with the energies of quartz crystals. It sounded like Caileen could benefit from some of their discoveries. She could introduce Caileen to her boss.

Orri shook his head.

The next time Maggie contacted Caileen, Adrian Zador was on the other side of the skull too. Caileen twisted her hands together. "I should have stopped talking then, but I didn't." Her voice rose at the end of the sentence. She continued to tell them how Zador convinced her how dangerous it was to have the fate of Atlantis resting on one crystal skull. What if something happened to that skull? If he could look at the skull, he might be able to find a way to duplicate it. Of course, the original would be safe with Caileen.

"Why didn't you come to me or Tya?"

Caileen flinched. "I don't know. I can't explain it."

"He's a dangerous man," said Adam.

Orri said nothing.

"I knew it sounded too good to be true, so I asked him what was in it for him," she said.

"And what was his answer?" Orri leaned his elbows on the desk.

Caileen swallowed hard. "He said with a copy of a skull like the thirteenth skull he could increase the positive energy on Earth. That would give him the ability to grow enough crops to feed all the starving people in his world. He asked how could I pass on such a win-win solution?" Caileen rubbed the side of her face with a shaking hand. "At that moment in time, I trusted him."

"How did he get the thirteenth skull?" Orri eyes narrowed. He knew as head librarian, Caileen had access to the Skull Room in the library where the council's skulls were stored, including the thirteenth skull.

"I didn't hand it over to him if that's what you are thinking. In my father's diary, he wrote about a portal he had found in the Egyptian archives. He believed it linked to a museum in New York City."

"This gets better and better." Orri stood up to pace again. "You gave him a way to get into Atlantis?"

"I didn't." Caileen stood. "The portal is protected! He couldn't get in unless I let him in."

"I was close to that portal when I returned to Atlantis," commented Adam. "What happened next?"

"I made sure Adrian was only in Atlantis for a very short time. He had a weird rectangle of glass with colorful pictures on it. Somehow, he used the device to take measurements of the skull. Then he left, I secured the portal to stop him returning and took the thirteenth skull to the Skull Room."

"How did you know it was the thirteenth skull?"

"Really, Orri, I think we all know the thirteenth skull has a place for the keystone." Caileen's voice rose with each word.

"Then how did he get his hands on the skull?" Orri's words matched her volume.

Tya appeared in the doorway. She looked back and forth between Caileen and Orri. A crease formed between her eyebrows. "Would someone like to tell me what is going on?"

Orri gestured to Caileen. "Are you going to tell her, or shall I?"

"I will." Caileen sat down.

Tya took a seat beside Adam with her eyes fixed on Caileen. She chewed the corner of her lip and nodded for her to continue.

A heaviness sat on Caileen's chest. "Adrian Zador tricked me, and he has the thirteenth skull. The skulls in the council room are fakes." Her eyes welled up again. "I'm so stupid."

"Oh, Caileen." Tya reached across the desk. "What happened?"

Caileen repeated her story to Tya. When she finished Tya remained silent for a moment. Caileen wondered if her best friend was going to walk away from her today too. "Don't worry, we'll work this out. Your real friends understand." Tya gave Orri a dirty look and turned back to Caileen.

Orri tapped his foot. "You still haven't explained what happened."

"A couple of light cycles later Zador asked me to meet him at the gate again. He had two copies, one for him and one for me, and wanted to make sure they were exact copies of the thirteenth skull.

"The meeting was just like before. But when I returned what I thought was the thirteen skull and its copy to the Skull Room, I discovered they were both copies. I don't know how he switched them," said Caileen. Her eyes welled up again. She swiped at them, but the tears flowed unchecked down her face. "I thought I was protecting Atlantis. This is all my fault."

Through her tears she saw Orri's jaw tighten and a muscle on his cheek twitch.

Adam cleared his throat. "Are you finished talking to Zador?"

Caileen gazed at Adam. "I am. I promise." She turned her eyes back to Orri. "By the Creator's words, I promise."

Adam looked at Orri. "At least we know the prophecies are fake."

"Do we?" Orri raised an eyebrow. "What if Zador really did make a copy of the thirteenth skull? Could one of those prophecies be real?"

"You don't believe that, do you?" Tya tilted her head.

Orri shrugged. "I don't know what to believe anymore. What is real? What is fake? What is good?" He glanced at Caileen. "What is evil?"

What right did he have to judge her? Caileen surged to her feet. "Are you saying I'm evil?"

"If the sandal fits," he snapped back.

"And who was my father's puppet the last time Atlantis was in trouble?"

"I didn't know what was happening. You." Orri jabbed a finger at Caileen. "You knew what Adrian Zador was capable of and *you* let him trick you."

"And I don't need you to tell me how..." Caileen's voice wavered, and she swallowed before continuing, "How stupid I've been. But it would sure be nice if you could admit you've been wrong too instead of judging me."

"Perhaps Caileen can talk to Zador when we have a plan to get the skull back," suggested Adam, hoping to change the way the conversation was going.

"Can we trust her?" said Orri.

"Jeez, Orri! Stop it!" Tya snapped.

"I know it's my fault. I will do anything to get the thirteenth skull back." She gazed at all three of them.

Tya stood and looked at the rest of them. "If we fight among ourselves Zador wins. I don't want that, do you Orri?"

Chapter Ten

The boys agreed with Caileen and Tya to keep the story of the replacement skulls between the four of them until they figured out what to do. As they left Caileen's office, Orri gave her a hug and Caileen leaned her head against his chest.

The intimacy of the moment made Adam turn his head. He didn't understand how Orri could be so mad at Caileen one moment and then behave like that. He lifted his gaze to see Tya watching him with sad eyes. Did she want him to hug her? That didn't make sense to Adam, he had no idea if he would he ever figure out how to act around girls.

Adam sat on his tidy bed. He stuffed a pillow behind his back and leaned against the wall. Orri sprawled across his unmade mattress, a pillow bunched up under his head, and tunics, clean and dirty, lay scattered over the bottom of the bed and the floor. The corner of Adam's mouth lifted. Some things never changed.

"Do you believe Caileen will keep her word?" Adam kept his tone casual, even though the answer to the question impacted everything they would do.

Orri played with the edge of his blanket before looking up. "I've known her all my life. She is a good person. If I don't believe that, then everything I've ever known about her would be a lie." He let out a breath. "What she did with Zador could destroy Atlantis." He raised his eyes. "And she understands that. If we are going to work together, then we have to trust her."

Adam had doubts about both girls. He had left Atlantis for a while and his relationships were not the same as before. "I'm not as sure as you are, but we don't have a choice. She is our only connection to Adrian Zador, and the thirteenth skull."

"I believe in her. That's all that matters." Orri's eyes drilled into him.

"Okay." Adam held his hands up. "Caileen will help us but we don't know where the skull is."

"That's true," said Orri.

"I researched Adrian about a year ago. The head office for his company, Farscope Foundation, is in New York City," said Adam.

Orri swung his legs over the edge of the bed and sat up. "Why would you do that?"

Adam hesitated. He didn't want to tell Orri what had happened with his biological father. "I was interested in finding out what Zador's company did." He held Orri's gaze with wide eyes hoping the older boy wouldn't probe any further.

Orri's mouth tightened. "If we're going to work together, you have to trust me too. What are you not telling me?"

Adam pulled his knees up to his chest. It was a huge leap of faith to open up to the older boy. But Orri was right, he didn't have a choice. "You remember James McKenzie, the man we met in Salem…"

"You mean, the man you brought back to Atlantis. Your biological father," Orri corrected.

"Yeah, him. I looked him up on the Internet…"

"The what net?"

"It's like a big library you can go to anytime. It's not important. Anyway, I discovered he works for Farscope Foundation, Zador's company."

"Why were you interested in him?" Orri leaned back on his elbows but continued to watch Adam.

Adam felt his cheeks burn. Orri's persistence made it hard to avoid telling the whole truth. "I was curious."

"About what?"

"Haven't you ever been curious about something?" His voice rang out, loud and harsh in the space between them.

Orri said nothing.

"I wanted to get to know him." Adam hugged his knees tighter. He remembered the words James had said to him. "It's not a good time for me to be a father. Forget about me." A wave of heat spread across Adam's face. "It doesn't matter, he wanted nothing to do with me."

"I can't imagine how that would have felt." Orri's quiet voice caught Adam's attention. The older boy gazed unseeing at the floor between their beds.

Adam couldn't form the words to thank Orri but telling him the truth added another positive layer to their relationship.

"So, you think Adrian Zador has the thirteenth skull in New York?" asked Orri.

Relief flooded through Adam. Conversations that involved his feelings had never been easy. "I do." He leaned back against the wall again. A vision of the Egyptian temple flashed across his mind, and he remembered seeing a face he recognized. "Right before I came here, I was in New York at a museum. I saw James in the Egyptian section, near the famous gate called the Temple of Dendur."

"That's the portal to you used to get to Atlantis, isn't it?"

Adam nodded.

Orri stood up to pace in the space at the bottom of their beds. "We could use the portal to get to the thirteenth skull."

The hair on Adam's arms lifted up, and a shiver ran through him. A moment later his bed rocked back and forth. He clung to the edge of the mattress to avoid being thrown to the floor.

Orri flopped onto his mattress and both beds slid back and forth across the room. Deafening noise, that sounded like boulders grinding together. Dust rained down from the ceiling. Adam closed his eyes and tightened his grip.

The earthquake stopped as suddenly as it had started.

"That's the second quake in two days," observed Orri in a quiet voice. "It's getting worse."

"We need to see what the damage is," said Adam as he rose to his feet.

"No!" Orri grabbed his arm. "We must stay here. We don't know where the black hole will appear."

The sound of feet running pounded in the hallway outside their room.

"Other people are out there. I'm going too." Adam pulled away from Orri and opened the door.

Dust choked the air in the hallway. In the haze Adam saw two council members run past, Madhuri and Rute. It surprised him how fast the two of them were moving. Adam put his hand over his nose and mouth and sprinted after them.

The closer he got to the council room, the more fallen bricks and broken doors he had to dodge. He was near the last corner before the council room when a frigid wind sucked his breath away. Then a silent vacuum yanked him toward a massive hole of nothingness. His fingers scrabbled against the wall as he slid down the hallway, each second drawing him nearer to certain death.

The stone surface of the wall opened into a doorway, and Adam clutched the door frame so tightly he thought his fingers would break. His feet struggled to find leverage as he twisted his body into the room. Grabbing the door, he leaned against it to push it closed, but the door fought back until it opened wide enough for Orri, Noor, and Alima to fall into the room. Orri and the others scrambled to their feet, and everyone pushed to close the door.

"I thought you were staying in the room," Adam panted.

Orri's chest heaved as he gulped for air. "I couldn't let you kill yourself."

The only sound in the room was the four of them gasping like they had just run a race. After a couple of minutes, Adam pressed his ear against the wooden door. "I can hear voices. I think it's safe to go out now." He opened the door a crack.

"Are you all right?" A woman who sounded like Madhuri asked.

"I think so." A shaky male voice answered.

"I've never seen anything like it," another commented. "The whole statue has disappeared."

"I can't remember a time when it wasn't there."

Adam stepped into the hallway with Orri right behind him. At the end of the hallway he could see the foyer of the temple. He walked toward it.

A crack zigzagged across the floor of the foyer. Chunks of the ceiling had fallen down leaving gaping holes where the black sky showed through. Most of the crystal sconces emitted no light. Even in the gloom Adam could see the statue of Nethuns was gone. Without the huge, golden statue the space appeared enormous. He glanced back to see Noor leaning against the wall, his hands clenched in front of his chest and his face a blank mask as if he didn't know how to react to what he saw. Alima stood beside him, shaking hands covering her mouth, and silent tears streamed down her face. Adam swallowed hard against the lump in his throat.

The tears on Noor's face froze. Adam turned his gaze to Alima, and she stood unmoving too.

"This is crazy." The words came out of Orri's mouth in a whisper, like he was afraid to say anything.

Adam understood the feeling. He was scared any movement would cause something terrible to happen.

Then Adam blinked, and they were back in the hallway walking toward the empty foyer. "What just happened?" He murmured to Orri.

"It's like time rewound for just a moment," Orri replied.

The phrase 'time rewound' triggered a memory in Adam's brain. "Noor said that time is like a piece of fabric. And sometimes the fabric folds back on itself causing time to reset to an earlier place." Adam stopped. He realized what fabric folding back on itself was.

Orri looked at him. "That's a time loop." They said in unison.

This time when Adam looked back, Noor stood behind Alima. He gave her shoulders a quick squeeze. She glanced at Noor with a tight smile on her lips, then wiped her palms across her face and gazed around.

The time loop was only a few seconds and it didn't seem to cause any problems. Were all time loops like that? Adam wondered.

"Is anyone hurt? Is anyone… m-m-missing?"

"Over here," Rute shouted and waved. Alima rushed to her.

Noor stared at the empty floor, and Raine came to stand by him.

Adam overheard Raine say, "We must call another council meeting."

Noor glanced at Raine.

"Noor. Can you hear me?"

"Yes, yes. In the morning. Can you let everyone know?"

Chapter Eleven

The next morning, Adam and Orri walked down the hall toward the council room where Raine had requested everyone meet. When they got back to their room last night, they had said nothing to each other. Adam didn't know how to talk about what had happened, so the silence continued this morning.

The way Noor had looked played over and over in Adam's head. The devastation he witnessed on his grandfather's face confirmed how critical the situation was. He had to do something.

Adam's shoulders stiffened as the fate of Atlantis pressed down on him. Once again, he had agreed to save the fabled city, and like last time, things were going from bad to worse. He didn't know if they could retrieve the missing artifacts in time to save the city that once again was beginning to feel like his second home. That thought gave him a pang of guilt. He already had a home... on Earth. Just like last time, if he failed to save Atlantis would he ever see his family again? A heaviness pressed on his chest.

The dust from the earthquake had settled and each step they took was recorded in the powdery carpet covering the granite floor.

They stepped into the light-filled foyer. The holes in the roof now showed blue sky instead of darkness, and the brightness highlighted the stark details. Dust didn't soften this scene. All the granules had been sucked into the emptiness of the black hole. A jagged black crack snaked across the marble floor where the tiles had pulled together after the black hole collapsed in on itself. The hideous scar reminded him of what had been lost. A girl was dead, and parts of Atlantis were disappearing too. How long would it be before something else was taken by the black holes? Again Adam sagged under the enormity of the task. Atlantis would be destroyed if they didn't save it.

Something on the floor caught his attention. He bent down and picked up a small egg-shaped piece of gold. Turning it over he saw the eye from the statue of Nethuns glistening in his palm. His stomach clenched as he thought about holding Noor's eye in his hand even if it was only the statue of him. He moved to put the golden orb back, but a warmth radiated from the eye and his hand shifted on its own to shove it into his pocket.

He inspected his fingers and palm wondering how he had lost control of his own hand. What's going on? He closed his fingers into a fist. They seemed to work now. Checking the side of his pants he couldn't find the opening to the pocket. Weird.

Adam glanced at Orri to see if he had noticed what had happened. Orri's breath shuddered in and out as he blinked hard. The sadness Adam saw in the sixteen-year-old's face made his problems seem shallow by comparison. He put his hand on Orri's shoulder and tilted his head toward the council room. "Let's go in."

Orri closed his eyes for a moment. "Yeah," he agreed in a quiet voice.

Most of the council members sat around the table talking amongst themselves in small groups. Tya and Caileen sat quietly beside each other. Adam and Orri took the empty seats on either side.

When Tya turned to Adam, her eyes were red and swollen. He never knew how to handle crying girls. His sisters said he was not sensitive enough, or he was condescending. Either way, he couldn't win. His chest ached. Right now, he'd give anything to be dealing with a crying sister instead of what was happening in Atlantis.

A hush fell over the room when Noor walked in leaning on Alima's arm. She helped him to sit down before taking the chair next to him.

Noor looked around the table and sat up straighter. Adam noticed the slight movement transformed him from an old man to a leader.

"The black hole last night has us all on edge," said Noor. "We must remain calm until we can figure out what is happening and then stop it."

Thuan jumped to his feet. "Remain calm? We don't need calm! We need action."

Raine glared at Thuan. "What kind of action are you proposing?"

Thuan plopped into his seat and crossed his arms over his chest. "Well, isn't that what we came here to talk about?"

"I have looked back at the time research the Incas did when Atlantis was located at Machu Picchu." A deep crease appeared between Raine's eyebrows. "According to their records, it is a possibility that inter-dimensional travel is causing the earthquakes and black holes." He looked around the table, "If I am correct it means we can't blame young Adam for the latest black hole. Someone else must be traveling between Atlantis and Earth."

Noor's shoulders curled in again and he clasped his hands so tightly his knuckles turned white. The confident leader of a moment ago disappeared, and Adam wondered what his grandfather was thinking.

Rute rose to her feet. "We have had two more black holes, and no time loops since Noor brought it to our attention when the gate in the outer ring disappeared." Her eyes zeroed in on Raine. "Can you explain that? Or are the time loops in Noor's imagination?"

Adam frowned at Orri. Why hadn't anyone told him about the destruction of the portal he used the last time he came to Atlantis?

Orri shrugged and fixed his gaze on Noor.

"There are many things we don't know the answers to." Raine nodded at them. "I discovered that Machu Picchu experienced similar problems. But parts of those archives were lost when Atlantis moved to the thirteenth dimension. I could not find out why the destruction is happening." Raine's eyes flicked to Noor before continuing. "I dislike drawing conclusions without solid evidence, but I think everything is connected to the movement of people or artifacts across inter-dimensional lines."

A murmur of comments ran through the room. Thuan still had his arms crossed over his chest, Andros whispered in Madhuri's ear, and Alima gazed at Raine with her eyes narrowed. If the tension in the room pulled any tighter, the fabric of this moment would rip.

Adam thought he saw something out of the corner of his eye. He peered into the foyer. Everything appeared the same, but a tingle quivered through his body. That had happened last night. Just before the tremor.

Alima jumped up and stared at something outside the door. "Oh no," she exclaimed and bolted into the foyer.

Noor's eyes followed Alima's exit and then he disappeared from the council room. Adam blinked. "What happened to Noor?"

"Horatio must have called him," said Orri.

"How do you know?"

"When something happens in the library Horatio can summon Noor," said Orri. "Noor rarely vanishes, so that's the only explanation."

Adam remembered when he had transported himself out of the library. The noise of all the skulls talking at once was too much to handle. Noor had appeared beside him very quickly. Maybe Horatio had called him then.

Raine and the rest of the council rushed out the door.

"I've got a bad feeling about this," said Adam as they raced out of the chamber behind everyone else.

"We all do." Orri threw the words over his shoulder, showing Adam his admission was unnecessary.

"But I felt it before Alima stood up. It's another black hole."

"No way. If the black holes happen that close together it won't take long for Atlantis to disappear."

"You heard Raine. Travel between Atlantis and Earth causes black holes. Someone is travelling, and we have to figure out who."

Chapter Twelve

Horatio's urgent call landed Noor in the hallway leading to the library doors. Evidence of the tremor lay scattered in the corridor. A wave of dizziness washed over him, and he leaned against the wall.

Every time he saw fallen stones and twisted floors coated in dust his heart broke a little more. Dark energy was destroying his beautiful home one fallen brick at a time, and he did not know how to stop it without causing even more damage.

Since the skulls had appeared in the council chambers Noor had reached out with his mind to the thirteenth skull, one of the two skulls, several times. Each time his call had gone unanswered. Despite Alima's efforts to boost his energy levels, his energy remained dangerously low. If he didn't re-establish his connection to the thirteenth skull soon, there would be no way to heal himself.

Noor moved down the hallway again. His legs shook, and he left a hand on the wall to steady himself. Moving toward the library, the sound of his sandals on the stone floor echoed in the space.

It was quiet. Too quiet. Normally he could hear the skulls in the library talking. Now he heard nothing except his heart pounding against his ribs.

Pushing open the buckled gold doors he saw what lay beyond and crumpled to his knees.

"No," the word stuck in his throat. Where tall racks of crystal skulls had once stood there was nothing but a dark mark zigzagging across the floor. At the edge of the bare area, broken shelves and crystal skulls lay scattered about.

This couldn't happen. The library was protected.

What have I done? He curled into a heap on the floor.

I caused this. The consequences of the thought crushed his heart in a tight-fisted grip.

"I know it looks bad, but most of the library is still here. Let me help you." Horatio's huge hand gripped his shoulder, bringing Noor back to reality.

Horatio reminded him Atlantis relied on him to lead the council. Pull yourself together, he thought. He drew on his failing energy and sat up. "I am okay," he murmured, trying to convince himself it was true and to reassure Horatio.

The big man pulled him to his feet and wrapped him in a bear hug. Noor felt Horatio using his limited skills to send healing energy into his devastated mind and body. Horatio whispered, "You are strong, always stronger than you think you are."

At the sound of voices in the hallway Horatio stepped back. "You're better now?" he asked.

"I am." Noor bowed his head. "Thank you."

Alima rushed up. "What happened?"

Noor stepped to the side. She gasped. Her eyes filled with tears when she looked up at him. "Oh, Noor." The barely audible words slipped through her lips.

Noor stared down at her and watched her eyes change from a pale grey to a dark and stormy color. "It is only one section of the library. We will rebuild." Her words echoed Horatio's and gave him hope. Maybe they would survive this. He would have hugged her, but the rest of the council filled the hallway.

The others poured into the doorway, and their voices blended in a communal outrage. Noor turned to view the scene again. An ache formed in his chest. Clenching his jaw he willed it away.

He stepped into the space with care, afraid he might cause more damage. Usually the library smelled fresh and earthy, but now there was an old dusty smell in the ravaged space. The scar across the floor looked no different from the one in the foyer, except here the loss of knowledge might take years to rebuild.

He picked up a pink quartz skull and cradled it in his hand. "N... Neth... Nethuns is the god of the sea. Six horses..." The skull fell silent.

Noor stroked its smooth head hoping to hear more. After a moment, he gently set it back on the floor. Pain filled his entire torso, and he crossed his arms across his chest.

Raine stepped to the front of the group and yelled, "Quiet!" The talking subsided. "The destruction must end. What has happened here shows why we have to stop the inter-dimensional travel, or all that will be left of Atlantis is a dark scar across an empty city. I will set up a skull that will connect to your individual skull pendants. If you leave this dimension without the consent of the council, I will know it." Raine glanced at Noor. "And with the council's agreement, we will punish the guilty person.

Noor swallowed against the lump forming in his throat. *Does he know I'm the one who caused this?*

Vannen's dark red eyebrows jutted out over his eyes. "What right do you have to decide what we should do?

"Somebody has to decide what to do!" Thuan shouted.

"Enough." Noor moved beside Raine. "We are a democracy. The council makes decisions together." His voice sounded feeble in his ears. All eyes concentrated on him, some with concern and others with scorn. "Raine has made a..." He glanced down at his friend. "Motion. State your opinions and then I will call a vote."

"The council knows the consequences of inter-dimensional travel. It can't be one of us." Rute's eyebrows drew together. "I feel you are invading our privacy by tracking us."

"But it is obvious someone is travelling," said Croston. "So if you are not travelling, why would you argue against this?"

Rute tipped her head in agreement.

Noor appreciated Croston's logic. *I won't travel across dimensions anymore,* he silently promised.

"Does anyone else have something to say?" No one spoke. "Then let's vote." Noor looked right, and Alima's skull pendant lit up. Beside her Rute's tiny skull glowed. When the vote came back to him, his skull lit up. Noor wondered why the only skulls that remained dark were Caileen's and Adam's. "The majority rules and the motion is approved. Raine will monitor all inter-dimensional travel."

Noor took a step back to lean against the twisted gold door. He inhaled deeply and continued, "We know the only way we can be free of dark energy is to move Atlantis and begin again. But we need the keystone that is in Adrian Zador's possession." Noor focused on the four young people gathered to one side of the group. "We must look to the prophecies to guide us."

"If I may speak," Madhuri's wispy voice asked.

"Go ahead." Noor nodded. Madhuri had been on the council since Orri's mother, Delanna, disappeared. Madhuri's inability to grasp how the council operated often annoyed him.

"You would think after all this time she would know what to do," muttered Thuan loud enough for everyone to hear.

I'm not the only one she irritates, thought Noor.

Madhuri spoke as if she hadn't heard the comment. "We need to decide if we will follow the prophecies or not."

"Is that a motion?" Raine prompted before Noor could stop him.

Madhuri's wide eyes scanned the group. "Oh... yes, it is."

The library was so quiet a feather floating to the floor would be heard. Why? Why did the silly woman choose now to ask a question that would rock the foundations of their existence? And how could Raine have helped her?

Andros stepped to the front of the group. "Is Raine running this council instead of Noor?" His voice was so venomous everyone fell silent.

All eyes focused on Noor and Raine. Andros had been questioning Noor's actions for a while and Noor knew if this continued the rest of the council would doubt his ability to lead.

Putting a hand on Raine's arm to stop him from responding Noor stepped away from Alima's support. He stared down at the shorter man until Andros dropped his gaze to the floor.

Pulling himself up to his full height Noor declared, "I am the leader of this council. If you are questioning my leadership, you know what to do." Looking around at everyone else he asked, "Are there any questions?"

No one spoke and Noor continued. "Now. This is too big of a topic to call for an immediate vote." He glared at Raine. "We will meet in the council chambers in one time segment for voting. You can state your concerns then."

Noor watched Andros leave the library. What was Andros trying to do? Noor wondered.

He maintained his stance until everyone except Alima left the library. The second the others were out of sight, Noor sagged against her.

"Let's get you to the healing center. We both need to recharge our energies," said Alima.

Chapter Thirteen

Alima had restored Noor's energy as much as possible. When he and Alima entered the council room the rest of the council was already sitting around the table. They sat down, and the conversation stopped.

"Now is the time to express any concerns you have about the prophecies," said Noor in a clear, loud voice.

"Atlantis needs us to act now! We cannot spend time investigating which prophecy to follow. I believe the prophecies are false," Raine declared. "It is time to stop following them and make our own decisions!"

Thuan shouted, "I agree."

"So do I," said Adam.

"I agree with Adam," added Andros.

Rute stood up her red curls bouncing as she pointed at Andros. "It was just yesterday you wanted the boy gone. Now you value his opinion?"

Noor watched in dismay as the comments flew back and forth.

"The prophecies guide us, we debate, and Noor leads us." Alima raised her voice, "This is no time to be fighting amongst ourselves." She hooked her hand onto Noor's elbow.

Noor squeezed her hand and squared his shoulders. He had to get them to see reason. "We have two prophecies. One states saving Atlantis must be shared and the other says the trio is no more and each alone will come to see. That does not mean they have to work alone to realize their potential. All it is saying is they will each come to their own conclusions about Atlantis." His voice wavered, and he licked his parched lips before continuing, "Therefore we can follow both prophecies and I see no reason to get rid of them."

His stomach tightened as he observed the group. They whispered to each other in small clusters. He could see his desperate explanation was not swaying any of the votes against following the prophecies.

Which way would the vote go? In all his years of leadership he had never seen a division over the prophecies. They followed the prophecies. Period.

He couldn't call a vote. It would destroy Atlantis. But he couldn't delay it either, that would only intensify the rift.

Noor raised a hand for silence. "Does anyone have anything to add to the discussion?"

No one spoke.

Noor took a deep breath. He had no choice. Great Creator please guide them to the right decision, he silently pleaded. "We have a motion. Those in favor of following the prophecies will light their pendant." He paused, reluctant to say the words that could forever change the council. "And those against following the prophecies, their pendants will remain dark. I..." He cleared his throat and slowly spoke the words, "I call a vote."

Alima's skull lit up, but beside her Rute's skull remained dark. Noor frowned. He had not expected that. Thuan's pendant was dark and Andros shook his head too. No surprise there. Vannen and Croston both had skulls that glowed. Madhuri avoided Noor's gaze and her pendant did not light up. He should have known which way she would vote. Noor took a deep breath to quell the fear rippling through him.

Raine stared at him, Noor knew his old friend would not agree with keeping the prophecies and his skull remained dark. Five against and three in favor. It came down to the four young people and him. Noor's stomach rolled. Adam shook his head. Orri met his gaze, and a light shone from his pendant.

The corner of Noor's mouth lifted at Orri's vote. Now there was hope, surely both girls would choose in favor of the prophecies with him and that was enough to carry the vote. Caileen smiled and her skull glowed. Tya gazed at the floor.

No, Noor wanted to shout. The Tya he knew believed in the prophecies, she loved rules. His fingers clutched the edge of the table. How could this be happening?

"Tya, we need your vote," Alima urged in a soft voice.

"I think she has cast her vote," said Madhuri.

With her mouth set in a thin line Tya's wide blue eyes met his, and her skull remained dark.

Noor's pendant flickered to life even though his vote changed nothing. "The motion is against..." He licked his parched lips. "Following the prophecies."

He stared at the table with a numb mind. He had followed the prophecies and the original laws for thousands of years. He had no idea what to do now.

The noise of the council members discussing the vote buzzed in his ears, but Noor could not determine what they were saying. He had to try one more time to stop this disgraceful decision. "Let us not forget the original laws. We must honor the decision of the council, but first, we must honor the Creator and follow his words. Is that what we have done?"

"Nothing has changed. We are honoring the Creator by saving Atlantis." Raine's voice quelled all the others. "We are not committing murder, stealing, coveting what is not ours, or lying, so we are not breaking any of the original laws."

Raine glared at Noor. "Our priority is to stop the black holes and the time loops."

Alima frowned and shook her head. "No. We need to get the keystone, so we can move Atlantis as soon as possible."

Watching his two oldest friends face off because he failed to lead stirred something deep within Noor. He had hurt too many people with his lies, he would not let them lose each other. "Both ideas are good." The words came out with little conviction. "Raine and Alima, can you find a solution to the problems together?" Were his words enough to subdue the unrest?

Raine tipped his head in agreement. "Tya and I can dig deeper into the Inca archives for clues to help us solve the mystery." Raine turned his gaze to Alima and asked, "Can you and Caileen come up with a plan to get the keystone back? We will meet later today to decide how to proceed."

I am a silly old fool, Noor thought. I deserve to have my guidance questioned if I had not gone to Earth to find Adrian Zador the last two black holes would not have happened.

Chapter Fourteen

James sat behind the ultra-modern glass desk in his office. Adrian leaned back in the chair across from him.

"You asked me to look into possible gateways into Atlantis. To do that I've developed a timeline of all the places I believe Atlantis has existed," said James.

His boss wore an uninterested expression on his face, but he didn't interrupt.

"The earliest evidence of Atlantis is on a continent in the middle of the Atlantic Ocean about 9500 BC. Volcanic eruptions and tsunamis destroyed that land mass."

Adrian pulled his buzzing phone out of his pocket and James paused. When he silenced the phone, James continued.

"There is also evidence of Atlantis being near Cuba around 5000 BC, and off the coast of southern Greece around 3000 BC. Rising water destroyed both places, so there isn't a doorway to Atlantis there either."

"What does this have to do with entering Atlantis now," asked Adrian, still looking at his phone.

James ground his teeth. He knew Adrian liked his information in uncluttered bites. About as much info as would fit on the screen of his cell phone, but he wanted Adrian to understand how much research he'd done. James rushed on. "Every time something happened to destroy the location of Atlantis, evidence of the fabled land would show up somewhere else in the world. I believe Atlantis somehow moved from place to place. Some of the locations Atlantis has existed are still here today. Like the pyramids of Egypt and the ruins of Machu Picchu."

Adrian shoved his phone in his pocket and glanced up.

Now I have his attention, thought James. He pushed a picture of a limestone wall covered in symbols across the desk. "This is Egyptian, and it talks of a special door." He slid another picture next to the first one. "This is the special door and it's a portal to Atlantis."

Adrian tapped his finger on the picture of the portal. "Do you know how to open the portal?"

"I do." James swallowed the lump in his throat. He knew Atlantis had existed in Egypt during the time the pyramids were built, but because of Adrian's rush to find Atlantis he had ignored all his scientific training. At best, the rest of the information was an educated guess. He didn't want to think about how Adrian would react if his theories were wrong.

"The portal is in the Metropolitan Museum of Art," said Adrian. "Have you been to see it?"

"I've viewed it with the curator." James leaned forward. "How do you know where the portal is?"

"That is none of your business." Adrian lowered his eyebrows. "Is the curator aware of the connection to Atlantis?"

"No." James shook his head. "I told him I was studying Egyptian writing."

"Arrange to look at the portal after hours. I'll handle the rest." Adrian stood up and walked out.

James sighed. He'd spent months piecing together a timeline that made sense. Figuring out what was myth and what was truth. He developed a theory he could back up with evidence, but Adrian didn't care. No 'Wow, you worked hard'. No 'Good job, James'. Just show me the artifacts.

Adrian's lack of people skills wasn't the only thing that bothered him. Nothing stopped Adrian from getting what he wanted. James believed his boss might even be capable of murder if it suited his purpose. But if he could help Adrian use the crystal skull to grow enough food to feed all the starving people in the world, then maybe it would all be worth it.

A shiver rolled across his shoulders that had nothing to do with the air conditioning in the office. James heaved another sigh and scrubbed his face with his hands. As the leading expert in his field, he could fly all over the world, talk to universities and museums and have any specialist he wanted to consult with return his phone calls. He had dreamed of finding the ancient civilization of Atlantis, and now with his professional goal within reach instead of being fulfilled he felt hollow inside. An empty shell of a man going through the motions of life. No matter how much he crammed his days with work the void continued to be there.

Had it been fourteen years since his wife drowned while diving near Cuba? The research they had done trying to find Atlantis seemed like a lifetime ago. Natalie loved the ancient civilization as much as he did. He wished she could be here now to see how far he'd come.

A tight band of pain squeezed his ribs. His wife wasn't the only thing he'd lost. Adam, the son he'd given up for adoption after his wife's death, found him about a year ago. He had told the young man he didn't have time in his life for a child. The hurt on Adam's face almost made him change his mind. But his gut feeling was stronger. Something told him that to keep the boy safe he must send him away. His gut still told him he must keep Adam safe. He would give up everything to make sure Adrian never found out about Adam.

Chapter Fifteen

The boys left the council chambers together. They walked side by side in silence. Halfway down the hallway, Orri yanked Adam into a small alcove. Through clenched teeth he whispered, "Why did you vote against tracking the skull pendants?" The scowl on his face deepened. "Didn't you realize Noor and Raine would be suspicious?"

"I wasn't the only one who voted against the motion. Caileen did too." Adam stared at the older boy. "I want to fight the destruction on my own terms. What if Caileen is still talking to Zador? Maybe we should ask her why she voted the way she did."

"No," Orri shook his head. "Caileen wouldn't be talking to Zador when she promised not to talk to him."

"She still has the gold skull. What if Zador contacted her?"

Orri's shoulders sagged. "I hadn't thought of that."

It wasn't the reaction Adam expected. Orri's attitude had changed in the space of one breath and the Orri who believed in Caileen was back. He did care about Caileen. "Let's talk to her," Adam said in a calmer voice. "Before we jump to any conclusions."

The corner of Orri's mouth lifted and he nodded. "She's supposed to go to the archives to work with Alima, but maybe she went to her office first." He walked down the hall with a determination in his step. Adam hoped Caileen wouldn't disappoint him again.

The door to Caileen's office wasn't quite closed, and Orri walked in without knocking. "Why did you vote against the motion for Raine to track our skull pendants?"

Caileen let out a hiss of breath. "Come in and shut the door."

Adam sat in the chair beside Tya and Orri stood with his back against the closed door.

"I'll answer your question in a minute, we have more important things to talk about. Someone else is crossing inter-dimensional lines."

"And it's not you?" Orri watched Caileen closely, as if he was afraid she would confirm his worst fear.

"Really, Orri? Of course it's not her." Tya paused for a moment, and in a quieter voice she said, "We think it's Noor."

Adam's body tensed. Noor wasn't perfect, but no way would he deliberately put Atlantis in danger. "Why would he travel to Earth?"

"Noor's responsible for keeping Atlantis safe, and he is devastated about what's happening." Caileen pressed her lips together before continuing. "Maybe he tried to stop it on his own."

Orri tipped his head in agreement. "He might believe he was helping Atlantis, like you thought you were," he said the words in a surprisingly kind voice.

Tears welled up in Caileen's eyes. She wiped them away and nodded.

"Have you told Noor about the replacement skulls?" Tya asked.

Relieved at Tya's redirection of the conversation Adam replied, "No, I'm not sure he would believe us, and if he did, the knowledge might kill him. He told me he relies on what he believes is the thirteenth skull to keep his energy levels up. We need to get the real thirteenth skull and the keystone first."

"You'll have trouble getting them because Raine is tracking our skull pendants. Not only will he know when we cross interdimensional lines, he'll probably know where we are all the time. So, if we're meeting." Caileen gestured at the rest of them. "Raine knows it. If we're in the restricted library vaults, Raine knows that too." She gazed at Orri. "To answer your question, I voted against the motion because I don't want to be watched. We have to save Atlantis, and we may end up doing things that will be questioned by the council."

"That makes sense." A small smile slipped onto Orri's lips. "And thanks for voting to keep the prophecies, it's the right choice. We have always been guided by the prophecies and Noor." His eyes shifted to Tya, and the smile disappeared. "I know Adam voted against keeping the prophecies because he doesn't believe in them. What I don't understand is why did you vote that way?"

Tya lifted her chin and stated in her signature know-it-all voice. "Because both prophecies are wrong. What's important is saving Atlantis, and the four of us working together can do that. Not the three of us as the first prophecy says, or alone as the second one says." She glanced at Caileen. "From the research we've done so far, it may be possible to use one of the replacement skulls instead of the thirteenth skull, and then we wouldn't need the thirteenth skull or the keystone."

"How do you know which skull is the right one?" Skepticism dripped from Orri's lips.

"We can't answer that question yet." Tya's cheeks flushed. "We need to figure some things out." The look on Orri's face showed he was about to make another sarcastic comment but Tya stopped him. "We know where to start. My Nan researched the Machu Picchu location of Atlantis. They had a copy of the thirteenth skull, so we can too. We also know from experience how dangerous Zador is. This way we wouldn't need anything from him."

"Tya, why wouldn't we need a keystone?" Adam asked.

"The thirteenth skull didn't need a keystone until Cavan carved a slot for it. If we go back to a skull without a slot, like the Incas had, we shouldn't need a keystone."

"You won't know if any of this is true until you do more research. Right?

Tya nodded.

His mom always said, 'Accept the things you cannot change.' Adam's chest ached at the thought of her, but her advice made sense. "We can't change the way the council voted..." He concentrated on Tya's face. "You and Caileen spend most of your time in the library, and you'll be working with Alima and Raine. So you can work on your ideas. We'll look into rescuing the real thirteenth skull and the keystone as a backup plan. We're still working together, just in two teams instead of one." He wasn't about to admit to the girls they didn't have a plan anymore.

Tya shrugged and then tipped her head in reluctant agreement. Adam breathed a sigh of relief. Thanks Mom.

When Adam said the word 'team' Tya had touched her skull pendant. He remembered the last time they were a team. A good team. He fingered his skull pendant too.

Orri leaned back against the pillow on his bed. "Now what are we going to do? We can't use the portal unless we want to cause another black hole, and Raine is watching us so we can't do anything else."

"Raine's going to be busy in the library. Do you believe Raine is watching us in Atlantis?"

"I don't know, but do you want to take a chance he is?" Orri turned and looked at Adam. "Raine and the council would take our powers away if they caught us."

Adam sat on the edge of his bed and leaned forward. "Could we teleport from one side of the dimensional portal to the other? We wouldn't be going through the portal, so maybe we wouldn't cause a black hole."

"Raine believes inter-dimensional travel is the problem, and we would still be crossing dimensions. We are better off doing nothing instead of causing more destruction."

Every cell within Adam silently screamed *NO*, they must do something. They were expected to save Atlantis, but how? His mind scrambled for answers, but searching his limited knowledge of how energy worked, he found no solutions. He wished the thirteenth skull was still in Atlantis and able to help him.

As Adam sat there thinking the hair on his forearms prickled, and he wrapped his arms around his body. A golden light blurred his vision. Then the light softened, and he saw Noor's prone body with the glowing Egyptian gate in the background.

Adam opened his eyes. Orri stood beside him with a concerned look on his face. "What happened? You looked like a statue." Orri shivered. "It was like you weren't even here."

"I wasn't." Adam described his vision to Orri.

Orri reached out and squeezed Adam's shoulder.

Adam stared at Orri. "We need to help Noor. He's near the Egyptian portal."

"The portal is in the lost vaults, and I know where it is," said Orri.

Chapter Sixteen

Noor stepped into the empty area the black hole had created in the library. He avoided the dark crack and trod carefully around the broken skulls and rubble at the edge of the open space. His heart thudded heavily in his chest, and Noor rubbed his ribs to ease the discomfort. I caused this, he thought, and I must find a way to correct it.

Beyond the area of destruction the shelves of skulls still formed long rows the same way they always had. Noor could hear the voices of the skulls in this section although they were much quieter than usual. All the skulls in the library were connected and they felt the loss from the black hole just like he did. Drawing a deep breath, the air filling his nostrils smelled like earth after a rainfall, just the way the library should smell. The resilience of this space at the center of Atlantis gave him hope. We will survive.

He stopped in front of a human-sized blue crystal skull sitting on a stone stand. He laid his hand on top of the skull. The heavy wooden door behind the pedestal swung silently open.

After he stepped inside, he closed the door. The round table looked crowded. Usually there were thirteen skulls, one for each of the council members, now there were fourteen. Two larger than life-sized clear crystal skulls sat close together on the other side of the table. They were the skulls that had appeared in the council chamber. Noor couldn't see any difference between them.

He sat in the chair beside the twin skulls, and reached out to his skull, the thirteenth skull, with his mind. "Are you there, old friend?"

Both skulls glowed blue but only one voice answered. "I am here."

Noor felt waves of healing energy flow into him from the skulls. As he started to feel stronger, questions began to form. "Why didn't you answer me in the council chamber?"

"There is danger. We must be careful."

The answer made sense to him. "Why are there two of you?"

"Two are better than one to face the danger."

Noor accepted that explanation too. "But why are there two prophecies?"

"The leader of Atlantis knows the answer to that question."

Noor didn't know the answer. A dull pain pierced his side. Did that mean he was no longer fit to lead Atlantis? His hand clenched his skull pendant. Warmth filled the little skull with each beat of his heart. I am still a leader, he told himself. He let go of the pendant and stood up.

I will find the answer. No light shone from the skulls and he heard no acknowledgment of his words.

Noor's mind reached out to Raine and Alima. "Meet me in the skull room." He sent the message as clearly as if he had spoken it out loud. Again, he sat down in the chair with the two skulls in front of it.

A few minutes later, Raine and Alima entered the chamber and seated themselves at the table.

"What has happened," Raine asked to the point as always.

"I asked my skull why there are two prophecies." Noor indicated the skulls in front of him. "It said 'The leader of Atlantis knows the answer to that question.'"

"There are two skulls, Noor. Which one is the one that spoke to you?"

The condescending way Raine asked the question rankled Noor. "There are two of them because of the danger we face. The second one is a clone of my skull, the thirteenth skull." Noor threw the second statement in as if it was fact hoping to stop Raine's inquiries. "And no, I can't tell which one is talking to me."

"What a clever idea Noor," exclaimed Alima. "Why didn't you tell us you were going to clone your skull?"

Raine's eyes narrowed. "Did you clone the skull?"

Noor pinched his lips together. Great Creator! Why did he always find the hole in the story? "No," snapped Noor.

"And you do not know why there are two prophecies?" Raine's blue eyes focused on Noor but his words were gentle.

"No." Noor shook his head. "I do not. That is why I called you both here. I need help finding the answer."

Raine leaned on the table. "We voted to ignore the prophecies. It is time to let go."

"But how are we going to know what to do?" Alima frowned at the bald man sitting next to her.

"We are going to learn to think for ourselves." Raine thumped his fist on the table.

"Are you saying you have a plan and I should not worry about the prophecies?" Noor asked.

"Yes." Raine stood up. "Now, can I finish setting up the skull tracker?"

Noor felt a smile tug at the corner of his mouth. He nodded and Raine left the room.

Alima gracefully came to her feet. "Try not to worry, we are all in this together."

Noor watched Alima leave the room. What would she say if she knew what I had done, he wondered? We are not in this together. I created this mess. I must fix it.

How long Noor sat at the table absently rubbing the skulls he didn't know. He sifted through tangled memories stored in his brain searching for a solution. He was about to give up when an image of two life sized crystal skulls sitting beside each other on a circular stone table covered in symbols appeared in his mind.

When Atlantis had existed in Machu Picchu there were two skulls. One to join the energy of the council and one to store the leader's knowledge. This practice had been abandoned when Atlantis had moved to the thirteenth dimension. Now the Creators had provided two skulls to tell him what to do.

Noor shook his head. I can't believe what a senile old man I am. Looking at the skulls in front of him he had to choose which one should store his knowledge. He decided, for no particular reason, it was the one on the right. Placing his hands on either side of the skull he took a deep breath and formed a connection. The skull glowed blue as Noor streamed his knowledge into it. He expected the process would be an energy drain, instead it filled him with hope and determination. If something happened to him, his centuries of insight were safe.

Leaving the skull room Noor strode deeper into the library.

He stopped at a wall and pushed on a series of bricks. The wall swung open and he stood the top a narrow set of stairs plunging into darkness. Creating a glowing light ball, he began his decent to the Egyptian archives.

A short time later he stood in front of the Temple of Dendur. He never wanted to cause the kind of destruction his last trip had resulted in. His plan was to shapeshift into a crystal, and by using the portal as a place marker, he would be able to jump from one dimension to the other as scattered molecules.

He was sure this method would prevent any damage to the space-time continuum or cause a black hole. Once he was on the other side, he would have enough time to shift back into his body and find Adrian Zador. Why hadn't he thought of this sooner?

Lightness filled his chest and adrenaline coursed through his veins giving him a youthful vibe. He was going to save Atlantis.

Chapter Seventeen

Delanna pushed herself up from her hands and knees and wiped the sweat off her brow with the back of her hand. She had finished weeding the potato hills, now they would be busy harvesting the corn for the next few light cycles. Staring up at the forty levels of terraces above her on the hillside at Machu Picchu she rubbed the stiffness out of her back. The people of Atlantis had farmed all the terraces when Machu Picchu was at the height of its existence. With only three of them here, Irdel, Manata, and herself, they could grow all the produce they needed to survive on the lowest level.

For two hundred years Atlantis thrived here, in the ninth dimension. Then the people of Earth had become corrupted by the power of Atlantis once again, as they had in every location Atlantis had existed on Earth. When the council moved Atlantis away from Machu Picchu, they retreated even further from the people of Earth to the thirteenth dimension, limiting the access between Atlantis and Earth. The people of Earth had proven they would always fall prey to the power that Atlantis represented. Separation between the two had become necessary.

Somehow, Andros had found a way to reopen the portal between Atlantis and Machu Picchu again without the council knowing. Delanna knew he needed to learn how the ninth dimension worked if his plan to recreate Atlantis in this dimension was going to happen. A plan Delanna knew would bring harm to Atlantis and its people.

Andros had tried to use Delanna's skill as a Recognizer, to see into people's hearts and minds, in order to help him to find the right people to fight the current council and make him leader. When she'd refused to help, he'd kidnapped her and brought her to Machu Picchu so she wouldn't tell anyone about his plan.

She spent many light cycles wandering the ruins by herself, almost driving herself mad, waiting to discover what Andros had in store for her. When Andros brought Irdel and his granddaughter, Manata, to Machu Picchu Delanna knew he needed Irdel for his engineering skills. To build the vision of what Andros thought Atlantis should be. Delanna could see Andros' plans were slowly coming together. Each time he visited his smile was a little wider and his swagger a little bigger.

What he didn't understand was that this version of Atlantis was not as secure as he thought. Occasionally, they could hear the people of modern-day Earth in certain areas of the ancient city. Delanna hoped one day she could use this to her advantage, but she had not found a way yet.

Gazing toward the hut they shared, Delanna saw Irdel resting in a chair and Manata juggling pebbles with her energy. She had over a dozen small rocks in the air forming intricate patterns as she played with them.

"Great Creator," Delanna muttered as she rushed toward the girl.

Manata collected the stones in her palm and grinned at Delanna, her blue eyes sparkling.

"How many times have I told you to be careful when you use energy?" Delanna snapped.

The smile fell from Manata's face. "Many times. I'm sorry. I forget. I'm so full of energy it bursts out of me when I don't expect it." She dropped her gaze to the ground and rubbed the toe of her sandal in the dirt. "I'll try to remember."

"If Andros discovers how strong your energy skills are, he will force you to use your powers in ways you can't imagine. He might even use you to hurt other people. Do you want that?"

"I would never hurt anyone!" The girl gazed at Delanna and shook her head.

"I know you don't want to hurt anyone, that's why you can't let Andros find out."

Manata's eyes filled with tears.

Delanna didn't enjoy using fear to stop the young girl from exercising her gift. "Come on. Harvesting will give you something to do with those restless hands."

Delanna prayed Manata would remember to hide her energy. Andros showed up a lot more often these days.

Chapter Eighteen

A rush of wind smacked into Noor forcing him to stop. Golden light poured through the opening in the portal blinding him. He raised a hand to shade his eyes and squinted into the light. An outline of a person moved toward him. Time slowed for Noor as he watched the man in a dark business suit come into view. The man stopped just inside the room. His dark eyes scanned down Noor's body and returned back to his face. The corner of the man's mouth lifted into more of a sneer than a smile.

Noor needed no introduction to know this was Adrian Zador and he was standing in Atlantis. Goosebumps covered Noor's arms. How did he get here?

"Who are you?" Zador asked, his voice as full of scorn as his face.

Noor pulled his shoulders back and lifted his chin so he could look down his nose at the shorter man. "I am Noor, Leader of the Council of Atlantis." His strong voice echoed off the granite walls. "And you are Adrian Zador. Why are you in Atlantis?"

"I like a man who gets to the point quickly. I don't like wasting time." Zador slipped his hands into his pockets and leaned back on his heels. "I need the base for the crystal skull. Where is it?"

Noor stared into Zador's dark eyes. The only way he could describe them was soulless. Icy fingers crawled up the back of his neck. "What skull is that?"

Zador laughed. "You don't know?"

The chill spread through Noor's entire body. "My skull?" His question little more than a whisper.

Laughter filled the chamber again. "I didn't know it was your skull. Now that's an unexpected bonus."

Heat flashed through Noor's body and he ground his teeth. I must stop him. "You will not find the base. It is protected from men like you."

"I thought that is what you would say." Zador pulled his hand from his pocket and a beam of red light hit Noor in the chest.

Noor slumped to the floor. His chest burned, and his legs were numb. Where had Zador learned that?

"Now." Zador pointed a blood red stone at Noor's head. "Have you changed your mind?"

"Why do you need the base?" Noor gasped out the words trying to buy some time to recuperate.

"It is for a noble reason." Zador lowered the hand holding the stone. "With the energy generated from the skull and the base I can grow crops anywhere. No one in the world will face starvation again."

The feeling was returning to Noor's legs. He had to keep him talking a little longer.

Zador's left hand grasped the lapel on his jacket. He continued in a reasonable sounding voice. "I don't want to steal the crystals. I can replicate them and return the originals to you."

"I could say the same thing." Noor carefully shifted his position and rooted himself to the floor. "How are we going to solve this?" Noor said hoping to distract Zador while he gathered his energy. He felt the first wave of current flow into his body.

"I know the answer to that..."

Noor saw Zador's arm start to rise. Noor hadn't regained his full strength yet, but he was out of time. He sent a bolt of blue lightening at Zador's arm. The red stone fell out of Zador's grip and shot across the floor toward him. Noor reached for it, but the stone flew into Zador's uninjured hand. Zador must use the stone to amplify his energy.

Zador held his wounded arm close to his body but showed no other effects from the hit or from using energy. Expending energy in any form had a cost. The body's efforts had a limit and time was needed to recover from using energy. Noor realized Zador had somehow learned to use energy to get what he wanted with little effect on his body and his morals wouldn't stop him from reaching his goal. The biggest threat to the safety of Atlantis stood right in front of him. It was his job to stop him. Noor had fought battles like this before. He needed to maintain a defense while looking for an opportunity to defeat Zador.

A stream of red light came at Noor. He managed to throw up a shield just in time to block the beam from hurting him again. Several more shots of light hit the shield. The shield required less effort to maintain than firing the energy beams did. If Zador kept this up, Noor knew he would quickly exhaust himself.

Noor watched his opponent gasp for breath as he stood in front of the portal. What he needed to do was to push Zador back through the portal, then close it for good.

Noor dropped the shield and created a wall of blue flames in front of Zador. He began moving the wall back toward the gate. Zador was forced to take a step back.

Noor thought the businessman wouldn't be able to attack because he was busy shielding himself from the flames.

An unexpected red fireball shot over the wall and knocking Noor to the floor. The blue wall disintegrated when Noor hit the ground. He lay prone on the floor fighting to maintain consciousness.

Noor heard Adam's voice. "You don't know where the portal is, do you? It can't be down here."

"Looks like we might have some company," said Zador

"I hear a voice," Orri replied to Adam. "I do know where I'm going."

"Go back!" Noor croaked. "It is not safe."

"Oh, do come in. Perhaps you can save poor old Noor before it's too late," said Zador as he broke into an evil laugh.

Noor heard the boys coming toward him. "Go back! Save yourselves!" He begged.

"Hold on. We're coming," said Adam.

Noor's heart skipped a beat. I must protect them.

A blast of white light shot over top of Noor. The businessman jumped to the side and the blast missed him.

Noor struggled to a sitting position. He pulled everything he could from the ground beneath him. One hand grasped his skull pendant and the other sent a weak bolt of blue energy at Zador. The world slowed down. Noor watched his ray of blue light advance on Zador. The businessman held up his hand and the blue light turned around. It moved with precision back at him. His body was frozen in time. He could not move out of the way. Just before the light pierced his chest he screamed. "Nooooo!" He felt the ray sear into his chest stopping his scream and everything else.

Chapter Nineteen

"Go back! Save yourselves!" Noor begged.

The way Noor's voice sounded told Adam his grandfather was in trouble. The vision of Noor on the ground in front of the Temple of Dendur flashed before his eyes, and he scrambled through the jumbled mess with Orri on his heels.

"Hold on! We're coming!" shouted Adam as they reached the doorway.

Noor lay twisted on the floor like he had been discarded there by an angry child. The shoulder of his tunic had a black streak on it, and his face was almost as white as his clothes. Across the room beside the glowing portal stood Adrian Zador, the keystone visible in his hand. Adam's stomach twisted. How had he gotten here?

From behind Adam Orri shot a blast of white energy at Zador. The businessman swiveled to the side and the beam missed him.

Noor struggled to a seated position. With a shaking hand he directed a ray of blue energy at the businessman.

Adam watched the unsteady beam move across the space as he rushed toward his grandfather. Zador's lips curled into an evil smile, and he held the keystone up to reflect the beam back at Noor. Adam wasn't close enough to push Noor out of the way.

"Nooooo!" His grandfather screamed as the light pierced his chest and he slumped to the ground.

Pain stabbed Adam's chest as if he had been hit too. He stood frozen, staring down at Noor's crumpled body. The energy bolt left a charred hole in his grandfather's chest and blood oozed from the open wound. Adam swallowed the acid rising in his throat. His gaze moved to Noor's face. Seeing his closed eyes, slack mouth, and ashen skin made Adam swallow again.

"I'll help Noor. Get him!" Orri's yell snapped Adam out of his trance.

The smile on the businessman's face taunted him from across the room. Adam's hands formed into fists, and he gritted his teeth. Flinging an arm out, he grounded himself on the stone floor, opened his hand, and sent energy flying at Zador's head. His anger caused him to lose control and the energy formed into a crystal dagger. Zador flipped it around with a beam of red energy. The knife raced back at Adam. He managed to send the crystal crashing to the ground just before it reached him. Sweat drenched his body. When had Zador become so powerful?

The floor beneath Adam's feet rolled like the waves on the ocean, and he dropped to his knees beside Noor's prone body. Bricks rained down from the ceiling. Orri threw himself across Noor. Adam curled into a ball beside them and covered his head. Crossing inter-dimensional lines had caused this. Adam silently vowed the evil businessman would pay for his actions.

When the stones beneath him stopped moving Adam looked up to see Zador scrambling to his feet. The businessman took a step toward them but stumbled over a brick that had not been there a moment ago. Falling to his hands and knees he dropped the keystone.

The red stone disappeared. Adam tightened his fist around the smooth stone and shoved it into his pocket.

Zador crawled in a circle searching for his lost amulet. Orri sent a wave of white light, hitting the businessman on his shoulder.

Zador stumbled over pieces of the gate in his rush to get to the portal. "I'll be back. You can't stop me!" he shouted.

Adam glanced down at Noor lying perfectly still on the cold stone floor. Adrenaline boiled through his body. Zador must pay for what he'd done. "I'll stop you!" Adam growled through clenched teeth.

Orri stepped in front of Adam, blocking his view of the gate. "No! That is not the way to handle this."

"What makes you the expert?" Adam spat the words at the older boy and moved to step around him.

Orri's fingers pinched painfully into Adam's shoulders. "If we kill Zador we may never find the thirteenth skull."

"But…" Adam's body sagged. Orri was right.

Dropping his hands Orri turned allowing Adam to see the portal again. Zador staggered through the opening, and they watched his outline fade into the golden light pouring from the gateway.

"Help me," said Orri, as he sent massive beam of white energy at the gate.

Adam's red light joined with Orri's beam. A tiny spark of accomplishment flickered in Adam's mind at the thought of stopping Adrian Zador from ever being able to enter Atlantis again. The rumble of the gate crumbling filled the room, and a cloud of dust made it almost impossible to breathe. Exhausted, Adam dropped to the floor and pressed his face into the crook of his arm.

The noise subsided, and he lifted his gaze. Large chunks of stone filled the space where the portal had stood. A small beam of golden light streamed through a chink in the rubble. The sound of sobbing interrupted the quietness. Hoping it was Noor making the sound, Adam sat up. Orri's dust-coated form lay beside Noor; he stroked Noor's hand as tears poured down his cheeks.

Adam crawled to them. A thick layer of dust masked Noor's face. He reached out to brush it off, but his hand shook so much he couldn't do it. His fingers curled into a fist as he pulled them back.

Noor was dead. The thought punched him in the gut, air rushed out of his lungs and he gasped for breath. The tears came, choked out past the thickness in his throat as he lay prone on the floor.

Chapter Twenty

Sometime later, Adam felt a hand on his shoulder. He pushed himself to a seated position. "I can't believe he's gone. Noor is Atlantis," Adam said in a tear choked voice.

Orri nodded. "He will be missed, but we must let the council know what has happened." His voice sounded deeper than usual and calm, considering Noor had just died.

Adam gazed up into Orri's dusty face. His cheeks were streaked with tracks the tears had made in the dust, but his eyes were storm-less. Orri squeezed Adam's shoulder. The gesture reminded him of Noor and somehow, he found it comforting. "Who should we tell first?" Adam asked.

"Raine," Orri said with confidence and offered a hand to help him up.

Adam grabbed it, grateful for the assistance, and clambered to his feet.

"Anyone there?" Caileen's voice carried clearly from the outer room.

Orri's eyes widened, and he swiped his sleeve across his face. "Stay there," he shouted as he rushed to the door with Adam at his side.

"There was another tremor. It seemed like it was right under our feet. Are you okay?" Tya asked.

"We're okay," Orri replied.

Adam glanced at Orri. How were they going to explain the way they looked?

Caileen's eyes narrowed. "You don't look okay. What happened?" She moved to step past Orri.

He blocked her.

Tya stepped to the side. Adam put his arm out to stop her from going around him, but Tya stood on her toes to peer over his shoulder. "Noor! We have to help him."

It took all of Adam's strength to hold her back.

Orri put his arms around Caileen and pressed her face into his chest. "It's too late. You cannot change what has happened."

For a moment, Adam thought he heard Noor saying the words, but only Orri stood there.

Both girls stopped, and all three of stared at Orri.

"Please, you have let us see him," said Tya in a shaky voice.

"We need to say goodbye," Caileen added.

Orri nodded.

The girls walked together to Noor's prone form. Caileen knelt on one side of him, and Tya crouched on the other side. Tears streamed down their faces.

Adam turned away as a band of pain tightened around his chest. His feelings too raw to watch the girls.

After a time, Caileen and Tya joined them again.

"We need to talk about this, but not here," said Orri. This time he sounded more like himself. He put his arm around Caileen's shoulders and guided her away from the scene.

Adam glanced at Tya. Tears still leaked from the corners of her eyes. He slid his arm across her shoulders, the angry words they had said to each other forgotten for now. The awkwardness Adam felt was overpowered by his need to comfort her.

Footsteps echoed on the stairs.

Cold fingers crawled up Adam's neck and he glanced at Orri, his mouth forming a silent 'Who?'

Orri shook his head and stopped in the doorway.

Adam halted beside Orri and slid his arm away from Tya. The four of them blocked the view of the demolished gate.

Raine appeared at the bottom of the stairs. His eyes narrowed. "What are you doing down here?"

Orri stepped to one side allowing Raine a view of Noor's prone body.

Adam watched the waves of emotion flow across Raine's face. Shock. Anger. And finally, a sadness so deep he had been afraid the bald scientist would break down in front of them. Adam stared at the wall above Raine's head. Watching the scientist fall apart would be too much to bear.

Raine took a deep breath and muttered, "Silly old fool." Then he awkwardly thanked them and said he would tell everyone to gather in the council room at the beginning of the next light cycle.

The four of them followed Raine up the stairs. When they reached the top, Caileen pressed a brick beside the door frame and the stone door swung closed.

Orri raised an eyebrow but said nothing.

By the time they got to Caileen's office, the adrenaline from the fight had dissipated but energy still coursed through Adam. He glanced at Orri. The older boy could barely stand. His own lack of exhaustion felt strange, he should be beat. Orri must have used a lot of his energy trying to save Noor.

Caileen helped Orri into a chair, Tya slumped down beside him, and Adam leaned against the wall. Caileen sat in her chair behind the desk and scrubbed her face with her hands.

Watching Orri hunched over in the chair Adam knew there was no way the older boy could tell the story. He swallowed to wet his dry throat, and with a shaky voice he told Caileen and Tya what had happened. When he finished, tears streamed down the girls' faces again.

The wretchedness of what had happened landed on his shoulders, and Adam had to fight to remain standing. He didn't know what to do. Part of him wanted to comfort them, but his own heart was shattered too. How could he help Tya and Caileen if he was broken himself?

A groan escaped Orri's lips as he sat straighter. "How far have you two gotten in your research into using two skulls?"

Caileen rubbed her temples. "We were just starting. We don't have enough information yet. We can't tell the rest of the council until we figure out how Zador got into Atlantis this time. Someone on the council might have helped him."

"I agree," replied Orri.

Adam was about to question Orri's assumption of leadership when the older boy asked, "What do you think Adam?"

"Yeah, sounds good to me." Orri the diplomatic leader? Another side to the new Orri. He wouldn't have believed it if he hadn't seen it with his own eyes.

Caileen gazed down at Orri. "Are you okay?"

"Nothing a little rest won't cure." He offered a small smile.

Adam knew he wouldn't rest tonight. He doubted any of the others would either.

The silence on the walk back to their room hunkered down heavy and awkward between them. Adam didn't talk to Orri because he had no idea what to say, and Orri wasn't talking either. At the door to their room, Orri glanced at Adam. "I think I'll take a walk," he mumbled.

"Don't you want to rest before the council meeting?" Adam stared at the older boy. Orri looked like he was a thousand years old and could fall over at any moment.

"No." He shook his head and walked away.

One part of Adam was concerned about Orri, the other part was relieved to have time to himself.

Adam sat on his bed and leaned against the wall. He squeezed his eyes shut, but it didn't stop the scenes from popping up in his mind's eye. A crystal dagger shooting out of his outstretched hand. Noor's twisted body lying on the floor. Tear tracks carved in Orri's dust-covered cheeks. The snapshots left him shaking and sweating.

He opened his eyes, hoping that would stop the memories, but new images took shape on the wall in front of him instead. A vision of his grandfather on Earth, a man he barely knew, laid out in a satin-lined coffin with his face pale and waxy. No! Noor would never look like that. Then he could see Noor resting on the round council table with the rest of the council standing around him holding hands. He could feel and see the flow of energy in the room. Noor opened his eyes, sat up and smiled.

A vision of Noor's dust-covered body on the floor in the library archives replaced the smiling one. The body dissolved into ashes and a wisp of smoke rose from the pile of cinders. A cold shiver ran down Adam's spine.

He lay down, pulled the blanket up to his ears, and tried to think of other memories. Noor in the council chambers when Adam had first agreed to save Atlantis. Noor walking in the hallway to the library with him. Noor sitting in his office admitting he was his grandfather.

He wouldn't be who he was today if Noor hadn't been there for him. The hollowness in his chest grew until his entire body was an empty shell. He'd lost his grandfather too.

Curling up in a ball, he yanked the covers over his head. The tears he hadn't known he'd been holding back suddenly flowed again. The enormity of his loss burrowed deep into his soul. *How can I go on?*

When there were no more tears, Adam sat up and wiped his face. He needed to feel close to Noor, and he knew where to go: Noor's office. The room with the two familiar chairs and a view of Atlantis. Although the conversations Adam had in those two chairs weren't always easy, they had been one-on-one with Noor, and they had brought understanding between the two.

He was about to open the dark wooden door to Noor's office, when he heard voices on the other side.

"That old fool!" Raine stated in a loud voice. "What made him think he could fight Zador alone?" His voice cracked as he spoke the last word.

"I don't believe he is dead. I can still feel his energy," replied Alima in an almost normal voice.

Could he be alive? A little flutter of hope cut through Adam's sadness.

"His energy is part of everything in Atlantis. That is what you are feeling."

The truth of Raine's words resonated with Adam. Noor would never be really gone as long as Atlantis was here. He had to save Atlantis, now more than ever.

"Maybe he has suspended his molecules in space, and he will show up when we need him," said Alima.

"You saw his body. There is no way he could have suspended his molecules and left his body behind."

"You are right. I... I just want him to be here with us." Her voice wavered. After a small pause Alima spoke again, "When Noor fought Zador on his own he left us a message...."

"That he was crazy!" Raine interrupted.

"Raine, just listen for a moment." Alima sounded impatient. "He showed us we must work together like the second prophecy told us."

"I don't know how many times I have to say this, but we don't need the prophecies."

Raine's voice was so loud and harsh Adam cringed.

"With a strong leader, we will move forward without them." Raine finished in a quieter tone.

"That is why I wish Noor was here," Alima quietly replied.

He didn't want to hear any more, but where could he go? The roof was out. Orri might find him there. The library was out. Too many reminders of what had happened and Tya would be there. He remembered there was a park at the edge of the city surrounded by trees with a fountain in it. The Fountain of Eirene. No one would think to look for him there.

Adam's steps echoed as he walked through the empty foyer. The statue of Nethuns was gone, and so was the man who inspired it. Adam hurried to the top of the temple steps to escape more reminders of Noor's absence.

He walked with care through the broken streets of Atlantis until he saw his destination. The trees had blue-green leaves and a minty, pine scent that filled his senses. Some trees had toppled over, and he had to climb over them to get to the rutted grass. The soft sound of running water trickled into the air. In the middle of the small park stood a beautiful white marble fountain. The lower bowl of the fountain held three dolphins standing on their tails. With their noses they supported a large upper chalice. Water sprayed up from the middle of the upper bowl and flowed over the sides of the chalice. A zigzag crack marred the side of the vessel. Adam remembered the crack from his first visit to Atlantis and wondered how he could save Atlantis when everything seemed more hopeless than it did back then.

He stuffed his hands in his pockets, and his hand touched something. He pulled out the gold eye of Nethuns and the keystone. With everything else that had happened he'd forgotten they were there.

Rubbing the golden eye, it warmed to his touch, Adam saw an image of Noor's face the first time he met him. The tall man with long snow-white hair melting into his white tunic. His sculptured face had reminded Adam of a comic book superhero, except for the wrinkles showing his great age. Like the face of the man in the golden statue, only older. Adam had gazed up into the green eyes that were the same color as his own and he wanted to trust this man who appeared to be an ancient superman.

If Noor could die, then Atlantis was closer than ever to being destroyed. Adam squeezed his eyes shut. A brief ray of energy flowed into his body from the golden orb. It eased his pain a little. Adam gave it one last squeeze before he stuffed it back into his pocket.

He sat on the edge of the fountain and stared down at the keystone resting in his palm. The base for the thirteenth skull, the hand, was safely hidden in Atlantis. He now had the keystone that locked the hand and the skull together. The only piece missing was the skull. And Adrian Zador had that. They hadn't been able to defeat Zador this time. How could they do it next time?

Adam rubbed the stone in his palm with his thumb. It glowed, and he felt a warm wave enter his body. Zador had used the small oval stone like a skull pendant. He wondered how the businessman had learned to do that.

The keystone vibrated. Without thinking Adam gathered his energy and centered it into the stone. Water shot up from the fountain and rained down over him. He jumped up and shook himself.

The water brought back memories of all the mistakes he had made while learning to use energy the last time he was in

Atlantis. It reminded him he should have been paying attention to what he was doing.

He could see the twinkle in Noor's eyes when he was amused. The memory sparked a tiny bit of warmth in his chest. He could hear Noor's voice encouraging him. 'Concentrate. Try again.'

Adam looked at the fountain. He sent his energy into the stone again and visualized repairing the crack in the upper bowl. He watched the crack disappear. Adam imagined Noor's hand was on his shoulder and he heard the words, 'You can do it.'

Adam smiled. He already had the keystone. And only the four of them knew about the replacement skulls. Noor, even if he was only a memory, had guided him to finding a way to save Atlantis.

Remembering Noor had given him the strength to go on. Noor did exist, inside him. He would use what Noor had given him to do what needed to be done. He slid the keystone into his pocket.

Chapter Twenty-One

After the boys shut the door behind them, Caileen stared unseeing at the skulls on her desk. She rubbed her thumb over the face of her skull pendant. The familiarity of tiny features did nothing to soothe her agitated mind.

"I'm going back to the library," Tya said in a raspy voice.

"I'll be there in a few minutes," replied Caileen, not looking up.

As the office door closed, Caileen wrapped her arms around her body and curled into herself. What would her world be like without Noor? The thought tightened her throat. She had looked up to two people in her life, her father and Noor. They were all the family she had. The person she was today came from the two men who had loved her and mentored her. Now, Noor was dead, and her father banished from the Temple. She had no one. The thought spread a chill through her body and left a cold emptiness behind.

How could she carry on? Caileen squeezed her eyes shut. The light from the crystal lamp on her desk wove patterns on her closed lids. The images morphed into the image of Noor lying on the floor. It was her fault Noor was dead. She had brought Adrian Zador to Atlantis. Everything was her fault.

She pressed her palms over her mouth hoping to suppress the sound of her cries. The first sob came and then spasms rocked her body as her head fell onto her folded arms. She mourned for Atlantis, for Noor, and for herself.

Later Caileen walked down the aisles of skulls toward the center of the library where she knew Tya would be. Her face was hot and her eyes throbbed, but she didn't care. She must move forward. She couldn't lose Atlantis too.

Standing across the table from Tya, Caileen watched her friend listen to several skulls in quick succession. Tya the focused one, Tya the strong one, Tya the one who wouldn't do what she had done. Caileen swallowed hard against the sob rising again in her throat.

When Tya's hand paused for a second in midair Caileen said, "Hi."

Tya jumped and her gaze darted up from the skull on the table. "I didn't know you were there." Not taking her gaze from Caileen's face Tya stood up and wrapped her arms around Caileen.

"I know you think this is your fault, but it isn't." Caileen moved to pull away but Tya gently tightened the hug. "You are my friend, and I understand."

Caileen shook her head. "You wouldn't do anything that caused... someone to die." She thought she had finished crying, but she had to breathe deeply stop another flood of tears.

Tya stepped back. In a quiet voice she said, "I know I had something to do with my Nan's death."

The words hung between them. Caileen gazed into Tya's eyes and knew Tya believed that to be true.

"We all feel sorrow in our lives." Tya squeezed her eyes shut for a moment. "Nan once told me we must use the brokenness to give us the strength to move forward." Tya's mouth formed a tight smile. "Nan also gifted me with my love of the library." She looked over her shoulder. Then she faced Caileen again, she held her chin high and stated, "We can fix this. Together."

Caileen nodded, unable to form the words to thank Tya.

"Sit." Tya indicated the chair across from hers. "I recently found Nan's journal. Her last entries were about the hidden Inca archives." Tya's eyes focused on Caileen. "This will be hard for you to hear, but I have to tell you something about your father."

What had her father done now? Caileen pinched her lips together. Tya's grandmother had said use the brokenness to find strength. The words gave her something to cling to. She nodded.

"I think the Inca archives is where your father first discovered he could use the hidden knowledge for his benefit," said Tya, her voice soft and tentative. "And he was researching the Inca history of Atlantis just like Nan was."

"They were working together?"

"No." Tya shook her head. "Nan never mentioned your father. I believe they didn't know what the other one was doing." She chewed the corner of her mouth before continuing. "In her last entry, Nan wrote about discovering new information in the Inca archives she wanted to check out. She didn't say what she was looking for." Again, Tya paused.

Caileen's heart dropped into her stomach, but she had to hear what Tya struggled to say. "Please tell me," she prompted.

"After reading Nan's journal, I have new memories of that day." Tya stared at a spot in the middle of the table. "Now I remember following your father down the stairs into the Inca archives, and I remember..." Tya swallowed hard. "Finding Nan laying on the floor in a circular room made of stones. The room had two windows across from each other and a large stone on the floor. Cavan held me back, so I couldn't get to her." Tya raised her eyes to Caileen's. "The story he told the council isn't true. He didn't find us at a table in the library, he must have put us there to make it look like an accident."

"When did you figure this out?" Her words came out sharp and suspicious. Maybe more than she would have wanted, but it was tough to hear more accusations against her father.

"Just before Adam returned to Atlantis." Tya tugged at the corner of her lip again. "I should have said something, but so much was happening." Tya glanced at Caileen. "And I didn't know how to tell you without hurting you."

Caileen was about to accuse Tya of hurting her more by keeping a secret, but before the words came out she realized they had all kept things hidden, especially her. It was the secrets that were pulling Atlantis apart. "There are too many secrets in Atlantis," she said. "We have to tell the truth from now on."

Tya nodded. "I discovered something else in Nan's journal, she left detailed instructions about how to get into the Inca archives."

Caileen felt the corners of her lips tilt up. Her pain hadn't disappeared, but she knew they had a chance to save Atlantis.

Chapter Twenty-Two

When Orri wanted to get away from it all he usually headed for the popollama field, but today his feet led him to the council room. As he entered the round chamber, the heaviness of what had happened settled on his shoulders again, and the low light from the crystal sconces reinforced his somber mood.

How could I let Noor die? An uneasy lump rolled in his belly. He had tried using healing energy on him, but it was too late. Noor's life force had slipped through his fingers.

Thoughts of 'what if' had played in his head since they had forced Zador back the way he came. Orri ground his teeth. How had Zador found a way into Atlantis this time? How had he learned to work with energy? People on Earth could have the talent, but they had no one to teach them how to use it. And yet, Zador had skills and he knew what to do with them.

The four of them, not just him and Adam, must learn to be stronger, or they would never defeat Adrian Zador and find the thirteenth skull. His power as a Recognizer couldn't tell him if they could do it. The chill in the pit of his stomach spread through his whole body. If he didn't know the potential energy skills of the four, then the fate of Atlantis was on very shaky ground.

He rested his open hands on the council table. An ember of warmth entered his palms, Orri closed his fists around it somehow knowing this scrap of energy would somehow heal him. Opening his fingers, he stared at his hands. He must be going crazy, there was no way a tiny bit of energy would heal him.

Words came into his head. You are stronger than you think. You are a part of saving Atlantis. He peered around. The council room was empty. Did someone have a mind connection with him? He shivered. He had never liked someone else talking in his mind, ever since Cavan had tried to control him. It felt like all his inner thoughts and feelings had been exposed. "Is anyone here," he asked in a loud voice. Silence answered, in the room and in his mind. Orri shook his head.

He tilted his face toward the dark opening in the roof. A memory of the replacement skull hovering above the council table filled his thoughts. Adam said Noor had a connection with one of the replacement skulls.

Replacement skull? The question came across louder than normal and clear as if it was spoken out loud.

Orri stood up and spun around. "This isn't funny! Who are you?"

Other than his own scattered thoughts there was no answer again. What was going on? Could it be a skull talking? "Skull, is that you?" Orri asked out loud as he looked up at the roof. Nothing appeared or popped into his brain.

"Come out," he ordered. Nothing changed.

Orri sat down again and laid his hands on the table palms up. He drew the energy from the air into his body. Are you there?

The air above his head shimmered. A pair of crystal eye sockets became visible, followed by a nasal cavity and a grinning mouth. The rest of the head followed until a complete skull glowed in the air. This was one of the skulls which spoke the prophecies. Which one he didn't know.

Can you hear me? Orri asked without words.

Yes, the word materialized in his head.

Who are you?

I am your skull. The thought formed loud and clear in his mind.

What?

Remember, I can hear your thoughts when you project them. I have always been your skull.

Orri shook his head. That's crazy.

What is crazy?

Sorry. I'm not used to having my thoughts heard. Are you connected to anyone else?

Not now. I have information for you. Open your mind and I will send it to you.

"I don't like this," Orri muttered out loud.

You will be safe. I promise.

The unease in Orri's stomach didn't go away. He grounded himself in the chair, took a deep breath, and closed his eyes. Images flashed through his head so fast he couldn't make sense of them. Sitting at the council table and all the councillors looked much younger, a beautiful woman pulling him close, Adam's eyes glaring at him full of anger, flying over Atlantis with the black cloud on the horizon. They kept coming, pictures invading his mind. His chest heaved, and his breath came in short bursts. His body became heavy like the surrounding air had turned to concrete. He couldn't move. If another picture entered his brain, it would explode. It was happening too fast. Stop! Please stop. He slid down and darkness came.

"Orri, wake up." Alima's voice sounded far away.

He opened his eyes and saw a blurry Alima kneeling beside him with what seemed to be a concerned look on her face. "What happened?" Orri uttered in a scratchy voice.

"I am not sure. Raine and I came into the council room and found you on the floor."

Orri glanced over Alima's shoulder. Raine stood there with his eyebrows pulled together and his mouth turned down. Orri recognized the scowl on the scientist's face was sadness, not anger.

Alima rubbed Orri's hand. "Can you sit up?"

Orri pushed himself up. A wave of dizziness washed over him, and he closed his eyes for a moment.

"Not too fast. Take it slow," Alima soothed.

A headache bloomed into knife-twisting, stomach-churning agony. Orri reached up to clutch his head.

Alima placed her hands on top of his. Waves of warm soothing energy flowed into his brain. The pain lessened and Orri lowered his hands.

"Wait," said Alima. She placed her hands directly on the sides of his face. Orri breathed deeply as Alima's healing energy took away the last of the pain. He reached up and squeezed Alima's hand. An electric shock flew up his arm. He yanked his hand away and stared at Alima. What was happening?

Alima moved her hands from his face and narrowed her eyes. "What caused you so much pain?"

"I... I'm not sure," said Orri. He couldn't explain it, and he'd sound crazy if he tried to tell Alima what had happened. "I felt dizzy, and then the next moment you were leaning over me."

She nodded, but the frown remained on her face. "Grief can be overwhelming. Maybe that is why you passed out." Alima's voice cracked, and she blinked hard. "We are all deeply saddened by what has happened, and each of us reacts differently."

Unable to witness the anguish on Alima's face, Orri stared at the curved ceiling instead. The opening in the roof showed it was still dark outside. It had been a long dark cycle, and he knew what he needed to do.

Alima stood up slowly and offered her hand to him.

Orri took her hand and clambered to his feet. He looked down at the tiny woman beside him. Something felt familiar, like he had done this too many times to count. Maybe Alima was right, grief had caused all the strange feelings.

"It is almost time for the council to meet," she said in a brisk voice. "Are you ready?"

"No, but I have no choice." Orri rolled his shoulders back and took a seat at the council table.

Alima sat beside him and said, "You can do this."

Andros and Thuan walked in. "Raine, what possessed you to ask us to come here at this point in the time cycle," asked Andros. His long red hair, not tied in its usual ponytail, stood out at odd angles from his head.

An image formed in Orri's mind of a much younger Andros playing with energy balls that caused his hair to stand on end from the static. Orri blinked, and the vision disappeared. He was so exhausted he must be hallucinating.

"You will find out as soon as everyone arrives," Raine answered in a curt tone.

"Who died and made you the leader?" Thuan grumbled as he took a seat beside Andros.

Raine shook his head but said nothing.

Orri admired his restraint even if it was a typical Thuan comment.

Crosten, Vannen, Madhuri, and Rute entered together. They sat down without comment.

Caileen, Tya, and Adam came in last. Orri could see the effect of Noor's passing stamped on their faces.

Once everyone had sat down Raine rose to his feet. All eyes turned to the empty chair beside him. "I…"

Madhuri jumped up. "Wait, Noor hasn't arrived!"

"Noor is not coming! Sit down!" Raine snapped.

"Where is he?"

"What do you mean, not coming?"

The questions came out one on top of the other, each person speaking louder than the person before.

"Enough!" Raine pounded his fist on the table. "Sit down!"

"Noor must lead the meeting, or assign someone to take his place," stated Rute in a quiet voice.

"There is no easy way to say this." Raine shook his head and composed his face into a neutral expression. "Noor is dead." Each word came out precisely spoken and emotionless. No sound penetrated the absolute silence that filled the room.

Orri watched each of the council members process the information in their own way. Rute held herself still, Madhuri blinked hard, Andros pinched his lips together so tightly a white line appeared around his mouth, Thuan leaned his crossed arms on the table with his head hanging down, both Crosten and Vannen stared at a spot in the middle of the marble surface. Orri saw the shattered expressions on his friend's faces, and he knew he looked as bad as they did.

Through the opening in the roof the sky changed from inky black to bright blue. Time continued, and they had to move forward. The pain inside Orri subsided a tiny bit.

Alima gazed up, and the corners of her mouth tilted a little, softening the deep lines on her face. "He is still here. Noor always said the Time Crystal had an interesting sense of timing."

"Where did... did it happen?" Madhuri's voice wavered.

Orri knew, deep inside himself, that the story was his to tell. If Raine told the story, the council wouldn't trust the four of them. He rose to his feet and gazed around the table. He rolled his shoulders back and spoke in a calm tone. "Noor died in the library archives."

"Which archive?" Andros scowled.

This was not starting the way Orri wanted. If he wasn't careful with how he answered questions someone would accuse them of contributing to Noor's death. He had no choice. "There have been archives found from all the places that Atlantis has existed. Noor was in the Egyptian archives."

"How did Noor die?" Croston normally took the reasonable position in a discussion, but his narrowed eyes told Orri he wanted to get to the real reasons they all ended up in the Egyptian archives.

"What were you doing there?" Thuan leaned his elbows on the table.

"I was there too." Adam moved to stand beside Orri.

"The stories continue," Andros commented.

Out of the corner of his eye, Orri could see Adam's cheeks redden. "I'll handle this," Orri muttered.

Adam glanced at him and nodded before taking his seat again.

Gratitude surged through Orri because of the simple gesture. I can do this, he told himself. He lifted his chin. "Adam had a vision that Noor was in trouble."

Murmurs flowed around the table. Orri held up his hand to stop the noise. "Adam's visions have proved correct in the past, and this is no different." The lull in conversation eased some of the tightness in Orri's chest. "It is important you let me finish describing the events before we discuss them." He lowered his hand. "We found Noor fighting with Adrian Zador. The businessman entered Atlantis through the Egyptian gate, and he has learned how to use energy."

Orri looked around the table to make sure he had everyone's attention. "Adam and I were too late. Adrian killed Noor." Saying the words in this room somehow made it too real. He took a long breath in. "We sent Adrian Zador back to Earth and demolished the Egyptian portal. Atlantis is safe for now."

"Where are Noor's memories stored?" Rute asked.

"What do you mean?" Orri licked his dry lips.

"If Noor knew he was in danger, he would have transferred his knowledge into his crystal skull." Alima peered at Orri with steely grey eyes.

Orri glanced down at the table to avoid Alima's gaze. His thoughts slowed down as he processed the information. He remembered rushing to Noor's side in the Egyptian archives and holding his hand. Noor had opened his mouth, but no words came out. There had been no connection.

"Noor is still here," Madhuri raised her arms and gazed around the room. "I feel his presence. He continues to lead us."

"This is insane. We need a flesh and blood leader, not some ghost," Andros leaned on the table and pushed himself up. "I can lead. I know what to do."

"Andros would make a great leader," said Thuan.

"You cannot announce you want to be the leader of the council and expect it to happen. First, we must define the qualities we would like to see in our next leader." Croston's blue eyes darkened like the sea on a stormy night as he stared at Andros. "And then nominations are accepted based on merit."

"Croston is correct." Vannen bobbed his head, making his long hair sway back and forth.

Orri's stomach clenched. "Noor's body isn't cold yet. Now is not the time to think about a new leader."

Adam stood beside him again. "Orri is right. Our priority is protecting Atlantis."

Caileen and Tya came to their feet at the same time. Caileen spoke for both. "We agree with Orri."

"I have other safeguards in place to stop the inter-dimensional travel without a portal. Atlantis is safe for now," said Raine. "There is no need for hasty decisions."

"We shouldn't move too quickly." Rute scrambled to her feet. "After we have mourned Noor, we will have a clearer idea of what must be done."

"That makes the most sense," agreed Alima.

"Don't we need a vote?" asked Madhuri.

Raine stood. "There is nothing to vote on. If we don't save Atlantis, none of us will be here," he snapped. "I have moved Noor's body to the mausoleum until we can plan a formal service."

"Atlantis is our priority." Orri's voice filled the room, and all eyes turned to him. "We will save our home by collecting the artifacts needed for us to move the city. We should all get some rest and prepare for what is coming."

Orri gazed in amazement as one by one the councillors filed out of the council room. No one questioned his words.

Alima touched his arm. "You handled that well." Her eyes crinkled at the corners as her mouth curved into a smile. "I think you will make a great leader one day."

Orri smiled at her, thankful for her support.

Adam remained standing beside Orri after everyone had left. "Let's go for a walk," said Adam. "I want to talk to you about something."

Chapter Twenty-Three

"I know a place we can go," said Orri.

"You lead." After a couple of hallways, Adam knew where they were headed. "Why are you taking me to the library?"

"I'm not. You'll see," Orri said without looking back.

Before they turned the corner into the hallway leading to the library doors, Orri opened a plain wooden door on his right to reveal a set of stairs going up. Adam had never noticed this door before. Orri gestured for Adam to enter.

"What's at the top of the stairs?"

A confused look flitted across Orri's face, then he shook his head. "With all that has happened I forgot about your fear of heights."

Adam's jaw tightened. "We might as well go up on the roof."

"I am sorry."

Adam stared at the older boy, Orri didn't usually apologize. Then he saw deep lines carved under Orri's eyes and on either side of his mouth. He looked like a middle-aged man. "Are you okay?"

"I'm a little tired. I will go to see Alima for an energy boost later," replied Orri. "There is a place you can stand away from the edge." He tipped his head toward the stairs.

Adam sighed and plodded up the steps. At the top, a small gallery looked out over the library. He leaned against the wall and gazed into the distance to avoid looking down. From this vantage point, the shelves of skulls continued as far as the eye could see. The vastness of the knowledge stored here took his breath away. He understood why Orri had brought him here. He heard footsteps on the stairs and twisted to face Orri. "This is why we have to save Atlantis."

Orri slumped against the wall beside Adam and nodded. "What did you want to talk about?"

"I know how to get the thirteenth skull."

Orri lowered his eyebrows in a way Adam had never seen before. "Have you forgotten Raine is tracking our pendants?"

"We won't leave Atlantis," said Adam. "All we have to do is go back in time, before Caileen gave the skull to Zador, and bring it back with us to the present."

Orri's eyebrows shot up. If Adam hadn't known better, he would have thought the older boy was surprised. Then Orri put his hands on his hips. "No! We will change the future, including yours. That is not a solution."

"Changing the future might be a good thing," Adam replied in a quiet voice. "We might bring Noor back."

Orri collapsed against the wall again. "I hadn't considered that." He rubbed the side of his face.

Adam watched Orri, hoping the thought of saving Noor would change his mind.

Just when Adam couldn't stand the silence any longer Orri spoke. "If retrieving the thirteenth skull changes the future for the worse, promise me you will take it back and reset time. Then we will have to find another way to get it back."

Adam deliberately kept his tone light. "It will work, and we won't need to return it."

Orri stared deep into Adam's eyes. "Promise me."

The way Orri looked at him sent a shiver through Adam. "Okay, I'll do it." Why was he making such a big deal about this? Like it was life or death. "What's going on? You're hiding something."

"I can't explain it. I don't quite feel like myself." Orri shrugged. "It's probably because of all that has happened." He turned and gazed at Adam. "I'm not hiding anything from you."

Adam believed him. "Any ideas where the thirteenth skull would have been before Caileen took it?"

"The last time I saw it was in the skull room in the library archives. It is best to use my memory to guide us," Orri stated.

"The skull room?"

"That is where the council's skulls are stored. There is a special layer of protection on that room."

"Do you go down there a lot?" The vague sensation he had failed to catch an important detail returned.

"Um, no, not really. But if we go back in time, I know we will find the thirteenth skull there." Orri shifted his weight from one foot to the other.

"And you know how to find this room?" Adam stared at Orri.

Orri smiled "Yes. Follow me."

They said 'Hi' to Horatio as they passed him. The big man raised a hand in acknowledgment but didn't stand up. Noor's death had devastated the normally jovial man.

Someone had repaired the gold doors at the end of the hallway. Adam could hear the skulls in the library, but he didn't need to turn the noise down because the skulls spoke in muted voices. The passing of the leader of Atlantis had affected the skulls too. Orri pushed the doors open.

They had also cleared the empty area created by the black hole of broken skulls and rubble. Only the dark crack remained zigzagging across the floor. Adam trailed behind Orri as he stepped around the open area. He watched the older boy's shoulders curl in. The weight of what they had to do pressed on Adam as well.

Deep in the library, Orri stopped in front of a blue, human-sized crystal skull sitting on a pedestal. He wrapped his hand around the top of the skull, and the heavy wooden door behind the pedestal swung open.

They stepped inside and Orri closed the door. The sconces on the wall did little to shed light in the space. The ceiling was made of dark stone and it didn't curve up to an opening like the council room. The thirteen chairs that sat around a circular table were an exact match to council room furniture, but there was a musty, unused smell in this space.

A crystal skull sat on the table in front of each chair, except for Noor's chair where there were two larger-than-life crystal skulls.

Orri reached for Adam's hand. "Are you ready?"

Adam gripped Orri's fingers. Holding hands with the older boy wasn't creepy anymore. It was the best way for them to connect their energy. "Ready when you are."

"I will visualize where and when we are going." Orri drew a deep breath.

A memory of traveling with Noor flashed through Adam's mind. They needed to be careful to make sure they landed in the right time period. Adam centered himself and grounded his feet to the floor. A warm current flowed into him from Orri's hand. Another wave followed seconds after the first. This energy had a different tone to it, wiser, deeper, and somehow familiar.

Just as Adam connected to the second wave of energy it pulled back. Orri's energy flow stuttered and then stopped completely.

Adam let go of Orri's limp hand. "What happened?"

Orri's hands clenched into fists at his side. "There are too many unknowns. I am sure we will change the future."

"We don't have a choice. There aren't any other options," Adam snapped. "What's wrong with you?"

"I can't explain it." Orri looked up at the ceiling.

"Why?"

Orri crossed his arms over his chest. "I cannot tell you. I wish I could."

"You're acting weird." Adam stared at Orri and watched the older boy's normally grey eyes turn to green and then back to grey.

"There are two of us within this body." Orri's mouth said the words, but the voice sounded like Noor.

Adam had a falling sensation, like he had stepped off the edge of the gallery. Things were happening too fast for him to take in. When he heard Noor's laugh come from Orri's mouth his whole world shook. "That is the first time I have ever seen you at a loss for words."

Orri's eyes grew wide and his voice asked, "Noor?" He tilted his head to one side like he was listening intently. "No!" Orri frowned and shook his head. "You can't make me do this!" His eyes narrowed and widened again. "If there is no other way." He nodded, chewed on his bottom lip, then he nodded a couple more times but said nothing more. Orri slid onto a chair.

Adam rubbed the back of his neck. He couldn't stand it any longer, he had to know what was going on. "Noor, Orri, I don't care who, but could one of you let me know what's going on?"

Orri glanced up, his face pale and his forehead wrinkled. "I don't know what you're complaining about, I just found out too."

"Can one of you tell me the short version of what happened?"

Noor spoke again. "It has only happened once or twice in our history, but somehow I moved my essence into Orri's body when we were fighting Zador. I did not intend to do it, so I am not sure how it happened. When facing dangerous conditions, council members must store their memories in their crystal skull. I stored my memories in one of my skulls, I mean one of the replacement skulls. When Orri went to the council chambers after the fight, the replacement skull transferred my memories to his brain." Orri took a breath and Noor continued. "I had to wait for the right time to tell both of you. I wanted to tell Orri sooner, but I can see now this was the best way to tell you." Orri smiled.

Orri and Noor shared a body. Adam peered at the older boy as he turned away from him. That was just—creepy. A shiver crawled up the back of his neck. He had to be sure Noor really lived inside Orri. "Tell me where we were when you first told me you were my grandfather."

"We were sitting on the chairs in my office." Orri's eyes were wide and serious.

Noor wasn't dead! Adam's chest filled with warmth. His grandfather was alive! And he lived inside Orri. But... he couldn't talk to one without the other being there. Noor lived, but it wasn't the same. Adam's heart ached again.

Since he had returned to Atlantis, Orri had been working with him to save the city. Then Noor's death changed everything. Adam watched Orri's profile. Now, Noor lived and the three of them together were a wiser, stronger team. The thought released some tension in his body.

"Everything has changed, and nothing has changed," Noor spoke again.

Adam didn't know if he'd ever get used to Noor's voice coming out of Orri's mouth. He looked at the floor, hoping it might work better if he could hear Noor's voice without seeing where it came from.

Noor continued, "Adam, you know my essence is inside Orri, but Orri is still himself in every way."

"It's hard to wrap my head around it."

"I agree." Noor chuckled. "But nothing should change because of me." After a couple of seconds of silence Noor spoke again. "Orri, I will be in the background of your brain, who you are and how you respond to those around you should not change. If you feel the need for privacy, just ask and I will close the door to my space in your brain. If you want advice, ask for that too. I will try to be quiet although I may not be able to restrain myself in some circumstances."

"This is crazy." The strain of the situation was clear in Orri's voice. "I'm not used to someone sharing my brain. How can I continue to be myself?"

"If you would like me to shut the door all the time, I can do that," Noor replied in a soft tone. "Orri, if you had rejected my essence I would have died, but you let me into your physical body, and you saved my life. Your sacrifice is beyond words."

The solemn words hung in the space between the two boys. Adam looked up. Orri's hands pulled at his hair as he paced back and forth in the shadowy space. As the older boy went past him, Adam put his hand on Orri's arm. "Noor's right, you have made a great sacrifice, and because of that we can use Noor's knowledge and wisdom to help us save Atlantis."

Orri gazed at Adam with wide vacant eyes, he squeezed his eyes shut and took a step back. When he opened them he said, "Don't paint me as the hero, we all know how well that works."

"I hope we have both moved past that." A little laugh trickled from Adam's throat.

"Noor, I can't ask you to shut yourself away." Orri sighed. "We will have to work together to make this ... partnership successful."

They would all have to work together to figure this out, thought Adam. A warmth filled his chest. His grandfather was alive and could help them save Atlantis.

"One more thing," said Noor. "I will let Orri take the lead with the council. It is time for the younger generation to find their rightful place at the council table. You are ready to take control."

"Are you sure?" Adam didn't feel as confident as Noor sounded.

"I am sure," said Noor.

"I hope you're right," said Orri. "There is too much at stake for us to fail."

Orri took a deep breath. "We need to find another way to retrieve the thirteenth skull and the keystone," he continued in an obvious attempt to change the subject. "Maybe we should talk to the girls."

Adam put his hand in his pocket and rubbed the keystone. He pursed his lips and thought about lying. The sick feeling in his stomach told him it was time to tell the truth. He pulled his fist out of his pocket and opened it up. The red stone glowed in his palm. "We have the keystone."

Orri stared at the oval gem in Adam's hand. "I thought Zador picked it up." His voice had a hopeful tone to it.

"No." Adam shook his head. "I did."

"It's glowing." Orri leaned closer to Adam's outstretched hand. "Can I hold it?"

Adam hesitated for a second, and then placed the stone in Orri's palm.

"It feels a little warm. But I don't feel any energy from it." Orri gave it back to Adam.

The glow in the stone deepened. The red gleam colored Adam's hands and chest. "I can feel its power. I see how Zador used this to hurt Noor."

Orri took it again and the radiance softened. He laid his fingers over the stone and squeezed his eyes shut. "I still feel nothing. It's connected to you. You're special."

The words were an exact echo of what Noor used to say to him. "No, I'm not." Adam slid it into his pocket. "We need to find a place to hide it. Any ideas?"

Orri laughed, but the sound had an echo of Noor in it. "You still don't like being told you're special, do you?"

"Because I'm not."

"Noor is your grandfather, so he is inside you too." Orri tapped Adam's chest. "And that makes you special." One corner of his mouth tilted up. "I know where I can hide the stone. Do you trust me?"

"After all we've been through, I think I can."

"The stone will be protected there," said Orri. "It's a place I go often, but it would be suspicious if you went there." Orri held out his hand.

Adam passed the keystone to him.

"Thanks." Orri pocketed the stone. "I'll see you later."

Chapter Twenty-Four

After getting a much-needed healing energy session from Alima in the infirmary, Orri exited the temple. The bright blue sky overhead reminded him of when Atlantis hadn't been in danger, but the damage to the buildings on either side of the main boulevard told a different story. He walked briskly to the outer ring of the city. Since he had left the skull room, Noor had been so quiet Orri felt like his old self.

When he reached the last ring, he turned into a tight alley where narrow houses leaned toward each other almost touching at the top. The empty lane twisted and turned. The only light came from the windows of the houses. He stopped halfway down an alley and opened the door. The sweet smell of baking wafted to him. "Ya-ya, it's only me," he shouted.

"In the kitchen," his grandmother answered.

Orri walked down the hall to the back of the house. The peeling paint needed to be fixed but she wouldn't let him do it. He hadn't been home in a while, and he missed her company.

Before he was through the stone archway to the kitchen, she had him in a tight hug. Her head only came up to his chest, so he bent over to hug her back. He felt her warm energy flow into him, and he pulled in all she gave him.

She stepped back to gaze into his eyes. Her grey eyes twinkled in her wrinkled face, and her wavy grey hair hung loose down her back like a young girl's. She put her hands on her hips. "You look tired. And skinny too. Are you getting enough to eat? Pancha is not enough to feed a growing boy. You need real food."

"Ya-ya, I'm just in the door. Let me sit down before you grill me." Orri laughed and he felt Noor chuckle too.

"It is only because I love you. Now sit."

"I'm sitting." Orri pulled a chair out from the table. This table had been in his grandmother's kitchen as long as he could remember. The single pedestal had four lion's paws for its feet. It supported a thick stone tabletop. He used to sit under the table and pretend the table leg was a real lion who could talk to him.

Ya-ya placed a plate of sweet buns on the table and sat in a chair beside him. She waited until he had finished one bun before the questions started.

"Some houses in the second ring have been damaged by tremors. There is nothing here yet. Is there more damage at the temple?"

"Adam is back," said Orri, ignoring her question.

She reached out and squeezed his hand. "How do you feel about that?"

"You know me too well." Orri gazed into her eyes. "It's different this time. We're different. Adam and I—we're working together."

"I'm proud of you." Her eyes filled with tears.

"Ya-ya, what…"

"It's nothing," she interrupted him. "A silly old woman sees her little boy all grown up." She wiped her cheek with the hem of her tunic. "So, what brings you here?"

Orri shrugged. "To visit with you. It's been a while."

"I may be old, but I am not senile yet."

"I did come for a visit." Since he had been living at the Temple, Orri hadn't been able to see his grandmother as much as he would have liked to. He looked at her with what he hoped was an innocent look. "And I need you to keep something safe for me."

"Now was that so hard?"

Orri pulled the keystone out of his pocket and handed it to her.

She held it and rubbed it with her thumb. "This is special. I know just the place for it."

"Ya-ya, it's the keystone."

She raised an eyebrow.

"The council doesn't know we have it."

Both eyebrows shot up. "Is lying to the council a wise thing to do?"

"Someone on the council is causing the tremors and the black holes. We don't know who to trust."

She nodded, slipped the stone into her pocket, and reached for his hand.

The simple gesture released the tension in Orri's body and started the flow of words. He told her everything like he always had, including letting her know about the essence within him. Ya-ya had been on the council at one time and he knew her insights would help him.

"That has happened only a couple of times in our history." Her comment matched Noor's. "When it happens, it serves to protect the chain of knowledge from one leader to the next."

Orri jumped up. "No! I'm not a leader. I'm not ready."

"You are wiser than you know." She stood beside him and leaned in to give him a hug.

Orri wrapped his arms around her, and again, her energy flowed into him. "This time you are wrong. I'm too young. No one will vote for me to run the council."

"You will know what needs to be done when the time comes," she said as she walked with him to the door.

At the door, Orri squeezed her again, still praying she was wrong.

"I am here anytime you need me," said Ya-ya as she closed the door.

Orri stared at the closed door, Ya-ya knew something he didn't, and he knew from experience she wouldn't tell him before she was ready.

His feet found their own way while Orri thought about what needed to happen. Noor's presence still strangely quiet. *I know you are there,* thought Orri. *Can you help me?*

You do not know what you need help with yet. You have all you need to do what must be done. A soft chuckle tickled Orri's mind. *Do not worry. I am available to help when I am needed.*

Ya-ya's words had affected Noor too. Orri shook his head as he stepped onto the sports field. He loved the ball game and when his life got complicated, he could always find refuge here.

He didn't have time to play, he should be thinking about finding the thirteenth skull, but he had no idea what to do.

Orri wandered to center court where two stone rings, one on each side, were mounted on the wall just above his head. He remembered that when he first played the game the rings were beyond his reach. Younger children played with a lighter, softer ball, or popo, to make it easier. The hard rubber popo he used now weighed three pounds.

A popo had been left on the sidelines, Orri grabbed it and began bouncing it off his head, hips, thighs and shoulders. He enjoyed the exercise and something inside him remembered how good this felt. Orri smiled at the thought of Noor playing popollama.

Caileen stepped onto the field. Orri continued to practice. It was a good thing he knew the moves so well he could do them with his eyes closed or he would have fumbled the ball. When had she become so beautiful? Orri blushed when he remembered Noor could hear his thoughts.

Noor, I need some privacy, he asked, and a mental door softly closed, shutting out a part of his brain. He didn't think he would ever get used to sharing his body with Noor.

Caileen stopped in front of him. "Playing with all your friends?"

Orri snorted. "You've used that line before."

She looked up at him and smiled.

"I think the last time I commented, 'I thought you were my friend.'" Orri said in a husky voice.

"I am your friend." Her light green eyes widened. "Are you still my friend?"

Orri let the popo drop to the ground with a thud. He looked over Caileen's shoulder. The words 'It's complicated' almost came out of his mouth. He knew he could do better than that. Gazing down at her he reached for her hand. "Let's sit down," he said leading her over to the spectator seating.

Caileen sat on the stone bench. Orri let go of her hand and sat next to her with enough space between them to make sure they didn't accidentally touch.

Caileen twisted her hands in her lap. "You haven't answered my question." Her voice wobbled on the last word.

"I have always been your friend. That's not going to change." Orri squeezed her hands to still them. "But…"

"There's always a 'but'," Caileen said in a low voice.

"It will take time for me to have faith in you again," said Orri. "Because you didn't trust me."

"What's that supposed to mean?" Caileen frowned.

"If you trusted me, you would have shared what was going on with Adrian Zador," Orri answered in a flat tone as he looked down the field at a group of boys just coming onto the field. He felt a sense of relief that the conversation would end soon.

"You're right," said Caileen.

Orri turned his gaze back to Caileen. She sat frozen with her mouth half open like she was going to say something. "Caileen?" She didn't move. He touched her arm, and she didn't respond.

He peered at the boys at the other end of the field. They weren't moving either. *What is going on?* Why is everyone frozen except me? Somewhere in the back of his mind he knew time was being stretched thin. Then the boys moved again.

Caileen turned to him. "Playing with all your friends," she asked.

"What?"

Caileen put her hand on his and laughed. "You were so focused you didn't see me walking toward you. That's what I love about you. You're so passionate."

Inside Orri's head the question repeated. What the dootz is going on?

"I suppose I'm focused too," Caileen peeked at him through fluttering lashes.

Orri felt the warmth of a blush spread over his cheeks.

"I love the library, but someone could distract me if they wanted to," Caileen continued in a low voice. "Speaking of the library, Tya and I will start researching how the replacement skulls can help us."

Caileen noticed the boys approaching. She leaned over and gave him a quick peck on the cheek before standing up. "See you after the game." It was a statement, not a question.

Orri sat there with his mouth half open watching Caileen walk away. What had just happened? Caileen said they would *start* researching how the replacement skulls could help them, but they already had a theory about that.

Smave stopped in front of Orri and smirked. "You've been keeping secrets." Motioning his thumb at Caileen. "When did that happen?"

Orri shook his head. "I don't know."

"Atta boy! Keep her guessing." Ener shook his messy red hair off his face and leaned over to lightly punch Orri's shoulder. "Are you going to play?"

Orri shook his head. "I don't have time right now."

"Are you sure? It's still early," said Asuwar, the captain of the other team.

"Maybe another day." Orri watched the group put on their equipment. When they started warming up Orri remained on the bench staring down the field. The guys thought it was earlier in the light cycle than it was. He recalled Caileen's words after the pause. She had gone back to the beginning of their conversation, and even longer than that when she commented about her research. Time hadn't just stopped; it had rolled back for everyone but him. His heart thudded in his chest.

Chapter Twenty-Five

After giving the keystone to Orri, Adam wandered through the library to give himself some time to think. He tuned into what the skulls were saying as he wandered down the aisles.

"We live in a universe composed of original consciousness," said a large mottled green skull in a monotone voice. "We are dreaming the dream of Creation, each of us experiencing the universe from our own unique viewpoint," the skull finished, showing no enthusiasm for sharing the knowledge it held.

Adam couldn't listen anymore. He ran his hand through his hair. The effect of the last couple of days on the library was unmistakable. If the library was a person it would walk with stooped shoulders, arms hanging slack at their sides, and with a down-turned face.

He caught movement out of the corner of his eye. Adam turned to see someone wearing the white tunic of a council member with long dark hair disappearing around the end of an aisle. Andros. What was he doing so deep in the library?

A black skull still glowed from Andros touching it. Adam focused on the skull. In a tired voice it said, "Atlantis existed in Machu Picchu for 120 Earth years. At that time, part of Atlantis also existed in the ninth dimension. An open portal joined the two versions of Atlantis."

What did that mean? And why would Andros need that information?

Adam walked down a couple of aisles trying to figure out what Andros was up to. He turned a corner and there was Tya sitting in her favorite spot. His traitorous feet had led him here with no conscious input from him. Concentrating on her face so he wouldn't get distracted by the rest of her, Adam noticed her eyes were still puffy and red. He wanted to help her, but he wasn't sure what to say. He couldn't tell her Noor was still alive.

Tya glanced up and her eyes widened. "How long have you been standing there?"

"Only a minute, I didn't want to disturb you." Adam gestured to the skulls scattered on the table. "Have you found anything?"

"I'm having trouble concentrating." Tya shook her head. "It is hard to go on without Noor." Her voice broke at the end of the sentence.

"Orri tried to save him." Adam swallowed hard. "But we were too late."

"It was good that someone was with him at the end," she said with a sniffle.

Adam watched the tears forming in her eyes. "On Earth, when someone dies there is usually some kind of memorial," said Adam, hoping to distract her. "What happens in Atlantis?"

"We gather with the body, talk about their lives and watch as the members of the council create an energy fire to send the body back into the universe. So, as Raine would say, the energy in the universe never changes." Tya didn't look like she was about to cry anymore. "But we have to save Atlantis first." Tya took a deep breath and met his gaze. "Can we talk?" The corner of her mouth tilted up a little as if she was unsure of his reaction.

"Tya, you said I didn't know what I was talking about because I left Atlantis." Adam shook his head. "I wanted to come back, but I couldn't."

"I didn't know that." Tya huffed and crossed her arms.

Adam noticed her bottom lip jutted out a little and formed a cute pout. Great! Tya is mad at me and I think she's cute. Adam inspected his fingernails and tried to focus.

"I'm sorry. Can you sit down?"

Adam raised his eyes to see her gesturing toward a chair. "Sure." Maybe she won't be so distracting if I sit down.

"I don't know why I said those things." Tya played with a ring on her thumb. "Remember the last time you were here?" Her voice wavered, but she didn't look up.

"Yeah. We did some cool stuff together," replied Adam.

"And we wanted the same thing. To save Atlantis." She chewed the corner of her lip. "I want that again."

"Us to be the same or to save Atlantis?"

"Both," she watched him with wide eyes. Almost as if she was begging him to agree with her.

"We're on the same page with the saving Atlantis part. But we are not the same people anymore. And we don't agree on what needs to be done. I want to find the thirteenth skull and you want to use one of the replacement skulls," said Adam.

Tya's face became so still she looked like a mannequin. He waited for her to speak, but then realized there were no sounds coming from the skulls either. He touched the skull closest to him on the table. It didn't make a sound. A sick feeling formed in the bottom of Adam's stomach. What the heck was happening here? He stood up.

Tya reached a hand toward him, her eyes bright and her face lit up with a smile. "I'm so glad you're back. It's going to be wonderful being together again. We'll be a great team!"

"Tya, what are you talking about?"

She frowned at him. "Don't be silly. You know what I'm talking about. I called you back to Atlantis with the thirteenth skull." Tya tilted her head. "We talked, and we decided to work together just like last time. Remember."

Adam couldn't believe what he was hearing. How could Tya not remember the conversation from a minute ago? Then the explanation hit him. This is what a time loop looks like.

What do I do now? My sister would say, 'fake it till you make it'. Adam sat down and lifted the corners of his mouth hoping Tya recognized it as a smile instead of masking his confusion. I must be desperate. I'm taking advice from my sister. "Sorry, traveling here must have done something to my brain," said Adam. "I remember now, we were a team."

"Can you help me with the research?" asked Tya.

"I have a better idea."

Tya narrowed her eyes at him.

"I need to find Orri and get him to work with us too. The power of three. Right?"

She nodded and she smiled again.

Adam rushed on before she could speak. "Can you start without me? You're better at this than I am."

"You're just trying to get out of working in the library."

"Okay, you caught me." This time he grinned at her. "But can we do it my way? Please."

"You could always talk me into doing it your way." She shrugged. "I guess some things don't change. Okay. You'll come back to the library later?"

"Sure. See you later." He stood up and once he was out of Tya's sight he bolted out of the library.

Adam knew Orri's special place was the popollama field. He headed there as quickly as he could. When he got to the arena, Orri was sitting on the sidelines and several others were playing on the turf. He knew there were other people living in the city, but now it sunk in how different life at the Temple was from everyday life in Atlantis.

Orri stood up and came to him. "Let's get out of here. We need to talk."

As soon as they were away from the boys on the field Adam spoke. "Something strange happened when I was with Tya."

Orri's eyebrows lifted. "You felt the time loop too?"

"Yeah. It was weird. Tya acted like I had just arrived in Atlantis. She was excited about us being a team again." Adam rolled his shoulders to get rid of the chill crawling down his back.

"Caileen hadn't started researching yet, my teammates froze for a couple of minutes, and then they thought we were playing on a different day. I think we have lost a couple of days."

"I don't know what that means. How have things changed?" Adam paused for a moment. "Is Noor still with you?"

"Yes." Orri paused. "Noor, I'd like you to listen to this."

"I'm here," said Noor.

Orri told Noor about the time loops. "I think that means whatever caused the time loop is only affecting some of what has happened in the last few days. We don't know what is different ..."

Orri didn't need to finish the sentence. Adam understood the pressure of saving Atlantis just got more complicated.

"We need to talk," said Noor. "I have a place where I go to think."

After leaving the field, they walked through the city in silence. Atlantis was constructed in concentric circles, and Noor led them to the outer ring. The crowds thinned when they reached their destination. Stopping at a bench overlooking the canal, Orri gestured for Adam to take a seat, and Orri leaned against a lamppost.

Adam swallowed hard at the thought of this beautiful scene disappearing, and his thoughts returned to changing time. "There have been two time loops now and we still don't know how they affect timelines. What do we need to do?"

"I was thinking about that as we walked here. We are starting to think alike." The corner of Orri's mouth lifted.

Adam shook his head and smiled too.

"Any travel not following a prophecy or having council approval causes rifts in the space/time continuum," said Noor. "Both black holes and time loops are rifts in the continuum. Time loops are explained by something called Changed Timeline Theory. It works like this: a person traveling to another dimension would continue to exist in the old dimension but his actions in the other dimension would change the timeline in the old dimension."

Noor paused for a moment and Orri rubbed his skull pendant.

"Do you have to do that?" Adam nodded at Orri's hand on his pendant.

"Sorry. Old habit." Orri lowered his hand.

"I know. It's still creepy when you do it," said Adam. Last time he was in Atlantis, Cavan had manipulated Orri through his skull pendant, and Orri had a tendency to rub it when Cavan was controlling him.

Adam stared at the water in the canal. "Zador coming to Atlantis must have caused the last time loop. Maybe we weren't affected because we were there when it happened."

Orri rubbed his chin. This gesture reminded Adam of Noor.

"It's a good theory," said Orri in his own voice.

"We still need to get the thirteenth skull, and we have to cross inter-dimensional lines to get it."

Orri sat on the bench and turned to Adam. "That would cause another time loop. It is not an option."

What had the skull in the library said? Something about a different dimension ... "When Atlantis was located in Machu Picchu, the city was also located in the ninth dimension." Adam watched Orri. "What does that mean?"

Orri rested his elbow on his knee. Cupping his chin with his hand, he stared across the canal. "That's it!" One side of his mouth lifted. "A long time ago Atlanteans began to realize their civilization had to change to stay on Earth. The city of Atlantis was located at Machu Picchu and the temple existed separately in the ninth dimension. Travel between Earth and the ninth dimension is easier because Atlantis existed in both places at the same time." He stood up.

"Then we could cross into Machu Picchu through the portal and still be in Atlantis." Adam gazed at Orri. "Do you know where the portal is?"

"I do," said Noor.

"Now we need Adrian Zador to go to Machu Picchu." Adam paused. "Noor, can we tell Caileen about the time loop?"

"You can, but she might not believe you," replied Noor.

"Maybe it's better for me to talk to Caileen," Adam looked at Orri.

Orri nodded. "You have less history with her."

"I'll find out where she is in her timeline, and then explain to her what has happened."

The sky went black and the streetlights glowed.

"It has been a very long day." Orri leaned both arms on his knees and clasped his hands.

Adam noticed Orri's hands were shaking before he interlaced his fingers. Exhaustion flowed through him too. They were in no shape to do anything tonight. His stomach rolled in sickening waves; saving Atlantis would have to wait until they had the energy to execute the plan. One more day wouldn't make a difference, would it? "Let's get some rest and I'll talk to Caileen at first light."

Chapter Twenty-Six

Delanna sat by the fire spinning the llama wool into yarn for her weaving frame. Her fingers did the repetitive actions without her thinking about the work.

Delanna believed she had been here for almost ten Earth years. Manata had been a young girl when she came to Machu Picchu, and now, she'd become a beautiful young woman.

Thinking of Manata reminded her of her son Orri, and her heart ached. She tried not to think about him because it troubled her too much, and she needed to keep her guard up if she was going to foil Andros's plan and escape.

Several times since he had first brought her here, she had tried to escape through the portal Andros used to travel between Earth and Atlantis. Each time she discovered where the portal to Atlantis was hidden, he moved the doorway to another location.

Eventually Delanna devised a plan where she infused a pebble with energy, and she could track its movements throughout the city.

She slipped the pebble into Andros' pocket. By using the trail left by the tracker, Delanna shadowed him when he left their hut. The tracker allowed her to follow him while staying out of sight as she pursued him across the central plaza to the Temple of the Sun. This was the temple where the winter and summer solstice aligned with the windows, and the rays of sun hit the altar in the middle of the temple. Here the original residents of Machu Picchu had paid homage to the Sun god and marked the passing of the seasons.

Peeking through the window of the temple, she watched him tap a stone in the middle of the wall and the rocks moved aside to create a doorway. Andros stepped through the portal and pushed a stone on the other side to close the opening. A shadow of the doorway remained for a few seconds after he used it. The shadow disappeared before she could reach it, but her heart skipped a beat because she knew this was their way out.

The next time Andros visited, Delanna, Irdel, and Manata were ready. When Andros slipped across the central area to the Sacred Plaza this time, the three followed. When the shadow doorway appeared after Andros had returned to Atlantis, Delanna used her energy to reopen the door. The stones slid silently apart, and she stepped through the portal with the other two close behind. The tall shelving piled high with skulls told her the portal lead to the library in Atlantis. She let out a breath she didn't know she had been holding and gestured for Irdel and Manata to follow her.

They slipped down the closest aisle and turned a corner at the end.

Andros stepped in front of Delanna causing her to shriek and take a step backwards. He squinted at her. "How did you get here?"

Delanna's breath came in short spurts. They had made it this far. She would not let him imprison them again. "You left the door open."

His eyes narrowed into slits. "Don't lie to me! You did something." He grabbed Manata's arm and pulled her in front of him. His arm wrapped around her waist and his other hand clutched her throat. "Tell me what you did, or I will kill her."

The young girl stared at Delanna, her eyes wide and her face pale, silently begging her to do something. Irdel grabbed Manata's sleeve and held tight.

"I followed you," Delanna snapped. "Irdel and Manata did nothing. I am the one you should punish. Let them go."

"You know I cannot do that. They would tell the council what I have done." Andros chuckled.

The smug sound made Delanna shiver.

He walked back toward the door dragging Manata and Irdel with him. "Time to go back to Machu Picchu." He touched several stones, and the portal opened again. He nodded at Irdel.

The engineer looked at Delanna. She inclined her head, knowing they had no choice. Irdel's eyes softened, and she knew he didn't blame her for what happened. He stepped through the doorway into the sun of Machu Picchu.

Andros shoved Manata through the portal and closed the doorway.

Delanna clenched her fists. "They are innocent! I planned this."

"Do not worry you will join them soon." His words came out bold and sure.

She knew he enjoyed playing with her, but she would not beg him to save herself.

Andros continued. "If you attempt to escape again, I will make sure Orri loses all his powers. He'll be disgraced and thrown off the council."

Fury boiled inside her and she gritted her teeth to contain the angry words. She would not give Andros the satisfaction of confirming he had found the only way he could control her.

Andros opened the door again and showed the way with a sweep of his arm.

Delanna held her head high and walked through.

"If you follow me again, I will take care of Orri." The words 'take care,' were emphasized so there was no doubt what he meant.

Andros used her love for her son to trap her in his bizarre attempt to become the ruler of Atlantis. If she ever got out of this, she would make him pay, and pay in a big way.

The three of them sat around the small cooking fire in the hut enjoying their evening meal after a hard day of harvesting corn and planting the next cycle of crops. The thick stone walls and thatch roof kept the inside of the tiny house cool on hot days like this.

Delanna watched Irdel. The old man's hand shook when he scooped up the sweet corn, and several morsels fell to the ground. "I'll give you some healing energy after we are done here," she said.

Irdel raised his eyes to hers and nodded.

"Can you teach me to do that?" Manata asked.

The stone wall of the hut shimmered and disappeared. Andros stepped through and touched a rock beside the opening. The wall became whole again. "What is Delanna going to teach you?"

Manata stared open-mouthed at Andros.

These unexpected entrances from the thirteenth dimension had Delanna on edge. Andros could appear anytime and at any place on the ancient hillside of Machu Picchu. "She wants to learn how to cook the corn to keep its sweetness." Delanna lifted the corners of her mouth hoping Andros would interpret the action as a smile and not fear.

Andros reached into Manata's bowl with his fingers. He stuffed a handful of corn into his mouth and chewed. "You are right, it is sweet," he said with his mouth still full. "I hope you will grow corn as sweet as this in Chichen Itza."

Delanna had to swallow her gasp. Chichen Itza was where Atlantis existed before the fabled land had moved to Machu Picchu. She must find out what he was planning. After setting her bowl on the ground, she stood. In a calm voice, she asked, "Would you like to come for a walk with me?"

"Of course." He grinned. Grabbing her hand, he tucked it into the crook of his arm.

It took all Delanna's willpower not to yank her hand away. She guided them out the doorway of the hut and across the field to a stone bench overlooking the setting sun.

"This is very nice," Andros commented, patting her hand with his calloused one. "I like it when you are agreeable. It makes things much more civilized, don't you think?" He turned toward her and this time his whole mouth bowed into a smile.

Every time the man's lips curved up a shiver ran down Delanna's spine. *What does he want?* Instead of answering, she tried to smile not trusting herself to talk.

Andros stood, stuffed his hands into his pant pockets, and puffed out his chest. "I am very close to discovering how to establish a connection in the ninth dimension. When that is done, I will move Atlantis to Chichen Itza."

Delanna came to her feet so quickly her long grey curls swirled around her shoulders. "It takes the combined energy of the entire council to move Atlantis." Before she could stop herself, she poked a finger at his chest. "You are not the leader of the council! And Noor would never allow this!"

Andros showed his teeth in a wolfish grin. "Noor is dead."

"You're lying!"

Andros placed a hand on his chest. "Why would I lie about that?"

Something about the way Andros asked the question made her believe him. Delanna took a step back and collapsed onto the bench. Noor had been on the council for longer than anyone could remember. How would Atlantis go on without him? Her hands shook as she clasped them in her lap.

"And with my help, your son will be the next leader of the council." The toothy smile was back on Andros' face.

A sick feeling rolled in Delanna's stomach. "Why would you want Orri to lead?"

"Orri has more support than I do, and he will do what I want. After all, he wouldn't want something bad to happen to his mother."

Delanna knew he had them both. She would willingly sacrifice herself to stop Andros, and perhaps Orri would be willing to do the same. She couldn't take the chance Orri would sacrifice himself for her. Andros knew that.

Chapter Twenty-Seven

The next morning, Adam got up early while Orri was still sleeping. He had discovered that each hallway in the Temple was unique, and now that he had figured out how they were linked, he was getting lost less.

Today would be the day they saved Atlantis, he told himself as he raised his fist to knock on the partially open door of Caileen's office.

"I can't do it." Caileen's voice trembled as she spoke the words.

Adam lowered his hand. Who was she talking to?

"You will find my stone and the base for the skull or I will destroy Atlantis." Adam knew the angry voice belonged to Adrian Zador. The person Caileen had sworn she wouldn't talk to.

No, that wasn't right; because of the time loop, she didn't know she had made that promise.

"I don't know where those artifacts are. I need time to find them," Caileen begged.

Adam peeked around the door. Caileen had her hands on either side of a baseball sized, gold-colored skull.

"You have one day. Bring the artifacts to Machu Picchu," Zador said calmly, because he knew Caileen had no choice. "If I don't hear from you, I will destroy Atlantis."

"Please don't do anything. I will find what you need."

Adam could tell by the look on her face that Caileen believed the threat was real.

Caileen stood up and Adam quickly slipped back down the hallway and ducked into the first available room. With his ear on the door, he listened to her walk down the hallway and take the path through the courtyard.

Adrian Zador had solved their problem. He was going to Machu Picchu. But something told Adam he needed to take the skull on Caileen's desk.

Opening the door, he checked both ways to make sure the coast was clear, then slipped down the hall and into Caileen's office. Adam grabbed the ordinary looking gold colored skull off the desk. Caileen would know the skull was missing the minute she walked into her office. He had no idea how he would explain it, but he'd worry about that later.

As he reached for the door, Adam heard footsteps in the hall. He ducked behind Caileen's desk and held his breath.

The door hinge squeaked. Someone stood in the entrance to the office, their breath coming in noisy wheezes.

The pounding of his heart filled Adam's ears. It was so loud he thought the person in the doorway must be able to hear him.

Then, whoever it was, left the way they came.

Adam breathed a sigh of relief and rushed to the door in time to see Andros turn the corner to the courtyard.

That was the second time in two days he'd seen the counselor sneaking around. What was he up to?

Adam crossed the courtyard and watched Andros go into the hallway leading to the library. He followed the counselor at a safe distance to avoid being discovered. Stopping at the next corner he peered around it to see Andros standing in front of Horatio.

The big man didn't move to let Andros past. "Hello, Andros. You've been coming to the library a lot in the last couple of days. What are you researching?"

"That's none of your business," snarled Andros. "Let me through."

Horatio didn't move. "It is my job to protect the library, and now..." The big man's mouth quivered, then he stood tall and rolled his shoulders back. "Now that Noor is gone, I have the authority to ask where you're going in the library."

Horatio knew Noor was gone, and Andros didn't question Horatio accusing him of coming to the library in the last couple of days. Now, Adam knew of four people that were not affected by the time loop. He wondered how they were connected.

Andros scowled. "Who gave you the right to ask questions?"

"Someone who cares about saving Atlantis."

"So Raine is overstepping his bounds again." The counselor pushed his shoulder against Horatio's massive chest.

Still holding his position, Horatio commented, "The more you resist answering me, the more I think you are doing somethin' you shouldn't be doing."

Andros peered up at Horatio, then he shook his head. "I'm meeting with Caileen if you must know."

Horatio stepped to the side and gestured for Andros to pass.

Adam tucked the gold skull in the crook of his arm, walked down the hallway, and stopped in front of Horatio. "I bet you don't have to guess who I'm coming to see."

Horatio laughed. "Say 'Hi' to Tya for me," he said as he handed Adam a cookie.

Adam stuffed the cookie into his pocket and hurried down the corridor to the big gold doors. Stepping through the doors he hoped to catch a glimpse of Andros, but he saw no one. Moving left, he peered down each of the aisles.

Nothing.

Then he ran in the other direction, still no sign of Andros.

The library was too big to search every aisle for the counselor. He didn't know how he would find Andros. Every fiber in Adam's body told him Andros was up to no good. Was it possible Andros had something to do with the destruction happening in Atlantis?

"Where is Andros?" Adam asked hoping one of the library skulls knew the answer.

Silence.

Adam leaned against the shelves at the end of a row. He reached up and rubbed the head of his skull pendant, he needed help to find Andros, but had no idea who to ask.

The small skull resting on his chest glowed and sent a warm wave of energy into his body. "Visualize finding Andros and I will link to his skull pendant," a strange whispery voice said.

Adam knew where the words came from even though he hadn't heard his pendant speak since he had first come to Atlantis more than two years ago. He had picked the tiny skull out of the bowl filled with many skulls, and then the little green skull had confirmed Adam had made the right choice. He looked down at the skull cradled in his palm. Why was it talking to him after all this time?

"I have always been ready to help you, but you never asked." The skull sounded offended that his assistance hadn't been requested. "Follow the lights on the floor, I know where his skull is."

Adam stared at the blinking lights moving down the aisle in front of him and began to walk.

"I didn't know I could ask for your help," said Adam. Raine had taught them how to channel energy through the pendant but had never mentioned it had other uses. That was probably because the trio only had one lesson with Raine.

"They should remove whoever trained you from the council."

The corner of Adam's mouth lifted as he imagined Raine's reaction to the skull's indignant statement.

A thought swirled in Adam's brain. Every time he had needed help in Atlantis someone gave it to him. A skull would speak to him, or a vision would show him what to do. Was he really a hero? He thought of himself as a fraud. When he thought of everything he'd done in Atlantis, it had all happened by luck.

The skull's soft voice spoke again, "You are special, and the prophecies were created to guide you."

Noor thought he was special too. His throat constricted at the memory of his grandfather saying those words.

What if the skull and Noor were right, the prophecies were created for him to follow? Destiny, not choice, ruled his world. The battle never changed. His jaw tensed. Would he ever get a chance to prove he had the strength to save Atlantis?

"Ordinarily the pendants are only linked when it is time to move Atlantis, but this is a special circumstance," the skull lectured. "That is how I can find Andros."

The lights in the floor glowed brighter. Adam didn't have a choice, even though the rebel inside him still wanted to refuse. He wasn't the kid he was two years ago, so he followed the lights deep into the library. They led him to a table set in front of a rough, grey stone wall. On the table lay a blue skull pendant.

"That pendant belongs to Andros," said Adam's skull.

Adam grabbed the chain and cradled the small skull in his palm. "Where is Andros," he asked the skull.

It didn't respond, just rested inertly in his hand.

The pendant on his chest glowed again. "Andros has disconnected himself from his pendant. It isn't able to tell you where he has gone."

Adam gazed at the shelves of skulls surrounding the table wondering where Andros had gone. His eyes were drawn to a large black skull. "Machu Picchu was the location of Atlantis from 1450 in Earth years to 1572 in Earth years." It went on to describe the buildings and the layout of the ancient city. Adam lost interest in what the skull was saying. His eyes wandered over the other shelves in the aisle.

Another skull two rows over lit up. "The Temple of Nethuns existed in the ninth dimension during the time Atlantis was in Machu Picchu. The people of Atlantis remained on Earth and the council was protected in an alternate dimension."

Orri had said he knew a way to travel to Machu Picchu in the ninth dimension. If Andros was going to Machu Picchu and he was still causing the black holes, then their theory about travelling using the ninth dimension was wrong.

A ruby red skull on a shelf below the blue skull shone. "The gateway between Machu Picchu and Atlantis has been closed since Atlantis has moved to the thirteenth dimension."

A mottled grey and white skull further down the aisle spoke in a gruff voice interrupted. "Not true. The gateway is open again."

Adam remembered they had used the portal to Machu Picchu when he was in Atlantis two years ago.

The ruby skull repeated its information in a louder voice and was once more stopped by the grey one. "The gateway to Machu Picchu has been open since Adam of Earth first came to Atlantis."

Shaking his head, Adam muted the discussion. A library on Earth might have conflicting information, but the books never got into an argument with each other. Maybe that was why he liked this library better than the ones at home.

Adrian Zador was going to Machu Picchu. They had to stop him from getting what he wanted. If their actions caused another black hole to take part of Atlantis, it was a better option than all of Atlantis being destroyed.

Adam shoved the blue pendant into his pocket hoping the skull pendant might help them find out what Andros was up to, and with the gold skull still tucked in the crook of his arm he rushed out of the library.

Chapter Twenty-Eight

Adam entered their room to find Orri sprawled face down on his bed. When he sat on the edge of his bed, Orri stirred and then struggled to pull himself into a half-sitting position against the wall.

It was clear the older boy had no energy. Hadn't he slept last night when they got back to their room? "What's wrong with you?"

"Nothing. I am all right." Orri ran his hands through his hair.

Adam squinted at Orri. "You look like you are a thousand years old."

A small smile trickled across Orri's mouth. "Tell me what happened with Caileen."

Even with Noor inside him, Orri shouldn't look this bad. Something wasn't right.

Orri stared at Adam. "Stop speculating what is wrong with me and tell me about Caileen."

Adam could hear Noor in Orri's tone. He wasn't going to let that stop him from finding out what his roommate was up to. "Not until you tell me what you did to make you so exhausted."

Orri sighed. "I practiced shapeshifting. I can make myself look and sound like Caileen." His mouth almost moved into a grin, but he couldn't hold the expression.

"And the cost of doing it?"

"I am a little tired," said Orri.

"Hmmm." Adam made a noncommittal sound. He watched Orri process it and then react.

"What does that mean?"

"Just look at yourself. You can hardly move. Does Noor think this is a good idea?"

"Noor is leaving this up to me to decide what to do, and I would use it if we had a way to talk to Zador."

Adam's chest tightened. He did have a way and he knew Orri would use it.

Orri carefully straightened and stared at him. "You do have a way, don't you?"

"It could kill you," Adam argued.

Orri said nothing as he continued to observe him.

Adam didn't like the way the conversation had flipped. "I overheard Caileen talking to Zador using the gold skull." Adam held up his hand to stop Orri from interrupting. "I stole it."

"You've got it!" Orri scowled at him. "Where is it?"

Adam set it on the bedside table. "I didn't talk to her." He filled Orri in on what he had overheard in Caileen's office and what happened with Andros in the library. When he finished talking, he pulled Andros's pendant out of his pocket and dropped it on the bedside table too.

Orri's eyes narrowed as he fingered the chain on the tiny skull. "Why would he leave his skull pendant? The time loop has reset time back to before Raine started tracking the pendants.

"Do you know why Andros would be going to Machu Picchu?" Adam asked.

"No." Orri twisted his torso and swung his legs over the side of the bed. When he was finally sitting upright, he was panting like he had run a race. "But it looks like we need to go there too."

Someone knocked on the door.

Orri shoved the gold skull and Andros's pendant under his pillow.

"I will keep your secret, for now," Adam muttered as he stood up and opened the door.

Caileen and Tya stood in the hall.

"Can we come in?" Caileen asked.

"Sure. I guess." Adam opened the door wider.

Orri straightened the blankets at the end of his bed and gestured to Caileen. She sat down and squeezed her hands together in her lap. Tya perched on the much tidier end of Adam's bed. Adam closed the door and leaned back against the wall.

Caileen twisted her hands. "I need to tell you both something." Her eyes flickered to Orri and away again. "Adrian Zador contacted me." She spoke the words all in one breath.

Adam realised Caileen and Tya had probably lost the last three days because of the time loop. They didn't remember earlier talks between the four of them. He turned to Caileen and even though he knew the answer he asked, "What did Zador say to you?"

"He demanded I find the hand and the keystone and bring them to Machu Picchu, or he will destroy Atlantis." Caileen's voice wavered. "We don't have the keystone."

"Caileen, it doesn't matter what Zador said," Tya spoke gently to her friend before looking at the boys. "We've found a solution that could save Atlantis."

Adam pulled a chair out of the corner, turned it around, sat down, and nodded for her to continue.

"We worked all night and we've found something," Tya gestured at Caileen. "The Incas copied the thirteenth skull and both skulls worked. If one of the replacement skulls is actually a real copy, we can use it to save Atlantis."

"Maybe I can talk to one of the replacement skulls to see how much it knows," said Adam. "Then we can decide what to do."

"And if we make a mistake, what happens to Atlantis?" Orri shook his head. "I don't like this solution."

Orri's statement hung in the air between them. That was the problem, there was no way of knowing if they were helping or hurting Atlantis until it was too late. Adam could see by the looks on their faces they were all thinking the same thing.

"I could talk to Adrian Zador and convince him to exchange the replica with the real thirteenth skull," said Caileen. "Then I will pretend to give him the real hand, but it will be a copy we've made. The only problem is I don't know what to do about the keystone. Why doesn't he have it?"

Adam exchanged a look with Orri who shook his head. Adam agreed, they shouldn't tell the girls about the keystone for the same reason Adam didn't know where it was hidden. Caileen would want to barter with Zador. He knew that was never going to work. "I don't know," said Adam. "But whatever we do with Zador is going to involve him coming to Atlantis, and that will cause another black hole."

"So we're back to the replacement skulls," said Orri.

"I think it's a good idea." Adam glanced at the girls.

"I say Adam talks to the replacement skull," said Tya.

"I agree." Caileen nodded again.

Adam knew what Orri's solution to the problem was. A solution that could kill him and cause further damage to Atlantis. How much more destruction could the city take? Adam's eyes fixed on Orri's.

"I guess majority rules," said Orri, like he agreed with the decision.

"I need to grab something to eat," said Adam. "Let's meet in the council room in five minutes."

Orri frowned at him. "Your Earth time doesn't mean anything here. Let's meet in one time segment."

Caileen and Tya agreed and left.

Adam grabbed a couple pancha from the bowl on the nightstand. He popped both into his mouth. The taste of tomato soup and grilled cheese filled his mouth. He looked at Orri. "Are you really with us?"

"I said I was, didn't I?"

"You did." Adam walked to the door. "Are you coming?"

Orri pulled his dirty shirt over his head. "Yeah. I need a clean tunic and then I'll be there."

Chapter Twenty-Nine

For years James had done what his boss wanted because it allowed him to study Atlantis, and he believed in Adrian's dream to save all the starving people in the world. He looked around the lush atrium on the top floor of the Farscope Foundation building. Vegetables of all kinds grew next to trees laden with fruit. James watched the flashes of color as butterflies, birds and bees danced from one flower to the next. Water trickled in a stream hidden from sight by thick foliage, and fish splashed in ponds fed by the running water. This was all possible because Adrian had discovered how to harness the power of crystals to grow this garden of Eden.

Adrian had heard about a very special jade knife in the museum's Egyptian art exhibit and had ordered James to get it. The museum curator had been happy to lend it to him to study it. This was one of those times when Adrian's influence had not been an advantage.

The green jade knife was known as a chi stone, and it brought the strength of a warrior to the person who possessed it. When James had held the small dagger, his conscience disappeared, and he wanted to act knowing he had the strength to accomplish anything he desired. When he set the powerful artifact down cold fingers of fear slithered down his spine. James knew he must stop Adrian from using the knife to hurt Atlantis. The artifact was safely hidden in his lab, and if he could stall for a couple of days maybe he could figure out what to do.

Adrian strode down the path in the atrium. He stopped in front of where James was sitting. "Do you have the chi stone yet?"

"I haven't finished researching it." His heart thudded in his chest. "I'm not sure it will accomplish what you want it to. Can you give me some time to do more research?"

"That isn't for you to decide. Give me the knife." The way Adrian made the statement sent icicles down the archeologist's back.

"It's a warrior stone. History tells us the last person who used it died a violent death, brought on by his overestimation of his physical abilities."

"I don't need it to increase my strength."

James swallowed a lump in his throat threatening to choke him. He didn't know what had happened when Adrian had used the Egyptian portal, but his boss had come back with his suit covered in dust and what looked like burn marks on his shoulder. "You said you couldn't use the Egyptian portal again. How are you going to get into Atlantis?"

Adrian narrowed his eyes. "I pay you to answer my questions, not to ask me questions." He leaned forward. "You work for me. Give. Me. The. Knife."

Adrian's cold stare drilled into James leaving no doubt legends about the jade warrior knife were true and Adrian wouldn't think twice about killing anyone who stood in his way. "It's in my lab."

"Get it."

Now James realized Adrian wanted to steal the powerful crystal energy from Atlantis, not to save the world, but to use it for his own corrupt purposes. He must protect Atlantis from his boss.

He nodded and exited the atrium. Why hadn't he told Adrian he didn't have the knife, or it had no powers? Or come up with any excuse to give him more time to stop his boss. He stared into the eye scanner beside the entrance to his lab, the door unlocked, and he walked in. He leaned against the closed door and listened to the electronic lock close with a click. He was a coward, and his actions would lead to the destruction of Atlantis.

Chapter Thirty

Orri felt guilty about lying to Adam and the girls, but Noor thought it was necessary.

"No one else needs to be involved," thought Noor.

"Are we any different than Cavan or anyone else who has acted on their own to suit their needs?" Orri silently questioned Noor. "The last time you did this you almost lost your life."

"We are not doing this for personal gain." Noor's outrage showed in the tone of his thoughts. "We are saving Atlantis!"

Orri didn't respond.

"I am not acting on my own; you are coming with me. Together we will be stronger."

Noor's attempt at logic was weak at best. "That doesn't make me feel any better about this."

"Can you think of another way?" Noor asked in a calmer voice.

"Why are you so against using the replacement skulls?"

"I don't trust Zador and he is the one who created the replacement skulls. I am sure that is not the correct solution." Noor paused. When Orri remained quiet he continued. "We know we cannot avoid doing more damage to Atlantis. By minimizing the amount of time Zador is in Atlantis and keeping contact down to just the two of us we should lower the amount of damage."

"I hope we are able to save Atlantis without hurting anyone else," thought Orri before going quiet.

Orri struggled into a new tunic and grabbed a couple pancha, chewing slowly he pulled as much energy as he could from the small white balls. Taking a deep breath, he picked up three more.

It wasn't the best way to restore his energy, but it would have to do for now. He grabbed the gold skull on his way out of the room.

He jogged to the library. The pace seemed slow to Orri, but Noor hadn't moved this fast in a long time.

Orri slowed down to walk past Horatio, so he didn't call attention to himself. Noor would lead them to the Machu Picchu archives located in the library, and in those archives, they would find the portal.

The last time Orri traveled to the sacred place they had used the dimensional portal in Machu Picchu by accident. After rushing down the stairs into the archive section, Orri stopped waiting for Noor to show him where to go.

"Do we have enough energy to succeed?" Noor asked.

If Noor was so convinced this was the only way to save Atlantis it didn't matter what he thought. "We must save Atlantis." The tone in Orri's thought clearly showed he wasn't happy about the situation.

Orri walked down the orderly row of skulls in front of him. Noor showed him where to turn and led him deep into the library archives. The crystal lights were set further apart giving a gloomy aura to the space. A layer of dust covered everything on the shelves, whole skulls were mixed with broken ones. Then the lights were gone.

Even in the darkness, Orri knew the row continued. He didn't need Noor to guide him now. Forming a light ball he placed it above his head. High brick walls rose on either side leading to a dark opening. The air smelled of burnt wood, and at the doorway a grey powder littered the floor. Orri bent down and touched it. Ashes.

How could he have forgotten the lady trapped in the door on their last trip to Machu Picchu? He, along with Adam and Tya, had freed her by burning the door. But the doorway wasn't in Atlantis last time, it was in Machu Picchu. What was happening?

"This doorway is the link between the dimensions. It is on both sides of the portal," answered Noor. "If you go through it in Atlantis, you don't go through it on Earth. And the opposite is also true. It is because Atlantis existed in both places and needed to be protected from unwanted visitors from Earth when it was in the ninth dimension."

Noor sounded like Tya, thought Orri. He heard Noor chuckle as he stepped through the portal with his light ball casting a blue glow over the area. The room hadn't changed since they were last here, it was still a jumble of artifacts as if someone had shoved everything they didn't need into the space. Swords, bows, arrows, pottery urns, with a scattering of gold and silver jewellery.

Spotting a section of a marble column in the junk, he pushed it upright and maneuvered it nearer to the wall in front of the doorway. Orri set the gold colored crystal skull on top of the column. Taking a deep breath, he centered himself and began the process of shapeshifting. It seemed easier this time. Maybe it was his imagination or perhaps because he could focus on the knowledge the pain would pass. His body changed first, his hips widened, his chest blossomed, and his shoulders shrank. The face was the most painful part of the transformation as every bone shifted and changed to form Caileen's face. Orri ground his teeth together so he wouldn't cry out.

Orri rolled Caileen's shoulders back and placed her hands on either side of skull. "Hello. Is anyone there?" Caileen's voice came smoothly out of her mouth, startling him.

"Have you found the artifacts?" Zador's voice questioned almost immediately, as if he'd been waiting for her to speak.

His heartbeat quickened. Thoughts scrambled through Noor's head. Why hadn't he thought about this? What should he say? "Not exactly," said Caileen.

"What? Do you have my stone and the base or not?"

He had an idea, and with a deep breath his heart slowed down. "I know where the base is but I'm not sure about the stone's location. Do you have a connection with it? If you do, you could come to Atlantis and find it."

"I'll be right there."

Orri heard Zador stand up and walk away from his skull. All he had to do was go through one more doorway and then he could force Zador to tell him where the thirteenth skull was.

Orri's knees felt weak.

Noor thought it was from relief until he took a step. No! They were running out of energy. They couldn't stop now. They were so close.

Carefully Orri made his way to the dark grey brick wall at the back of the space where the blue glow from the light ball revealed an archway closed with a grey stone door.

Orri scanned the brick wall beside the door and almost dropped to his knees. Hold on! Orri moved his arm toward the wall hoping Noor would be able to tell him what to do.

His hands slowly touched a series of bricks. One moved to the side revealing the outline of a handprint. Orri held a hand up. It was too small.

"Now what?" Orri asked.

Noor's thoughts were sluggish too. The energy drain was affecting him as well. Think. Think.

Pain sliced through Orri's chest. His head felt like it would explode. I'm losing Caileen's molecular integrity.

"No! Hang on," begged Noor.

Orri, not Caileen, lay flat out on the stone floor. He couldn't feel his arms and legs. His body weighed more than a granite building block. He could see the outline of the hand on the wall above his head. If he could have smiled, he would have. The outline was the same size as his hand.

He rolled over and pushed himself to his hands and knees. Leaning on the wall Orri staggered to his feet. When he placed his hand on the outline a doorway opened. A rush of wind pushed him back to his knees. He squinted when a bright flash of light filled the doorway and a man came into view. Adrian Zador.

Orri clutched the side of the doorway and tried to stand up straighter. Why hadn't he rested for a moment?

Adrian stopped in front of Orri with his mouth curled into a tight-lipped smile.

Orri frowned at the green stone knife in Zador's hand. Where did that come from? Orri could feel the huge amount of power the small artifact contained.

"I was expecting Caileen, but it is good to see you again." Adrian held out his hand. Noor remembered the particulars of the Earth greeting. Orri held out his hand before he realized the danger of the action. Zador gripped it and squeezed. A wave of ice-cold energy shot up Orri's arm and into his body. He slumped to the ground. His last conscious thought was a silent scream as he heard the businessman step over him.

Chapter Thirty-One

Adam met the girls in the council chambers.

"Where's Orri?" Caileen asked.

"He said he'll be here after he changes his tunic."

"Is he mad at me?" Caileen's voice cracked.

"He's worried about you because the council could punish you for what you've done." Adam wanted to make sure she understood. "You could lose your place on the council or worse."

Caileen gazed at him with eyes pooled with sorrow. "I know, but now I can see how easily it happened to my father." She crossed her arms over her ribs and looked away. "Can we talk about something else?"

"Come sit down." Tya indicated the chairs around the table. "Let's talk about how we are going to find out if one of the replacement skulls is a replica of the thirteenth skull."

Once they sat down Tya focused on him. "Adam, do you have any ideas?"

"The last time I tried to contact the real thirteenth skull both replacement skulls showed up. They were not friendly. But if we work together, we might be able to figure out if one is a real copy."

A shiver ran down Adam's neck. How long does it take to change a shirt? "There's no point talking about this without Orri. I'll go check on him."

"We'll go with you." Caileen stood up.

Adam thought about refusing, and then he realized if Orri was in trouble the girls would be able to help.

The three of them ran to the boys' room. No Orri. Now Adam's whole body felt cold.

Dashing down the halls they made it to the library in record time. "Is Orri here?" Caileen asked Horatio.

"Yeah. He came in not long ago. I thought it was strange, you know, Orri coming to the library by himself."

"Thanks, Horatio." Caileen led as they bolted past the big man.

Inside the golden doors to the library, Adam rubbed his skull pendant. "Where's Orri?"

Tya frowned at Adam. "I forgot you can hear your skull pendant talk, but I didn't know he could answer questions."

"That was the lesson we missed with Raine," Adam replied.

The tiny skull led them through the aisles of the library. Adam knew Orri was up to something he didn't want the council to know about. A lump formed in Adam's stomach.

"We have to find him before he kills himself." Caileen's words echoed what Adam felt.

Adam's pendant continued to lead them into a dark corner where they had to create light balls to show them the way. They walked down a corridor with high brick walls. "Are you sure Orri went this way?" he asked the tiny skull on his chest.

"Go to the doorway, you will find him there."

"According to my dad's notes, this is the portal to Machu Picchu." A line appeared between Caileen's eyebrows.

"Why is Orri coming here?" Tya wondered.

"I think we're about to find out," said Adam.

The smell of burning wood filled Adam's senses and stirred something in his memory, but Caileen kept moving so he didn't have time to think about it.

Caileen stepped across the threshold and gasped.

Adam moved beside her and saw the gold skull on top of a chunk of marble. His heart skipped a beat. This was bad, really bad.

"Oh no." Tya's eyes were wide.

"Orri, what are you doing?" Caileen's hands were fisted at her sides.

Adam surveyed the junk filled room, this was where they had fought Adrian Zador and lost the keystone. At the back of the room, something was leaning against the wall in front of an opening.

A gust of wind nearly knocked him over. Adam hugged a pillar to remain standing and the girls clung to him. Bright lights filled the opening, blinding him for a moment. Spots of light danced before his eyes as he saw a man shake hands with Orri. Adam rubbed his eyes. When he opened them, he watched Orri slump to the floor as if the bones in his body had melted.

Orri, what have you done? Adam recognized the man and his breath caught in his throat. He grabbed Caileen's arm to stop her running to Orri. Tya stood beside Caileen.

The evil businessman stepped over Orri.

Orri groaned.

Good, at least I know he's not dead, Adam thought. Why didn't he listen?

Zador sauntered over and stopped in front of Adam. "Ah, the boy who stole my keystone. And I remember the girl with the red hair, but who are you?" He pointed at Caileen.

"I'm sure you know my voice."

Zador raised an eyebrow. "Thank you for coming to our little party."

He raised his hand and stood with his palm facing toward Adam.

Adam shivered as a cold wave rolled down his body. He tried to swallow but his mouth was too dry. The cold surge was coming from Zador.

The girls tried to move in front of Adam, but Zador held them back with the other hand.

"Where have you hidden it?" The question came out as a reasonable request.

"I didn't hide it," said Adam, glad he could tell the truth.

"But you must know where it is." The businessman's mouth tilted up at the corners, but his eyes were as cold as the wave of energy that continued to scanned Adam's body.

Orri was right about not telling me where he hid the stone. Adam smiled back. "No. I don't."

The smile, if you could call it that, was gone from Zador's lips. An icy fist reached into Adam's belly and twisted his insides cruelly. The pain filled his senses and he screamed.

Orri groaned again.

The girls held hands and pushed against the invisible barrier holding them back.

Zador glanced over his shoulder, lessening his grip on Adam.

Adam grounded himself to the stones beneath his feet and channeled every ounce of power he could draw from the floor into his body. With his hands he drew a line on the floor in front of Zador and it ignited into flames barely a foot high.

"Is that the best you can do?" Zador laughed.

The laughter kindled a burning sensation in Adam's chest.

Caileen grabbed his hand. Adam could feel her energy and Tya's connect to his. He pulled everything into his free hand and the flames on the floor flared into a wall of twisting heat.

Zador jumped back clutching his burnt hands.

Adam watched the other man through the flames. He couldn't believe it when Zador blew on his blistered hands and they healed. Where had he learned to do that?

Zador smiled at Adam and turned to Orri laying on the floor.

"No!" Adam screamed.

Orri's body twitched like a puppet jerked on a string.

Easing to the side to get a clear view of Orri, Adam formed an energy shield around his friend's body and the twitching stopped.

Adam's heart pounded, and his body quivered. He knew he couldn't protect Orri and block Zador at the same time.

"Protect Orri." Adam nodded at Tya. She broke the connection and formed her own energy shield around Orri.

"Stay with me," he ordered Caileen. Adam's energy combined with Caileen's and filled his body again. Rolling the wall of flames into an enormous fireball he flung it at Zador. The evil man put threw up his hands and the ball exploded just in front of him. Sparks burned holes in his suit. The shield protecting Orri wavered in the heat from the fireball but Tya re-established the protection.

Adam knew they were using a huge amount of energy to fight Zador. How had the evil man become so strong? It didn't matter, they had to save Atlantis. "You can't stop us," he yelled and tossed another smaller fireball at the evil man.

This one lit Zador's jacket sleeve on fire and he scrambled to pull the burning clothing off his body. A green stone knife fell out of the jacket's pocket, and Zador grabbed it.

The waves of icy energy flowing off Zador continued to diminish their energy at an alarming rate. Adam's arm shook, and Caileen's grip on his hand tightened sending more energy into his body. He knew they had one last chance to stop Zador. All he could conjure up was a tennis ball sized fireball. He hurled it at the man and hoped it was enough.

Zador pivoted to face Adam right before the fireball impacted his chest and the green stone knife fell to the floor again. Zador's eyes opened wide and he fell backward onto the stone floor.

Adam's arms and legs turned to jelly, he collapsed on the floor. He heard a groan but couldn't tell if it came from him or Orri.

Chapter Thirty-Two

"Adam! Wake up!"

Why was Tya in his room?

"Wake up." Tya yelled again. Adam covered his ears.

His hand was pulled away. "Come on! I know you can hear me!"

This time his head pounded from the noise.

"Please wake up," Tya pleaded in a soft voice.

Adam opened his eyes. He was on the floor in a room lit by the light balls hovering over Tya and Caileen's heads. The memories flooded back. "Is everyone okay?"

"You and Orri took the worst of it," said Tya. "I'm tired and Caileen is, too. We'll be fine after we have rested."

Adam pushed himself onto his elbows. Orri was sitting with Caileen. Zador lay motionless by the portal. "Is he… is he dead?"

"I'm not sure," said Tya. "And I don't want to touch him to find out. He deserved what you and Caileen did to stop him, he caused of all the bad things that are happening to Atlantis."

"Help me sit up."

Tya supported his back as he eased himself up. The room wobbled in his vision and he leaned against her. After a moment he tried to pull away.

"It's okay," she said. "Relax."

The sight of Zador lying on the floor made Adam's stomach roll. He turned his head and his gaze settled on Orri. "I thought you were dead."

"It's not that bad. I'll live." Orri's pale face showed how close he had come to the other option. He lifted one shoulder in an attempt at nonchalance. "You were right. I shouldn't have done it, especially not alone."

"Why did you?" Adam pressed his lips together to avoid yelling at Orri.

"Something inside me was sure using the replacement skulls wouldn't work. I did it because I saw no other way, and I didn't want anyone else to be hurt."

Adam knew Orri was referring to Noor. Orri shouldn't have done what he did, but Adam understood what had happened. Thinking of Noor, Adam slid his hand into his pocket and rubbed the bronze eye. Warmth flowed through his body leaving him feeling stronger.

Caileen pulled away from Orri. "You lied to us! You said you agreed with us," her voice full of outrage.

Forgetting his irritation with Orri, Adam turned on Caileen, "You're calling Orri..."

Tya's fingers dug into his arm causing Adam to stop speaking. "We pushed Orri into agreeing with us. He isn't the first person to act on his own." Tya squeezed his arm again. "But we can't let Adrian Zador trick us into giving him what he wants."

Orri gazed at Caileen. "Any time Zador contacts Atlantis someone ends up lying about it. It doesn't make what I did right. Can you forgive me?"

"I'm sorry, I shouldn't be angry with you, I started this." Caileen's eyes filled with tears and Orri hugged her tight.

Feeling Tya's body close to his and watching Orri and Caileen, Adam suddenly needed to focus on saving Atlantis. "I made a mistake too." When three pairs of eyes turned relief flooded through him. "I was trying to stop Zador from hurting Orri, and I didn't get him to tell me where the thirteenth skull is."

"Or the keystone," said Caileen.

"The keystone is hidden in Atlantis." The words slipped out of Adam's mouth as if all lying had become impossible. Orri grinned at him, and some heaviness disappeared from his chest.

Tya nodded at Zador. "He must be dead; we're all telling the truth."

"Doesn't matter whether he's dead or alive, he can't help us, so there's no point leaving him here," said Caileen. "Tya can you help me move him across through the portal?"

Orri moved to stand up.

Caileen put her hand on Orri's shoulder to stop him. "Stay there, you and Adam need to conserve your energy."

The girls dragged Adrian's body across the threshold and quickly returned to the Atlantis side. On the way back to the boys, Tya picked up the green jade knife. "What is this?"

"Zador's energy was very powerful. Maybe he used it to give him energy," answered Adam.

Tya slipped the knife into her pocket. "We can find a safe place in the library to archive it, and then it won't be used for evil purposes again."

Caileen helped Orri to his feet so his hand could press against the outline. The door began to close, but before it shut completely, it stopped moving and the light on the other side disappeared.

The empty darkness roared as the black hole opened up.

"Run!" Adam scrambled to his feet and grabbed Tya's hand. The black vacuum of empty space made every step agonizing. Knowing they were fighting a losing battle, he wrapped his arm around a large marble column a few steps to the side of the opening and pulled Tya in. Grabbing Caileen's hand, Tya dragged the other two over. The four of them locked arms and clung to the heavy pillar. Gold and silver jewelry flew past their heads, then weapons, pieces of armor, and urns. Lastly, large chunks of marble and heavy stone objects slid across the floor toward the opening. Some pieces were too big for the gap and they crumbled against the wall next to them.

The grinding noise from the big pieces moving across the stone floor prevented Adam from talking to the others. He could feel Tya shaking beside him. On the other side, Orri's legs began to buckle. He didn't have the energy to move them to safety. Images of Alima and Raine finding their squashed bodies flashed through his mind. Adam's hands gripped his friend's fingers tighter, and he closed his eyes waiting for the end.

The noise stopped.

Still holding hands, all four of them dropped to the floor.

"I don't think I could have held on any longer," said Tya in a shaky voice.

Orri pulled his fingers out of Adam's grasp and leaned against Caileen. "I wouldn't have made it without all of you."

"I'm grateful we were all together," added Caileen.

"We make a great team." Adam smiled waiting for the others to comment.

Tya punched him in the shoulder. "You are not doing that corny speech, are you?"

"We didn't buy it last time, so don't waste our time now." Orri's eyes twinkled for a moment and then he sighed. "I don't know about the rest of you, but I need to go to bed."

For the walk back to the boy's room, Caileen supported Orri, and Tya wrapped Adam's arm over her shoulder. The smell of her hair tickled his nose and the warmth of her body next to his added a lightness to his step. When Tya tilted her head and offered him her quirky smile Adam knew he wouldn't be pulling away from her until he had to.

"I've never been so tired," said Orri, lying down on his bed. He let Caileen pull the blanket over him.

Adam knew Orri felt exhausted, but the older boy seemed to play on it to keep Caileen's attention. Taking his cues from his friend, Adam let Tya cover him up.

"Are you okay?" she asked. "Should I get Alima?"

"No!" Adam and Orri said in unison.

"It will be bad enough trying to explain what happened in the morning," Orri shuddered and pulled the blanket tighter. "I don't want to deal with Alima's questions tonight."

"Me neither," said Adam. He wanted more of Tya's warmth, but facing questions from Alima forced him to agree with Orri.

"We'll be better in the morning. We need to get some sleep." Orri smiled at Caileen and closed his eyes.

"All right... good night." Caileen dimmed the light and both girls left the room.

Adam waited for the sound of the girl's footsteps to fade away, before he whispered, "You awake?"

Orri touched the crystal lamp on the bedside table between their beds. "I should have listened to you." He tucked his arm under his head. "I overestimated my skills, and shapeshifting used more energy than I expected. I don't know what would have happened if you hadn't come when you did."

Adam knew if he had the power to shapeshift he would have done it too. But he wasn't about to let Orri off the hook that easily. "Yeah, Adam the hero to the rescue again."

Orri chuckled. "This never gets old for you does it?"

"Nope. I've got sisters. I can be a real pain when I want to be." Adam missed his sisters. He hoped he would see them soon. He blinked hard to clear the unexpected tears in his eyes. "I'm glad you didn't tell me where the keystone is hidden. Zador couldn't trick the information out of me."

Adam could see Zador's body on the floor. The girls had dragged his body through the portal before the black hole, but Adam didn't know if Zador had survived or not. The thought pressed down on him. What if he had killed Zador?

"Adam."

He blinked again and noticed Orri watching him. The dark circles under Orri's eyes were darker than ever.

"It's my fault, not yours." Orri swung his legs over the side of the bed and leaned forward. "I should have dealt with him."

Adam sat up and licked his dry lips. "It doesn't matter who did it. We're supposed to be the good guys. Good guys don't kill people."

Orri's grey eyes had a hint of green in them as they drilled into him. "Listen, there is no true good or evil, no black or white. Each side has a little of the other side in it. Some have more bad than good, they are a darker grey. And some have more good than bad, they are a lighter grey." He continued to stare at Adam, and Adam squirmed under the scrutiny. "Today you did something that had to be done. It doesn't make you a bad guy."

Adam looked down and closed his eyes, the tears spilling down his cheeks. Like a drowning man, he clung to Orri's reasoning. I'll do better next time. I have to.

"We still need to find the thirteenth skull," said Orri.

Adam rubbed his hand over his face, glad the subject had changed. "I know you don't want to hear this, but I think we might be able to use the replacement skulls."

"And if we're wrong? What happens to Atlantis?" Orri shook his head. "Didn't we learn anything today? We can't afford any more mistakes."

The last thing Adam wanted was another mistake. "That's true."

Orri slid down onto his mattress laying on his side facing Adam. His face was very pale. "Can we figure out what to do tomorrow?"

"Yeah," agreed Adam plumping his pillow before laying down again. "Where's Caileen's skull?"

"It must have been sucked into the black hole."

"That skull was linked to Farscope Foundation's offices in New York. Maybe Zador kept the thirteenth skull there too."

A deep crease formed between Orri's eyebrows. "I think today taught us we need to work as a team. We can work on this tomorrow."

"I agree. We need to do what's best for the team."

Orri was asleep before Adam finished talking. Adam slid his hand into his pocket and rubbed the golden eye. Warm energy flowed through him like just last time. He sat up. Fractured thoughts whirled through his mind. Was Zador dead? Have I killed him? His stomach rolled in sickening waves. He had only wanted to stop him from hurting Atlantis.

What if he lost control again? There had been a few close calls because of his inability to manage his talent, but what if he was responsible for another tragic mistake? Who would he hurt or kill next time? Cold fingers of dread crawled through Adam's body. He couldn't let that happen.

Justifying his actions and flawed reasoning didn't make what he was going to do right. He knew it was crazy, but he wouldn't put his friends in danger again. Adam swung his legs over the side of the bed.

He tiptoed out of the room carrying his sandals. After closing the door without making a sound, he shoved his feet into his sandals and headed for the library. A clear image of Adrian Zador laying beside the Machu Picchu gate came to mind. *No!* He squeezed his eyes shut hoping to banish the vision. I can't think about that. I have to save Atlantis. Then he realized he couldn't use the portal. It had been destroyed. A sigh of relief flowed through him and he opened his eyes. Where could he go now?

The Fountain of Eirene called to him, no one would be there. In the glow from the streetlights he slipped through the silent city.

When Adam reached the park, he sat on the only stone bench still undamaged and stared down at the rutted grass in front of him. Aware of the cost of making another mistake, he reached into his pocket he pulled out the eye of Nethuns. His thumb slid back and forth across the gold orb, and the now familiar warmth flowed through his body.

What would Noor have done? He rubbed the orb again and even more warmth flowed into his body. His energy levels were the highest they had ever been. What if Alima was right? I have to save Atlantis by myself.

Adam firmly believed if Noor knew about Alima's vision he would've taken matters into his own hands and done what was best for Atlantis.

The park faded from his vision and a bright light appeared in front of him. Within the light a life-sized clear crystal skull formed. The thirteenth skull. It sat on a glass surface with a black chair behind it. The light above the crystal sparkled off the top of its head sending rainbows around the room.

Adam reached out with his mind and asked, "Where are you?"

The skull didn't answer.

Pulling energy from the ground beneath his feet, he sent it toward the vision. "Talk to me, please."

Again, no answer. The skull and the light faded, bringing Adam back to the park.

The furniture in the vision looked like it belonged in an office, and somehow it had seemed familiar. Then it hit him, the offices of the Farscope Foundation had furniture just like that when he had tried to contact James last year.

The vision confirmed the thirteenth skull was at the Farscope Foundation.

Taking a deep breath in, Adam made a decision. He was the only one connected to the thirteenth skull, so he was the only one that could bring it home. His actions would cause more physical damage to Atlantis, but then, he told himself, the city could be rebuilt. The fear that he would cause someone to die nudged at his thoughts. His stomach rolled, and nausea rose in his throat. He swallowed hard. This was the only possible solution.

"Do not travel," a whispery voice warned him.

Adam knew the voice and he looked down at the small skull glowing on his chest. "I have no choice, there isn't another way."

"It is not safe. You will be in danger."

"I understand, but I have to try. Will you help me?"

"I am your pendant and yours alone. I will obey your commands."

Adam could hear the anxiety in the small skull's voice. To ease the tight band around his chest he muttered to himself, "I can do this. I must save Atlantis."

Pulling on the memory of traveling to Earth with Tya. Adam conjured up a picture of the steps to the Metropolitan Museum of Art in New York City. He could hear the traffic and feel the cold breeze of a November day in Manhattan. Grounding himself he breathed in energy. Then he magnified it within his body. The park flickered and disappeared into total darkness. The sounds of the fountain faded into silence.

A rustling sound, like leaves in the wind trickled into the silence. A cool draft of air lifted him off the ground and pushed him forward. Far ahead, a pinpoint of light disrupted the darkness. The wind became warmer and stronger, moving him faster and faster. The sound grew into a raging storm, and the wind bucked and twisted, tossing him about.

Chapter Thirty-Three

"I don't want to wake up," grumbled Orri. He rolled over in an attempt to avoid the hand shaking his shoulder.

"Orri, get up." A vibration that felt like a swarm of bees flowed up his neck and into his head.

"Oww, I'm getting up. Give me a minute." He rolled back toward Adam's bed and opened one eye. Alima sat on the bed and by the look on her face she wasn't happy with him. Orri pulled himself into a seated position and scratched his head.

"What happened in the library?" Alima glared at him.

Orri looked away from the hard look and pressed his lips together, not sure how he could spin the story. It didn't sound good from any angle. They had kept too many secrets from the council. He rolled his shoulders back and glanced at Alima again. It was all about to blow up and he was the guy left holding the skull.

"Start at the beginning." Alima's normally kind eyes had an icy gleam to them. "And don't leave anything out."

"Maybe we should wait until Adam, Tya and Caileen are here," stuttered Orri. "It involves all of us."

"I will talk to them later. I am asking you. What happened?"

Orri heaved a sigh. He had no choice, so he might as well do what she asked. "To start with neither of Noor's skulls are the thirteenth skull."

Alima raised an eyebrow. "Go on."

Once Orri started talking the words spilled out: Caileen using the golden skull and being tricked by Zador, Adam getting the keystone when Zador battled Noor, Adam possibly killing the businessman to save him and Atlantis.

When Orri ran out of words, his body sagged like an empty sack and his gaze dropped to his lap. "I am sorry," he said in a deep voice that wasn't his own. His breath caught in his throat, he peeked at Alima's face but saw no recognition.

She reached for his hand, her grip was firm and the energy she sent through his body this time was soft and healing.

"That should help you." Alima patted his hand. "I felt a shift in the energy field tonight and that is how I found the mess in the library. You are very lucky. You could have destroyed Atlantis."

Orri lifted his head and met Alima's gaze again. "This was my fault. I'm the one who should be punished."

"That's very heroic, but I don't see it that way. The council will review the situation and decide how we should deal with what all of you have done, but that won't happen until after Adam has saved Atlantis."

He leaned forward, his hands pushing down on his knees. "What? He can't do it alone. We're a team!"

Alima stood up and placed a firm hand on his shoulder. He noticed her steely grey eyes were level with his, and this gave the tiny woman an advantage. Looking at the bed behind her to avoid her eyes, he noticed Adam's bed was tidy, so tidy Orri knew he hadn't slept in it. "Was the bed like that when you sat down?"

Alima glanced over her shoulder. "His bed was made ..." She swiveled back and her grip on his shoulder tightened. "Do you know where he is?"

Orri hands gripped the bedsheet by his side. "He's gone to save Atlantis, when he promised me we were a team."

"Listen to me." Alima gave him a sympathetic look. "I had a vision. I know Adam is supposed to save Atlantis by himself because I have seen it. He is doing what he is supposed to."

"Alima's visions are rarely wrong." Noor's thoughts filled Orri's mind.

Orri didn't want to hear Noor's opinion right now, especially when he agreed with Alima.

"My visions are usually correct," added Alima as if she had heard Noor.

No way could Adam do this alone. The existence of Atlantis was at stake. He had to change her mind. Maybe …

"Do not tell her I am inside you."

Great! Orri clenched his jaw and silently asked Noor, "What can I do to change her mind?"

Noor didn't answer.

Orri's fingers clenched. The brittleness throughout his body had reached a breaking point.

"I can feel how frustrated you are. Let Adam do what he needs to do." Noor's calm voice filled Orri's mind and flowed through his tense muscles. Some of the anger seeped out of him. He knew what Noor said was right.

"I will gather the rest of the council and let them know what has happened," Alima continued.

Orri surged to his feet. "I'll come with you."

"It is better if you do not attend." Alima grinned and brushed past him.

The amusement on her face made Orri's fingers curl into fists again.

Alima continued, "If the four of you are not at the meeting no votes can be proposed. All I want to do is fill them in on what is going on. I don't want them voting you off the council or something foolish like that." She walked to the door. "I can hear Raine grumbling already."

Noor chuckled. Orri clamped his lips together to keep the sound inside and sat down on the edge of the bed.

"You need to rest," said Alima and she closed the door behind her.

As soon as they were alone Noor's voice filled his head again. "Do not go after Adam. Sometimes it is best to step out of the way and let others follow their destiny."

"You really agree with Alima?" Forgetting he could talk to Noor in his mind Orri spoke out loud, getting louder with every word, and by the end of the sentence he was shouting.

"Yes. Your role is to lead Atlantis to safety." Noor's thoughts came out as a simple statement of truth, and it was enough to stop Orri from rushing to the door.

It wasn't what Orri had expected. He didn't know how to respond. "Lead?"

"Yes."

"How?" Orri shook his head.

"You will take my place on the council."

Noor was crazy. "I can't do that. No one would support me."

Noor chucked. "I am not crazy." After a moment he continued. "Do you remember when your mother disappeared?"

Orri closed his eyes. How could he forget. Images of that day still haunted his dreams. "What does that have to do with the support you believe I have?" He answered with his thoughts unable to get the words past the tightness in his throat.

Noor ignored the question. "You believe it was your fault, if you had not fallen asleep that day she would still be here."

"Yes."

"Orri, that is not true. Whoever took her caused you to lose consciousness." Noor's words were gentle and kind.

"How do you know that?" For a long time, Orri had thought he should have protected his mother that day. One statement from Noor wasn't going to change his mind.

"Because the person who took your mother didn't want you to see them. They abducted her to use her skills—she is a powerful recognizer. She knows how to show anyone with energy abilities the way to reach their full potential. Her only flaw is she doesn't see the dark side of people."

Orri ground his teeth. Why hadn't Noor told him sooner? All that time of torturing himself!

"Orri, I know we have hurt you." Noor made a sound like a slight breeze ruffling leaves.

The sound puzzled Orri, then he realized it was the thought version of a sigh.

Noor continued. "But it was important to keep the knowledge of this quiet. Whoever did this could hurt you too. I wanted to tell you sooner, but we have been busy saving Atlantis."

Orri shut Noor out of his thoughts. He didn't want to hear any more excuses. Noor and the council had covered up important details. They had lied to him! His heart pounded in his chest, he wanted to scream. He was just about to open the door and vent his anger at Noor when a cold breeze flowed down his body and his heart slowed down. He had lied too. He had withheld important information from the council. Although he didn't want to admit it, he was no different than Noor or the council. How had Atlantis become so full of lies?

Orri opened the barrier between his thoughts hoping for the truth. "Is my mother still alive?"

"I believe she is." Noor's answer held no hesitation. "According to Alima her energy signature can still be felt in Atlantis. If she had died, she would no longer have a presence here. My theory is your mother was taken by someone who needs her skills, so they will keep her alive to use her talents."

"One more thing before I leave you to your own thoughts," added Noor. "Your partnership with Adam has been noticed by some the council members. You have grown into a courageous and wise young man."

A soft click sounded when Noor closed the barrier between them.

Chapter Thirty-Four

The wind spiraled, sending Adam spinning in circles. He couldn't feel his arms or his legs, and in the darkness, he couldn't see if they were still attached to his body. Then his chest and torso became desensitized, he couldn't feel his breath anymore. He was dizzy and disorientated. He'd never experienced this on a trip before. What was happening?

"Help me!" His pendant shrilled by his ear.

"Stay with me," Adam managed to whisper.

The numbness crawled up Adam's neck, something that felt like sand particles brushed his cheeks, then he sensed a solid object passing near him. Adam's mind reached out and latched onto it.

He drew energy from his tiny skull, and fragment by fragment he attached small pieces of himself to the object. His scattered thoughts pulled together, he visualized his body whole and unharmed. A pinprick of light in the distance grew bigger and bigger.

Adam landed hard and toppled over, he drew a shaky breath in as he gazed down at his body. All the parts were in the right places. His breath came out as a sigh, "That's good."

The next intake of air made him cough. A smell, so intense it burned the back of his throat. Covering his nose and mouth with his hand he looked around. He lay beside an industrial garbage bin in a dirty alley. He could hear the sound of traffic nearby and felt a chill in the air. A loud scream sliced through his head and he turned to see a teenage girl dressed in a ragged hoodie and dirty jeans backing away from him.

"Wait! Where am I?" Adam croaked just before she reached the end of the alley.

The girl peered at him as if she didn't believe what she saw.

"Am I... in New York?"

"Yeah," the girl said as she dashed around the corner.

He had to get out of the alley. Adam pushed himself up to sitting and noticed his skull pendant lying on the ground beside him. Weird, the pendant had never come to Earth with him before. He reached for it, and the Eye of Nethuns dropped from his hand. Picking up the golden orb he rubbed it with his thumb —a warm energy flowed through him. The energy boost muted some of the heaviness of his limbs. He peered at the golden eye resting in his palm, a feeling that it had saved him trickling through his mind.

Sliding the orb into his pocket, he looped the chain of his skull pendant around his neck and tucked the tiny skull underneath his shirt. "Do you know what happened?" he asked the tiny skull.

"There was a protective shield around Atlantis. It almost disintegrated your physical being," the skull answered.

Adam's breath caught in his throat. He had pulled himself together from tiny pieces. He was lucky to be alive. Rubbing the golden eye Adam remembered Raine saying he had other protections in place. That could be a problem when he wanted to return to Atlantis, but there was no point worrying about that now.

He rubbed his forehead where a headache was forming. He breathed through his mouth to minimize the effects of the smell in the alley. He had almost died getting out of Atlantis and had no way of knowing if he could return. He tightened his jaw. Right now, he had to focus on retrieving the thirteenth skull.

Adam wore the clothes he had on when he left Earth. He noticed his backpack lying a couple of feet away. Standing up, he brushed the grime off his pants as best he could and grabbed the backpack, slinging it over one shoulder. Adam dug in a pocket and pulled out his cell phone. The time was an hour before he left Earth. His heart skipped a beat. He was in danger of changing his future. He had to be careful. Every action would cause a reaction in the timeline.

Somehow, he had managed to get here. Did that mean destiny brought him here? Adam shook his head. Wow! He never believed that thought would occur to him. Maybe Atlantis was changing him.

Adam checked phone again. It showed the same time as before. What was going on?

"You came here to find the thirteenth skull," his pendant answered.

He hadn't intended to pose the question to his pendant, but the tiny skull was right. His mission hadn't changed. He needed to find James.

Last year Adam had done research on the Internet to find out about his biological father, James McKenzie. The archaeologist was a well-known expert on ancient civilizations, especially Atlantis, and he worked for Adrian Zador. Adam had looked up the address of the Farscope Foundation offices in New York and hoped to find him in his office.

He emerged from the darkness of the alley and found a sunny fall day, cooler than usual for this time of year. Light glinted off the windows of the tall buildings and the smell of car exhaust filled his nose. A tour bus zoomed by him kicking up dust and debris in its wake. Adam preferred to be on an ocean beach, but New York had a hectic appeal all its own. He drank in the vibes of the busy city to further restore his energy levels.

It didn't take Adam long to find the Farscope Foundation building. He entered the skyscraper through the revolving door set in a wall of glass. The foyer rose three stories; its white marble floors and walls shone in the sunlight.

The only way into the skyscraper was through a gated security area. If you couldn't scan an identity card, you had to convince the guard you belonged there. Adam paused for a moment not sure what to do, his legs refused to move forward. He heard the grey-haired woman tell the guard she had an appointment. His knees unlocked. That would work.

Adam stepped up to the round bellied man at the gate. The man smiled, and he reminded Adam of a short Horatio. "I have an appointment with James McKenzie," said Adam doing his best to sound like he knew what he was talking about.

"Your name," the man asked.

"Adam Danburg."

He picked up the phone and dialed a number. "Hi, Samantha, I have a young man by the name of Adam Danburg to see Mr. McKenzie." The man listened. "You're sure?" He nodded in response to the answer and hung up the phone. He frowned at Adam. "I'm sorry, it appears you don't have an appointment and you are not listed as an approved visitor for this building."

Adam's stomach dropped. He had risked so much to do this. Last year, James had been giving a lecture at the university in Adam's hometown of Baltimore. Adam had gone to see him, only to get rejected by his biological father. He felt as if James McKenzie had just punched him in the stomach again. He ground his teeth and clenched his fists. He would not walk away this time, there was too much at stake.

Adam used his best imitation of a determined, mature voice. "It is a matter of life and death. I must speak to him."

"I see," said the guard. He turned and dialed the phone again.

Adam held his breath while the man passed on the information. The guard shook his head.

"Wait!" Adam held up his hand. "I have critical information from Mr. Zador that he needs to know."

"You hear that?" said the guard.

Adam's heart pounded. Please listen. Please, he begged silently.

A surprised look crossed the guard's face. "Okay, I'll send him up."

The man hung a visitor card around Adam's neck and opened the gate for him. He indicated a wide hallway behind them. "The elevators are there. Use the ones on the right side. Scan your card on the panel inside the elevator and press the forty button."

"Thank you." Adam rushed to the elevators before the man changed his mind.

Adam was the only person in the elevator when the door closed. He watched the floor numbers flash by on the display above his head. As the count got higher, Adam's chest tightened, and his breathing became shallow. He didn't need to see how high he was to have the fear descend on him with dizzying precision. He desperately hoped there wouldn't be a window anywhere near James McKenzie's office.

The elevator eased to a stop and the doors slid silently open. In front of him, a woman sat behind a desk. Adam assumed her name was Samantha.

She didn't smile at him when she stood up. "This way," she said. Adam followed her down a white marble hallway. A trickle of sweat ran down his back. He knew James didn't want him in his life, James had made that very clear last year. All Adam wanted from him was the thirteenth skull, and then they both could go on with their lives.

Samantha opened a floor-to-ceiling glass door and announced, "Adam Danburg."

When she stepped to the side, all Adam could see was Central Park, forty floors below him. The room spun, and he slumped against the door.

Someone caught him and helped him into a chair. Adam closed his eyes, leaned forward, and took several deep breaths like his mom had taught him to do. This was not the way he expected to meet James McKenzie again.

"There you are. I am so glad you came."

The words popped into Adam's mind, clear and concise. He couldn't believe it was true. Could the thirteenth skull be so close? Could it be that easy? "Are you the thirteenth skull?" he silently asked, hoping he wasn't mistaken.

The grating noise that passed for the skull's laugh filled his head.

"Where are you?"

"I am in a locked room. I must be near you because your energy is strong."

"I can transport you," said Adam. With a clear picture of the life-sized crystal skull in his mind, he focused on speeding up the resonance of the skull's energy. He felt it disappear. He opened his eyes and focused on the floor at his feet. Slowing the resonance down again and the skull appeared on the floor.

Adam reached down to pick up the skull.

After Samantha settled Adam in the chair, James sent her away and tried to keep the smile off his face. It wasn't funny really, but he recalled the times he had teased his wife about her crazy fear of heights. The familiar sadness from remembering her wiped the smile off his face and replaced it with an ache in his heart. He watched as Adam struggled to breathe. The boy looked so much like his mother. He desperately wanted to get to know him better, but he knew as long as he worked for Adrian it would be dangerous for Adam to be close to him.

The boy didn't seem to be recovering. James moved around the desk and crouched in front of him. He was about to touch Adam when a life-sized clear crystal skull popped into existence between the boy's feet. James knew by the rainbows radiating from the crystal this was Adrian's skull. James grabbed it at the same time as the boy opened his eyes and picked it up.

The crystal shifted back and forth between the two until James lost his balance and it crashed to the floor.

Chapter Thirty-Five

Adam stared at the pieces of the skull spread across the floor. A cold sweat covered his body. Atlantis couldn't be moved without the thirteenth skull. It would be broken apart just as the skull had been.

He caused this. Adam knew something had to go wrong. It always did with him. His stomach twisted in a painful knot. Maybe he wasn't destined to save Atlantis, but instead, destined to destroy it.

James let out a long breath. "I'll get a janitor to clean the mess up."

Adam's head snapped up. "No! You don't just throw away a powerful artifact." His body became as rigid as his clenched fists. Adam remembered going to meet James last year. He dreamed of discovering where he came from and why he had this strange connection to nature. But James had rejected him and told Adam to forget about him. The open wound from that day hadn't completely healed and today had ripped it wide open again.

Adam jumped up with his eyes riveted on James. "Or is that what you do. Throw away things when they don't serve your purpose anymore?"

"I was trying to protect you. My boss is a dangerous man," said James. "Maybe when this is over, you and I can start again."

"It's too late for that. You have no idea what you've done. Atlantis..." Adam's knees turned to jelly, forcing him to slump onto the chair.

A deep crease formed on James' forehead. "What about Atlantis?"

"I'm supposed to save Atlantis." A crushing need pushed down on Adam. He had to make this man suffer. This man who had destroyed so many things. "Adrian Zador is dead, and I killed him to protect Atlantis." Seeing the look of surprise on James' face fueled Adam to continue. "I could kill you too!"

James backed away. Moving around his desk without taking his eyes off Adam. "Adrian Zador is dead," he questioned in a shaky voice. "How?"

"He came to Atlantis through a portal. He attacked me and my friends, and I stopped him with a fireball," Adam spat the words at James.

"Through a portal?" James sat down. He leaned his elbows on the desk and placed his fingers on the side of his temples. "Did he get the base for the crystal skull?"

"The hand?" Adam shook his head. "No, he said he was looking for the keystone."

"What's that?"

"If you don't know, I'm not going to tell you."

"You're sure Adrian is dead?"

Adam wasn't going to admit he had no way of confirming it. "The fireball burned a big hole in his chest," he bluffed. "So yeah, I'm sure." Adam shook his head. He didn't like to think he might have killed someone but being a part of destroying Atlantis was too much to bear. "You just don't get it. You and Adrian Zador have destroyed Atlantis."

"No, that can't be! Atlantis has survived for thousands of years."

"The skull is broken." He spat the words at James. "If we don't have the skull, Atlantis can't be moved. If we don't move it, Atlantis will be destroyed."

The sound of Adam's breathing filled the space between him and James. Adam shook his head. It was no use, nothing he did would change what would happen now. His body slackened, and heaviness pressed down on him. No matter how much he wanted to, he couldn't save Atlantis.

"I'm sorry," James whispered.

Adam didn't know if James was sorry for contributing to the obliteration of Atlantis or the destruction of their relationship. In the end, it didn't matter what he was apologizing for.

James walked over and crouched down to pick up Adam's backpack. Opening the bag, he carefully placed the chunks of the crystal skull inside.

Adam watched him. Once the large chunks of crystal were in the backpack there was nothing left behind. No small shards. No crystal dust. Something inside him told him this might be important, but his brain couldn't make the connection.

James remain kneeling on the floor and lifted his head. "I know Atlantis has moved many times..."

"Why do you care about that?" Adam interrupted.

"I have spent most of my adult life researching ancient civilizations. Atlantis is very special to me for many reasons; one of them is because Atlantis brought you to me." James stood up and stared down at Adam. "I'm sure you don't care about my feelings."

Adam didn't want to hear any more. "I need to get back."

"Will I see you again?"

"I doubt it. We have nothing in common."

"Can I explain one thing?"

Adam watched the muscles in James' throat move up and down. "Sure." He knew it wouldn't change how he felt.

"I gave you up for adoption because I knew I couldn't be the father you needed. Every time I looked at your face, I saw your mother and my heart broke a little more."

It wasn't what Adam had expected. A deep sadness flowed into James' eyes and Adam had to swallow against the lump forming in his throat.

"When you came to see me last year, I sent you away again and I know I hurt you." James spoke softly, his pain and regret filled every word.

Adam clenched his jaw.

"I was afraid Adrian would use you to get me to agree to his crazy plans." James sighed. "It seems I might have been right about that."

James gazed deeply into his eyes. "You don't want to have anything to do with me and I understand that, but everything I have done was because I love you and wanted to keep you safe. I can't change the past, but I hope you understand why I did what I did."

Two years ago, another man had revealed his love for Adam and said the same words 'I can't change the past'. Noor's face flashed before Adam's eyes. He had learned to love and believe in Noor again. Could he learn to do the same with his biological father? Adam stared at James. He saw nothing but love in the hazel eyes watching him. Adam took a deep breath and a little crack formed in his defenses. Their relationship would take time to heal, but it wasn't dead anymore.

"I understand what happened and why." Adam saw the tension leave James. "I will contact you when I get back to Earth."

A crease formed between James' eyebrows. "What do you mean 'get back'?

"I have to return to Atlantis." Adam picked up his backpack and walked out of the office back to the elevator. After pushing the elevator button, he glanced over his shoulder. James stood in his office staring at him through the glass wall.

When Adam reached the sidewalk, he looked up and down Fifth Avenue, unsure of which way to turn. He shuddered at the thought of being shattered into a million pieces if he used teleportation to get back to Atlantis.

Standing against the building, the flow of people moved past him on the busy sidewalk. Adam's hand rubbed the golden eye in his pocket, and it sent a warm wave of energy flowing through his body. He pulled the eye out and stared at it nestled in his palm, trying to remember when the energy boosts had started. It was after Noor fought Adrian Zador.

A small smile tricked across his lips as he slipped the golden orb back into his pocket. The little piece of Noor reminded Adam that his grandfather and mentor would always be with him. Without thinking he headed toward the museum. Maybe returning to the Temple of Dendur would give him an idea of how to get back to Atlantis.

The round visitor sticker on Adam's backpack allowed him into the museum without question. He hurried through throngs of people in the well-lit foyer with its huge stone arches reaching high above the crowd. He got to the Egyptian section in time to see his class move away from the exhibit. Adam waited until the group turned a corner before he stepped up to the two massive stone pillars sitting on either side of the oblong doorway and topped with the brick lintel to form the Temple of Dendur.

The gate looked very different on the other side in Atlantis. Adam remembered the pile of broken stones rising to the roof blocking anyone from using the portal. The golden light that had flowed through the gateway was gone …no, there had been a small chink in the boulders letting the light shine through. Was the tiny opening big enough for him to travel through? He didn't know for sure, but he had to try.

Adam was about to pull energy into his body for the trip when he remembered travel from Earth to Atlantis caused time loops. There had been two time loops since he arrived in Atlantis. The one after the statue of Nethuns had disappeared had only set time back a few minutes, and neither him nor Orri were sure it had really happened. The time loop after Noor's death definitely affected his relationship with Tya and Orri's relationship with Caileen. It hadn't changed him and Orri, but everyone else in Atlantis had lost a couple of days.

He had no other option. He must return to Atlantis with the thirteenth skull, even if it was broken. So far, the time loops hadn't caused any real damage, he reasoned. What could go wrong? Then he remembered that he was prophesied to save Atlantis so maybe no time loop would happen. He hoped destiny was in his favor this time.

Adam rubbed the golden eye in his pocket and felt the smooth energy flow through his body like sunlight on a warm spring day. Gathering his thoughts, he began the now familiar process.

Chapter Thirty-Six

Adam landed at the bottom of the steps to the Temple, stumbled and sat down hard. His backpack thumped down beside him. His backpack? In Atlantis?

He wore the tunic and loose pants that were the standard clothing in Atlantis, but his backpack didn't fit into this world. Pulling the heavy bag into his lap he held his breath and tugged the zipper open. He pulled the edges of the pack out of the way. Light from a streetlight hit the crystal chunks and rainbows radiated from them. The pieces looked the same as they had when he packed them on Earth.

"Put me back together."

Adam knew that voice, he peered into the bag again. The rainbow light glowed brighter, filling the backpack with light. Now, he needed figure out how to reassemble the thirteenth skull. That should be easy, right? He let his breath out, nothing was easy. His mother said, 'If life was easy, you wouldn't learn anything.' His chest tightened. If his mom was here, she'd help him figure out what needed to be done, but mom wasn't here.

He closed the zipper, pushed himself to his feet, slung the pack over his shoulder, and sprinted up the stairs to the entrance to the temple.

His heart skipped a beat as he stared at the life-sized golden statue of Nethuns riding in a chariot pulled by six horses. The statue couldn't be here, it had fallen into a black hole. A cold chill slithered down his back. Had he caused a time loop?

Adam gazed at the face of the young man in the chariot. Noor's face. Something was wrong. He reached into his pocket and pulled out the eye missing from the statue. How far back had time moved? Was Noor back in his own body again? Hope warmed him.

He had to find Orri, Tya and Caileen. The only person Adam knew he could locate for sure was Tya. Even though it was dark outside, he hoped she was still in the library. Stuffing the golden eye back into his pocket he hurried to the library.

Horatio stood guard as usual, but the big man's face was pale, and his eyes were red rimmed. One corner of his mouth lifted for a moment, then it slipped down again. Was Noor dead? Not sure how to behave because of the possible timeline changes Adam let the guard take the lead. Horatio embraced him with a smothering hug, and when he finally stepped away he said, "I'm so...so very glad to see you again, young Adam."

"It's good to see you too," said Adam. "Are you okay?"

"I will be now you are back." Horatio did manage a wavering smile this time.

Adam shuffled his feet and nodded toward the door to the library. "Is she still in there?"

"Yes, she has been spending a lot of time here." Horatio leaned down to open the door. Adam expected a cookie as he passed through, but it wasn't offered. Then he remembered the cookie he had put in his left pocket. He pulled it out, and in two big bites he finished the cookie. Where am I in the timeline if I still had the cookie? Adam wondered.

He opened the gold doors and stopped. The scar on the open area of stone floor wasn't there. The shelves and the skulls were the same as they had always been. The chill invaded Adam's body again. What was going on?

Adam rushed down the aisles not paying any attention to the voices of the crystal skulls. He turned the corner into the open area where Tya usually worked, and three pairs of eyes stared up at him. Tya, Caileen and Orri.

Adam couldn't believe Orri was in the library. His stomach churned. Going back to Earth had definitely changed the timeline in Atlantis, but how?

"Hi." The normal greeting Adam had hoped for came out as a squeak.

"I thought I should let you sleep when traveling here almost killed you." Orri gestured for Adam to take the empty seat beside him.

Adam sat down and set his backpack on the floor. What was Orri talking about? Leaving Atlantis had almost killed him, not coming back. Did they think he had just arrived? He rubbed the back of his neck. "How long have I been back in Atlantis?"

Tya's eyes narrowed. "This is the second light cycle since you arrived. Don't you know that?"

"That isn't true." Adam put his elbows on the table and leaned forward. "I've actually been in Atlantis for five light cycles. I went back to Earth to get the thirteenth skull. Traveling to Earth almost killed me and must have caused a time loop."

Caileen and Tya glanced at Orri and he frowned.

The reactions were not what Adam expected, he looked from one to the other hoping someone would explain.

"There is no such thing as a time loop," grumbled Orri.

"We've had a couple black holes," said Tya. "We are meeting to come up with a plan. Caileen and I have already researched black holes and time loops, but Orri doesn't believe in time loops because there is no hard evidence," said Tya in a smug tone.

Only a couple of black holes? "Where was the last black hole," asked Adam.

"On the main street. A young girl was crushed by a gargoyle and then sucked into a black hole. Orri witnessed it."

"I was there too," said Adam. "That happened when I first got to Atlantis." They were looking at him like he was crazy, so he might as well ask the next strange question. "Is Noor alive?"

"How could you ask that? Of course he isn't." Tya crossed her arms over her chest.

Caileen blinked rapidly and her mouth trembled. Orri stared at Adam with slitted eyes.

The heaviness returned to his chest. "When did it happen?"

"At the last council meeting, Noor seemed different to me." Orri shook his head. "Nothing I could explain, but something wasn't right. When he left the meeting, I asked my skull pendant to track him, and I followed him to the Egyptian archives." He took a deep breath.

The memory of the scene in the Egyptian archives flashed through Adam's brain.

"I got there too late, I couldn't save him," Orri stated with an unemotional face.

Caileen's eyes brimmed with unshed tears. "Tya and I found them a time segment later."

Orri's composure baffled Adam. He remembered the older boy sitting beside Noor's body, his tears making tracks in the dust on his cheeks. That was before Orri knew Noor lived inside him. Adam's eyes drilled into Orri's, his gaze was calmly returned, then the corner of Orri's mouth lifted for a moment.

The little gesture told Adam Noor still lived, and he lived inside Orri. One quick glance at Caileen and Tya's sad faces stopped Adam from grinning. The girls didn't know.

"You seem to believe you have caused a time loop," Orri said in a skeptical voice.

"It's not the first one I've experienced, you and I felt a time loop happen before I went to Earth," Adam stared at Orri. "But you don't remember, and I don't have any proof."

Orri chewed the corner of his lip. "I might know what you're talking about. It's like there's a shadow that I can't quite see but I know it's there."

"Why didn't you say that sooner?" Caileen questioned.

Orri shrugged. "I didn't think it was important."

Caileen's nostrils flared.

Adam interrupted, hoping to prevent an argument between the two of them. "Can one of you tell me what has happened here in the last few light cycles?"

Caileen gestured at Orri.

"Tremors had been happening for a while, but they weren't causing any major damage and there was no black cloud like last time. Then the tremors got worse and the damage couldn't be repaired."

"We think that is evidence of time loops, but Orri disagrees," Tya added in her know-it-all voice.

Adam suppressed a smile when Orri continued without commenting on Tya's statement. Orri still liked to be right in any timeline.

"It wasn't until the first black hole destroyed part of the gate in the outer ring that the council began to worry. A council meeting was called two light cycles ago, and the thirteenth skull declared there were two prophecies. One says saving Atlantis must be shared and the other says the trio is no more and each alone will come to see. The council argued about the prophecies and nothing was decided. The black hole that killed the girl happened in the last light cycle and you showed up right after that."

"The prophecies are the same ones I remember," Adam commented. "But there were two replacement skulls that announced them because Adrian Zador had the thirteenth skull."

"Zador contacted me. I remembered how he tricked my father." Caileen shivered. "I wasn't going to let that happen to me, so I didn't do what he wanted me to."

Adam was speechless. No replacement skulls? Then why did he have to rescue the thirteenth skull from Zador?

Tya, misunderstanding his silence, reached across the table and gave his hand a quick squeeze. "I know how you must feel."

No, she didn't know. How could she? She wasn't living in an altered timeline.

"You were in bad shape when you got here, you muttered something about being shattered into a million pieces. Alima had to treat you in the infirmary." Tya touched his hand again. "You'll be okay when you've had a couple of light cycles to rest."

Adam pulled his hand out of Tya's reach, he stared at all three of them. He wasn't going to be okay. They didn't understand. "None of this makes sense," he pushed the words out through tight lips. "Some things that happened in my timeline aren't the same as yours, or they are the same, but happened in a different order. I don't understand what's happening." His whole body was shaking. He couldn't stay here anymore.

Standing up his foot brushed against his backpack on the floor. He had the thirteenth skull. If it was in the bag and still in pieces, then his timeline was the right one.

Grabbing the pack Adam placed it on the chair and tugged the zipper open. Inside the pieces of the skull glowed. Pulling out the pieces he placed them on the table. "I brought the thirteenth skull back from Earth. It has been broken and needs to be put back together. Where does that fit in your timeline?"

Caileen touched the fragment closest to her. Its glow deepened and a rainbow of colors reflected on the shelves surrounding them. "If our timeline is correct, we will find the whole thirteenth skull in the Skull Room."

After putting the crystal pieces into the backpack, Adam closed the zip. The floor vibrated under his feet and his heart pounded. He grabbed the edge of the table when the vibrations turned into waves.

"Under the table!" yelled Tya, tugging on his pant leg.

Adam crawled under the stone tabletop, huddling into the small space close to Orri, Caileen, and Tya. Floor stones scraped against each other, skulls rattled on the shelves, and the library walls groaned under the shifting weight of the building. Thick dust obliterated his vision. The noise made it impossible to talk. Covering his face, Adam wanted, above all else, for the tremors to stop.

The motion ceased. Adam's scalp prickled. Something wasn't right.

Orri crawled out and stood up. "Everything is okay here."

Coming out from under the table, Adam pulled the backpack with him. Nothing seemed out of place. Was it just a tremor? The silence in the library caught his attention, there were no skulls talking. He remembered the scene just inside the gold doors of the library in his timeline. Hugging his backpack to his chest he bolted down the closest aisle.

From somewhere behind him Orri yelled, "Where are you going?"

Adam didn't stop until he got to the end of a row where broken skulls lay scattered about, a few more steps brought him into the open area with the huge black scar across the middle of the stone floor. Alima stood on the other side of the open area with her hand across her mouth and tears rolling down her pale cheeks. Noor wasn't standing beside her. Adam hugged the heavy backpack closer to his aching chest. He still didn't know what to do.

Chapter Thirty-Seven

Caileen's breath caught in her throat as she peered around Orri at the devastation in her beloved library. The knowledge and history lost would take thousands of light cycles to correct. She took gulps of air fighting to hold down the rawness bubbling up in her throat. Orri turned toward her blocking the view of the destruction and wrapped his arms securely around her. The wall of tears she had been holding back flooded through her defenses and she sobbed against his chest. A dreadful keening sound assaulted her ears, then she realized the sound was coming from her.

When Raine shouted, "Quiet!" to get the council members to listen to him. Caileen lifted her head—the black hole had brought all the council members to the library. She pulled a cloth out of her pocket and noisily blew her nose. Wiping her tear-drenched face with her hands, she turned around. Orri tightened his arms around her again, and a warm wave of healing energy flowed into her body. She leaned back into him. What would she do without him?

Caileen watched in silence as the members of the council quarreled. She saw both sides of the debate without reacting. Her brain was not ready to take in what was happening.

When Raine announced he would track individual skulls, the fog lifted. She clenched her teeth. Before anyone on the council meddled in their findings, she and Tya needed to finish their research. Even though Raine had worked closely with them, he had no right to monitor what happened in her library.

Although the council was missing one member, Noor, nearly everyone agreed a vote was needed. When the vote came around to her, the tiny skull around her neck remained dark. Only Adam agreed with her. The majority voted in favor of Raine tracking the tiny skulls. Caileen decided her skull pendant would spend a lot of time sitting on her desk in the next few light cycles.

The council continued to argue, this time about following the prophecies. Without Noor the discussion wasn't debated as it should be, and the argument led to a vote. When Orri voted in favor of keeping the prophesies, Caileen glanced up and smiled up at him. Maybe he had been listening to what she'd said to him. After she had voted the last vote was Tya's, and her pendant remained dark. Caileen couldn't believe what she had just witnessed. The Tya she knew loved rules and believed in the prophecies. She would never vote against following them. Tya kept her head down, avoiding her stare.

Because the vote was a tie, with six for keeping the prophecies and six against, the council could do nothing until they elected a new leader. Caileen hoped the new leader would be in favor of following the prophecies that had guided them for centuries.

When the impromptu meeting was over, she turned to Orri, Adam, and Tya. "Let's go to the Skull Room." She turned and went down the closest aisle. Orri walked beside her, with Adam and Tya following. Further away from the devastation near the golden doors, the library showed few signs of damage. Caileen breathed in and the fresh smell of the library filled her senses. Maybe they could rebuild.

"Are you okay?" Orri asked in a low voice as they walked away.

"I will be once we get to the Skull Room."

Orri gripped her hand again and sent a wave of supportive energy. She tightened her hold on his hand.

Stopping in front of the human-sized blue crystal skull Caileen laid her hand on top. The heavy wooden door swung silently open. She prayed Noor's skull was where he had left it.

When they were all inside, she closed the door and turned to look at the table. On the round stone table, an exact replica of the one in the council room, sat twelve crystal skulls as unique as the people they represented. The thirteenth skull, Noor's skull, was gone.

Tya gasped and Caileen's heart skipped a beat, she had been so sure Adam was wrong. How could this happen? Her mind flipped from one thought to another, trying to understand what was going on. The only explanation was Adam's alternate timeline.

"Would Noor's skull be in the archives because he is, you know..." Tya's question faded into silence.

Caileen shook her head. "No, the skull would be part of his memorial service, but it should be here." She knew Tya understood that, but she recognized the younger girl had also been praying for a different answer.

Adam moved Noor's chair aside and carefully placed the chunks of crystal on the table. "We need to put Noor's skull back together." His hand brushed against the largest piece and it sparkled. "But I don't know how to do it, and if we screw this up, we won't be able to save Atlantis."

Orri placed a hand on Adam's shoulder and gave it a squeeze. "I have an idea." He stepped in front of Adam and moved the pieces of the crystal around.

When he moved back, instead of random chunks of crystal, the pieces now resembled the thirteenth skull, except for the large cracks marring its face.

Noor's skull wasn't lost. Caileen smiled at Orri, thankful she could depend on this level-headed version of the boy she had known her whole life. "Now molecular transformation can make the skull whole again." She gestured to Adam. "You were there when the skull was broken, so you must be the one to put it back together."

The color drained from Adam's face and he shook his head. "No. No. What about the power of three?"

"I agree with Caileen," said Orri.

"Caileen is part of this too. Shouldn't we repair the skull together?" Tya asked.

"I am not a part of the three, my responsibility is the library, and the information in the library is clear about this." Caileen watched Adam's face and continued. "The thirteenth skull was broken once before when Atlantis was located in Machu Picchu. The records say the person who broke the skull must be the one to make it whole again."

Adam's wide eyes saddened Caileen. She took a deep breath. She knew that what she was about to say would devastate him. "The information from that time also states if the person repairing the skull is born on Earth he must return to Earth because if he stays in Atlantis he will die."

Adam slumped onto Noor's chair and hung his head.

Tya knelt beside him. "I wish you could stay," she said in a shaky voice.

The lump in Adam's throat prevented him from speaking. The higher power in Atlantis sure had a warped sense of humor. He swallowed to clear his throat. "I know what I must do," he said, barely above a whisper. "How much time do I have in Atlantis after that?"

"The Machu Picchu archives stated the man who repaired the skull died of an energy imbalance, it doesn't say when he died. The healer attributed his death to remaining in the wrong dimension."

He only had one choice, so he might as well get it done. He knew molecular transformation could repair the skull. Adam stood in front of the pieces of crystal, and his muscles tensed. If he didn't get the vibrations correct the skull could melt into a pile of crystal goo.

Adam closed his eyes to banish the vision. He must get this right. In his mind, he focused on the image of the crystal skull, whole and filled with rainbows. He drew a deep breath and felt the shapes of the pieces as if he touched them with his fingers. Letting the vibrations of the crystal pieces echo within him, the pulse traveled to his brain and he could hear their slow, steady heartbeat. He increased the speed of the crystal's energy vibrations and opening his eyes he saw the pieces disappear.

He focused on the table in front of him again. He blinked, and an image of the cracked skull flashed through his mind. *No!* The hair lifted on the back of his neck.

He visualized the skull again, whole and glowing with rainbows of light. The faster beat of the crystals sounded in his head, and he slowed the molecular energy down to its original speed. The thirteenth skull came back into existence... with a huge crack running down the middle of its head and face.

Adam's hands curled into fists and he crumpled onto the chair.

Chapter Thirty-Eight

"Adam, it's okay." Tya moved toward him again.

He held up his hand to stop her saying anything else. This was all his fault. "No, no, it's not. Just look at it, the thirteenth skull doesn't have a crack down the middle." He pointed at the skull. The fissure made it resemble a grinning gargoyle.

"It doesn't matter what it looks like if it's working properly." Orri nodded at the skull. "Try to communicate with it."

He hadn't thought of that, maybe Orri's suggestion came from Noor. He hoped it was right. It had to be right. His mind reached out to the skull. "Are you there?"

A loud sound like rocks grinding together filled his head.

"Can you hear me?"

The sound came again, and Adam knew the skull was trying and failing to talk to him. The pieces talked to him, and now because of what he'd done this chunk of glass couldn't do what it needed to. A sick feeling filled his stomach. If the skull couldn't communicate with him, it couldn't join with the hand and the keystone. The three crystals needed to work together to move Atlantis to safety. The ancient city was doomed.

Orri watched him. "Can you talk to it?"

Adam shook his head. The weight of his actions pressed down on him. He couldn't try again, what if he screwed up even more? Sweat flowed down his back.

"Can you try to fix it again?" Tya asked.

"I don't want to cause more damage." Adam pinched his lips together.

Tya nodded, the other two looked at him and said nothing.

He had to find another solution. Last time the keystone was missing, and they couldn't move Atlantis. Caileen's father had discovered the Great Crystal. They had used the crystal to protect Atlantis. Could they use the Great Crystal again?

Adam knew this was an act of desperation, but he didn't know what else to do. "Do you remember where the Great Crystal is?"

"Yes." Caileen narrowed her eyes. "Why?"

"I think we need to go there, maybe we can find something to help us save Atlantis."

"Adam, we can't use the Great Crystal again," said Orri.

"We're not using it again! We're making sure it is still protecting Atlantis and maybe boost its power, so we have more time." They had to listen to him.

"No, that isn't the solution," Orri's voice was deep like Noor's.

Although Adam didn't want to admit it, he knew Orri was right. There had to be something he was missing. What was different from last time he came to Atlantis? His thoughts skipped through all that had happened since he got here, and then he had the answer. Time... time had changed, it had looped. If they could figure out why the time loops were happening, maybe he could go back in time and find the thirteenth skull in one piece. "What causes the time loops?

"When the black holes started, Raine, Tya, and I researched what could cause them," said Caileen. "We know the black holes are a result from a rift in the space time continuum, and our research has confirmed Raine's theory that black holes happen because someone goes from Atlantis to Earth using a portal."

Caileen fixed her gaze on him. "We also learned that time loops happen because someone travels across inter-dimensional lines without using a portal."

He had caused the last time loop.

"Is that what you did?" Caileen asked.

"Yes." Adam's voice wavered.

"You didn't know that. This isn't your fault." Tya placed her hand on this shoulder.

I wish I could say that was true, thought Adam. Everyone had done things they shouldn't, probably him most of all, but regret wasn't going to solve their problem. He looked at Caileen. "How do time loops work?"

"When you create a time loop, your specific actions generate a new timeline," Caileen stated. "We don't know if you erase the old timeline, or it continues to exist in a parallel universe."

"How many changes are caused by a new timeline?" Adam's voice was sharp.

"I know it frustrates you, but we are just telling you what we discovered," Caileen said softly, as if she comforted a small child. "The new timeline isn't about changes in comparison to the old timeline, the new timeline is a new reality, with new opportunities."

Adam didn't need the indulgent tone, the same tone his older sister used when she thought he was being a baby. He ground his teeth together.

A deep crease formed between Orri's eyebrows. "Adam, what is going on?"

Adam shrugged. How could he explain his feelings about being unable to fix anything and not having enough information to find another answer? A position Atlantis had put him in before, only this time it seemed worse than ever.

"Adam," said Orri in his deeper Noor-like voice. "You are grasping at straws. Stop. Breathe. Reach inside yourself, find your strength, and use it. I know you will make the right decision."

Adam rolled his eyes but took a deep breath as Orri had told him to. His thoughts slowed down, and he realized his actions didn't account for all that had happened to Atlantis in the last few days. Someone else must be involved too. He drew another deep breath.

He'd seen Andros sneaking around in the library before the time loop. That event might not be in the new timeline but might be important. He told them about Andros in the library.

"While researching time rifts, we discovered someone on the council has been secretly researching them too, but they had covered their tracks, so we didn't know who it was," said Caileen.

"Horatio will know if Andros is in the library," said Tya. "I'll go ask him."

Tya returned quickly. "He's here."

"Let's check the Machu Picchu archives," Caileen suggested.

They found him sitting at a table littered with skulls.

Andros glared at Orri. "What are you doing here?"

"Why are you spending so much time in the library?" Orri's voice was dangerously quiet.

"That is none of your business!" Andros spoke the words with such force spit flew across the table.

"Then I will ask the question when council meets later today. Let's see if they think it is none of our business." Orri sounded very reasonable, but the statement caused Andros to gasp.

Adam watched Andros rub his skull pendant. In this timeline, he hadn't left his pendant behind. Could he use his pendant to cross dimensional lines without a portal?

"I have been researching Machu Picchu, such an interesting time in our history." Andros made the statement as if he chatted with friends.

"Why would that be?" Orri continued with the same tone.

"I... well, I..."

Caileen smiled. "We've looked into the ninth dimension. It is fascinating, don't you think?"

"Ah yes, only a fellow researcher can understand." Andros tucked his long hair behind his ear.

"Machu Picchu is interesting place. Have you been there?" asked Orri.

Adam watched Orri and thought of a cat playing with a mouse. He realized they had done all the things they believed Andros was guilty of. Were they better than him?

"Of course not!" Andros sat up straight in his chair. "I would never put Atlantis in danger."

"But you have been to Earth." Orri's lips formed a straight line.

"No." Andros shook his head.

"Do you want to answer the question again?" Orri's voice was dangerously quiet.

Andros shook his head again. Then his face turned deep red. He grabbed his throat and made gurgling noises.

Orri held his fists close to his side. Adam noticed Orri's fingers tighten and Andros's movements became more agitated.

A line of sweat formed on Adam's back. This dangerous version of Orri reminded him of the old Orri.

Lines formed on Caileen's forehead. "Orri, please stop."

Andros pulled the neck of his tunic away from his throat and drew a shaky breath.

"Answer me!" Orri growled through clenched teeth.

"Yes. Yes. I have traveled to Earth." His eyes flicked back and forth between Orri and Caileen.

"Where?"

"Machu Picchu…" Andros clutched his throat.

Adam could see Orri struggled to control his emotions. "Take it easy."

"Let me handle this." Orri didn't take his eyes of Andros, but his hands relaxed enough for Andros to draw another breath. "Why?" Orri questioned.

"I researched Machu Picchu in the ninth dimension to duplicate those conditions in Mexico. I wanted to save Atlantis, but it is not working."

"What else are you not telling me?"

"Nothing. I swear!"

Orri leaned over and grabbed a fistful of Andros's tunic, pulling him up to standing. "Tell me!"

"Your mother is in an alternate dimension in Machu Picchu." Andros sobbed.

"Is she alive?"

"Yes! Please believe me! She is alive, and I need to go back there to protect her."

"Let me worry about that. You are not going anywhere."

Chapter Thirty-Nine

Orri clenched his fists to control his need to punch Andros. His mother saw the best in everyone, and Andros used that to his advantage. Saving Atlantis would have made her so happy it blinded her to everything else.

Just before his mother disappeared Orri knew she had changed. She smiled less, hugged less, and listened less. He thought she was angry with him, and he had blamed himself. Why didn't he see what was really happening? He must save her now, but first they had to save Atlantis.

Orri gripped Andros by the arm. "Adam, take hold of his other arm. Link your energy with his."

Adam looked at him with his eyebrows drawn together.

"If he attempts molecular transformation, we need to pull him back into his body." Orri tightened his fist on Andros' bicep enough to make him wince. "Don't be afraid to hurt him."

Adam nodded, although his frown didn't go away.

Orri didn't care what Adam thought. This man hadn't taken his mother from him. "We're taking him to Raine's lab."

Caileen watched him with wide eyes. "Tya and I will do some research on Mexico."

"Thanks," he replied.

A short time later, Orri opened the thick metal door to the lab without knocking. Raine glanced up and his eyes narrowed. He stepped around the table littered with skulls of all sizes, jars of murky liquids, and an odd assortment of small tools. "What is going on?"

Orri dragged Andros closer to Raine and Adam stepped back. "He kidnapped my mother and is probably responsible for the black holes."

"Why, Andros?" Raine's blue eyes had an unyielding gleam.

"It's not true! He is making it up. Let me go."

"Orri, could you pull that chair over here?" Raine nodded at a chair beside the table he had been working on. Gesturing to Andros he said, "Please, sit down."

Andros pulled his arm out of Orri's grip and settled on the chair.

Raine grabbed another chair and sat facing Andros. "Since Noor died Horatio has been reporting the activities in the library to me. I know you have been spending a lot of time in the library for the last two light cycles." Raine leaned forward. "What are you doing?"

"You do not understand..."

"If you can't tell me what you are doing, I'm inclined to believe Orri."

Orri's shoulders relaxed. Raine supported him.

"Someone had to do something." Andros's lip curled up. "That old fool Noor did not know what he was doing. I will be the one to rescue Atlantis."

Raine stood up and grabbed the front of Andros' tunic "That old fool was my friend." Raine's standing height matched Andros sitting in the chair, but the slow way he spoke left no doubt he would do whatever it took to protect Atlantis. "I can hold him in the lab. He is not going anywhere." Raine stepped back from the chair. A golden rope made several loops around Andros's wrists and the ends of the rope tied themselves into a tight knot.

"I will call a council meeting in the morning and we can decide his fate then." Raine turned to Orri. "I am surprised you left him in such good shape."

"I considered hitting him, but..." Orri shrugged. "I knew he would say I coerced him into confessing, and I didn't want that."

"Noor would be proud of you."

Orri could feel his cheeks getting warm.

Noor's voice inside his head spoke, "I am proud of you."

Noor's words added to the warmth.

In the hallway outside the lab Orri said, "I'm going to our room." He glanced at Adam. "Are you coming?"

"I'll meet you back there, I have to check out something first."

Orri grabbed Adam's arm. "I'll come with you. Where are we going?"

"To the Skull Room," Adam answered. "We can ask Noor to fix the thirteenth skull. It is his skull."

Once inside the Skull Room, Orri pulled out a chair next to his large blue crystal skull on the table. He nodded at the empty chair next to the thirteenth skull.

Adam sat down and remembered the conversations he had sitting across from Noor. His grandfather had always given him good advice. Would Orri do that now because Noor was inside him?

"You were brought to here to save Atlantis. We can't save her without the thirteenth skull. That means you have to make the skull whole." Orri's voice was gentle and wise.

Destiny still surrounded him in Atlantis. Adam no longer had the need to fight against it. "Do you ever wonder why things turn out the way they do?"

The corner of Orri's mouth lifted and his eyes lightened to a soft grey. "Maybe we meet our destiny on the route we took to avoid it."

"You sound like Noor." Adam shook his head. He must save the skull and save Atlantis, and once he did that Atlantis would send him home. "I know I can't stay here, but will I be able to come back later?"

"Haven't your experiences taught you anything? The consequences of our actions are complicated, predicting the future is a very hard to do."

His eyes probed Orri's. "I believe my time here isn't done."

"We will have to see what the future holds for you."

Orri's tone made it very clear that no matter how their friendship had improved, Atlantis would always be his priority.

Orri continued, "I know you love Atlantis, and I trust you would not knowingly put her in danger."

Adam stared at the older boy, and realized he trusted Orri the same way he had trusted Noor. They had both changed since he came back, and Noor's death had pushed them even closer together. Changing relationships, death, and trust had moved them to this place.

Orri gazed back at him without saying a word.

Adam smiled. "When did you get so smart?"

"I had a little help."

Not as much as you think you did. Adam could tell by the smile on Orri's face that Noor's words flowed into both their minds. Even though Noor was inside Orri, Adam realized he still had a connection to his grandfather.

"I could use some help fixing the thirteenth skull," said Adam.

"You must look at making the skull whole from a human perspective." Adam knew Noor's voice was in both their minds.

Orri's forehead wrinkled. "I don't know what that means."

Adam examined the fracture splitting the thirteenth skull's face and noticed the wound wasn't deep. If the skull had been human, they could stitch the injury closed. The tension in Adam's body slipped away. "He means the skull isn't just a crystal, it's more than that. We can't just fix it. We must heal it."

Orri smiled. "When did you get so smart?"

Adam laughed at his question coming back at him. "Let's see if I'm smart enough to heal the skull." He grounded himself to the floor beneath his feet and placed his hands on either side of the skull's face. A powerful force filled his body, and he concentrated the flow into his skull pendant. Breathing out, he sent the power into the thirteenth skull. The sides of the crack running through the skull's face moved closer together, but a line still marred the face and the fissure on the top of the skull remained unchanged.

"Can you hear me?" Adam asked the skull.

"Yes."

Adam's hands trembled. The skull could talk to him. That was good, but why had part of the crack not healed. "What did I do wrong?"

The skull spoke again. "The power together must be there."

Orri moved to stand next to him. "I don't think you did anything wrong."

His gaze flicked to Orri's face. He'd forgotten Orri with Noor inside him would be connected to the thirteenth skull too.

Orri placed his hands on top of Adam's and sent a gust of energy through him. Adam gathered his energy again and connected it with Orri's.

His body filled up again. He took a deep breath preparing to send the energy into the skull. A third force joined them. Adam knew it was Noor. When he breathed out, rainbows shot out of his fingertips filling the skull with light. When to glow faded, the thirteenth skull sat whole and unmarred on the table.

Adam dropped into the chair.

A wide grin split Orri's face. "You did it!"

"No." Adam shook his head. "We did it."

"Without you we would not have been able to heal the skull. You alone drew our energies together," Noor added.

"Noor's right," said Orri. "That is why you were brought back to Atlantis."

"The power together must be there," the skull repeated.

Adam leaned forward with his elbows on his knees. He should be happy, he'd saved Atlantis, but that meant he had to go home because he would die if he stayed here.

He wouldn't see Orri, Tya, or Caileen again. He wouldn't be able to talk to Noor. His energy skills would stay in Atlantis when he got home.

Adam missed his Mom and Dad, his friends, and even his sisters. He loved his life on Earth.

His chest tightened. He couldn't expect to have everything he wanted.

"Are you okay?" Orri asked.

Adam nodded and pushed himself to his feet. "Now that the skull's fixed we need to move Atlantis to safety."

Orri placed a hand on his shoulder. "I know it isn't easy for you. Is there anything you want to talk about?"

"No. I know what needs to be done."

"That is true, but it doesn't mean you have fully healed too."

Something tugged at Adam's heart. "When I left Atlantis last time, I felt used and abandoned. That isn't true, but it's the way I felt. What if I feel that way this time?"

"Most people could not understand themselves well enough to make a statement like that." Orri squeezed his shoulder. "You know who you are. If you feel the same this time, accept what you are feeling and know it will make you stronger." Orri pulled Adam into a hug. "You are braver than you believe."

Heat flushed Adam's cheeks, and he squirmed.

Orri continued to hold him in a tight embrace.

A soothing breeze flowed into him from Orri, and Adam knew he couldn't get out of this by fighting it. His shoulders relaxed and the tightness in his chest disappeared. He breathed in. Another grounded current from Noor surged into him and combined with his energy. His heart beat faster, his palms tingled, and his chest filled with warmth. The power of his energy would always be there even if his skills didn't work on Earth.

Again Atlantis had taught him some valuable lessons. He'd learned some things were beyond his control and he had to accept that. He'd also discovered he had the courage to change the things he could.

"I understand." Adam stepped back and smiled. "Let's go find the rest of the council. We must move Atlantis to safety."

Chapter Forty

They found Tya and Caileen were in their usual place in the library, and Orri told them the thirteenth skull was now healed.

Tya squealed and threw her arms around Adam's neck. Warmth bloomed in his cheeks as his arms circled her waist. He didn't like hugs, but this was different. Over Tya's shoulder Adam saw Orri kissing Caileen. He averted his eyes away from the private moment.

His heart was beating so fast he thought it would burst out of his chest. Tya moved closer, and the warmth spread through his whole body. She stood on her toes and her lips moved toward his cheek; he turned his head and their lips met. The softness of her mouth was the only thought in his brain. He closed his eyes.

Adam felt Tya move away from him. Opening his eyes, he stared into her wide blue eyes searching his face. When she moved back into his arms, all thoughts fled from his brain and his body took over.

Orri cleared his throat.

Tya pulled away from him again and Adam inwardly groaned at Orri's timing.

Orri cleared his throat again. Adam attempted to slow his breathing as he glared at the older boy. Then he saw Noor in the smile on Orri's face and his gaze dropped to the ground. He didn't know what was worse: Orri interrupting him or Noor watching him kiss a girl.

Orri asked the girls to retrieve the crystal hand from its hiding place in the library. He said they would get the keystone.

They all agreed to put the artifacts in the skull room and ask Horatio to keep them safe until the council meeting.

Adam followed Orri to the outer ring of Atlantis. When they turned into a small alley, Adam remembered Orri taking him to the temple after he had landed in Atlantis for the first time. The narrow houses and the twisting lanes no longer terrified him as they had that day.

Orri opened a door halfway down an alley. "Ya-ya, it's me," he shouted. "I brought someone to meet you."

A tiny woman with long grey hair flowing down her back and grey eyes set in a wrinkled face almost ran toward them. Orri had to take a step backward when she launched herself into his arms. "Ya-ya, it hasn't been that long since I was here." Orri chuckled.

She stepped back and gazed up at him. The smile on her face made Adam smile too.

Without saying a word, she turned and pulled Adam into her arms. The healing energy she sent into his chest pushed his worries away. Adam laughed and hugged her back.

Orri smiled. "Adam, this is my grandmother. Ya-ya, this is Adam."

"Orri has talked about you, and I feel I already know you." She shooed them down the narrow hallway in front of her. They entered a room with a stone table. The single leg under the middle of the table had lions' paws carved on it.

"Sit," Ya-ya ordered. "I have buns I baked this morning." A plate of buns sat on the table.

"Buns?" Adam had no idea there was real food in Atlantis.

"All you have been feeding him is pancha?" The tiny woman stood with her hands on her hips and one eyebrow raised at Orri.

Adam had seen Orri with the same look on his face.

Orri shrugged. "We've been busy, and we can't stay."

Ya-ya wrapped up two buns for each of them in a square of cloth, then handed the packages to the boys.

Adam couldn't wait. He took a big bite of the bun covered in honey. The soft flavorful morsel almost melted in his mouth. "These are so good," he said with his mouth full of bun. When he grabbed another sweet roll Ya-ya grinned.

"Now that you know where I live you can drop by for real food anytime."

Adam nodded, his mouth too stuffed to speak.

"I'm sorry. We don't have time for a visit," said Orri. "We need the keystone."

Adam expected an argument about not visiting, but she nodded before disappearing through a doorway. A moment later she returned and gently set the ruby stone on the table.

A warm glow filled the oval gem before it went dark, like it thanked Ya-ya for protecting it.

Orri reached out and clasped the old woman's hand. "One more thing, would you consider being on the council again?"

"Is the question coming from my grandson or from a council member?"

"Both." Orri let go of her hand. "But I wouldn't ask unless I thought the majority of the council would agree to it."

"When you have the agreement of the council then I will come back."

Orri hugged her. "Thank you."

"No matter what I will always love you."

"And I you," Orri replied before sliding the keystone into his pocket and walking back down the hallway.

Adam's chest tightened as he thought about his parents. He knew what it felt like to have unconditional love.

Ya-ya turned and hugged him. When she released him, Adam looked down at her. "Thank you for the buns."

Ya-ya smiled. "Anytime."

Adam followed Orri to the door. He glanced over his shoulder. He could see tears running down Ya-ya's face as she smiled. His chest tightened again.

The council assembled at the round table in the council room. When everyone sat down, Orri stood up and raised his hand for silence. This time the muttering stopped.

"You notice that Andros isn't with us. He will be here soon." Orri spoke in a strong, composed voice. "Please listen to what

Adam has to tell you before you ask questions." Orri inclined his head in Adam's direction and sat down.

Thuan leaned back in his chair and crossed his arms, Vannen set his elbows on the table and clasped his hands in front of his mouth, and all eyes around the table focused on Adam.

He stood and hoped he could relate his story so the council would listen to him. He told them about retrieving the thirteenth skull stolen by Adrien Zador, and about the skull getting broken. Gasps and mutters circled the table as butterflies fluttered in Adam's stomach. He glanced at Orri and the older boy nodded for him to continue.

Then he spoke about fixing the thirteenth skull after he returned to Atlantis. Alima, Tya, and Caileen smiled. Madhuri clapped and Raine joined her. Thuan, Vannen, Crosten, and Rute sat huddled with their heads close together.

Adam watched the non-believers and slipped his shaking hands into his pockets. He explained about the time loop he caused when he returned to Atlantis.

The room filled with noise because everyone talking at once.

"Noor has returned to us," Madhuri lifted her arms and stared at the blue sky showing through the opening in the roof.

"You are making that up, you just arrived," Thuan yelled as a vein pulsed on the side of his neck.

"Do we have any proof this has happened?" Crosten stared at Orri.

"That is a good point, Crosten," said Rute.

Raine stood up. "What the boy said is true. He came here to save Atlantis. That he is here is the only proof we need."

Adam's cheeks were warm as his eyes scanned the room. "How could I make up something that crazy?" He ran his hand through his hair. He didn't know how he could explain it any better so the council would understand.

"We need order to discuss this properly," Orri stated in a voice loud enough to cut through the uproar. He knew what it was like to have the council angry at your actions.

Thuan glared at Orri. "Who do you think you are telling people what to do?"

"I am trying to keep the meeting on track," Orri said with a firm tone.

"Maybe you are in cahoots with Earth boy." Thuan stood up and thrust his chest out.

"Considering you believe Adam just got here, I don't know how I'm in cahoots with him."

"Maybe you have been secretly meeting with him."

"You believe Adam has been here for more than two light cycles?" Orri had to stop a smile from appearing on his face. Thuan's face was so red Orri thought he might have a heart attack.

"That is not what I said!" He dropped onto his chair and continued to scowl at Orri.

Orri turned his gaze to Raine. He knew the scientist would be the next to offer his opinion.

"What has happened today only proves we should not be relying on prophecies to guide us. If they were of any use, we would have known about the rifts in time," said Raine, unaware of how predictable he was being.

Raine's statement started a new wave of comments around the table.

"The prophecies are essential."

"Adam causes problems every time he comes here, this time he has caused time to rip apart. What next?"

"I say we get rid of the prophecies and send Earth boy back to where he came from."

Orri rose to his feet. He nodded at Raine and the scientist left the council room. The comments continued around the table.

"If we send Adam away, we cannot move Atlantis."

"We must address our problems..."

"Silence!" Orri's deep voice echoed in the space. All eyes turned to him. "Now that I have your attention..."

"Use your control wisely," Noor's thought cautioned him.

"The prophecies have come true. The first prophecy 'The trio's power shall not be' is correct because it took four of us,

Adam, Tya, Caileen, and myself, to discover how to save Atlantis. The second prophecy states 'Saving Atlantis they will share' is also true because all of us have contributed to the knowledge we now have."

Raine came back into the council room with Andros. Raine pushed him onto the empty chair and the golden rope binding his wrists became visible. Andros hung his head, so his long, dark hair shielded his face.

Thuan pounded his fist on the table. "Why is Andros tied up? We should never treat a member of the council this way!"

"The golden rope is necessary," said Raine in a tone that showed Thuan should know this. "Andros has said he will try to escape."

"You never trusted Andros. This is your way of stopping him from being on this council."

Orri stared at Thuan. "He has been attempting to create a parallel dimension for Atlantis in Chichen Itza, Mexico, and he kidnapped my mother to take advantage of her skills."

Andros lifted his head and glared at Orri. "You will never find your mother without my help."

Orri turned his eyes away from Andros. He did want to find his mother, but first they had to save Atlantis. "I call a vote to suspend Andros's talents."

All the skull pendants at the table lit up except for Thuan's. Raine yanked Andros to his feet and pulled him over to the entrance of the round room. In the small space away from the stone table the council formed a circle around Andros. They linked hands, and Orri guided them to focus their energy on the man in the circle's center.

The room was quiet except for Andros's ragged breath. Then his body twisted and twitched as if pulled by invisible strings. His scream filled the chamber, and he slumped to the floor like a limp rag doll. The chain on his pendant snapped, and the tiny skull rolling across the stones made the only sound in the chamber.

He opened his eyes and gazed around. "Where am I? What happened?"

"You lost consciousness," said Alima as she helped him to sit up.

Orri swallowed the lump forming in his throat. Andros had been suspended, and that meant he might never find his mother.

"The sacrifices of a leader are never easy, but I am sure we will find your mother," Noor comforted.

A band tightened around Orri's chest. "I am not a leader," he thought. Noor didn't respond.

Alima asked Thuan and Vannen to assist Andros to the infirmary and the rest of the council took their seats around the table again.

"Suspending talents should be gentle," Madhuri's wide eyes seem puzzled.

Orri resisted an urge to shake his head. Madhuri was in a constant state of confusion. "How did she make it onto the council?" He thought and Noor chuckled.

"I have never seen a suspension cause so much pain," stated Rute. "Did we make a mistake?"

"We were forced into deciding to suspend Andros's talents." Crosten shook his head causing his light red hair to sway and pointed at Orri.

Orri leaned forward. "I only called for the vote. The decisions were yours alone."

Thuan and Vannen returned to their seats.

"The only reason the suspension hurt Andros was because he was unrepentant and resisted it," said Raine. "There are too many conflicts within the council. A divided council is not a strong council. We must come together and elect a new leader."

"We need two more council members before someone can be nominated," said Orri.

Chapter Forty-One

Orri took a deep breath. "Many of you have served on council a long time, and I would like to nominate a previous council member, Yirseva. She will replace Andros."

"She is your grandmother," said Vannen. "Wouldn't that be a conflict of interest?"

Adam blinked and his eyes widened.

Orri almost smiled. Adam only knew his grandmother as Ya-ya.

"Relatives and even spouses have served together on the council. I think Yirseva would make an excellent addition." Raine nodded at Orri.

"I have known Yirseva my whole life, her wisdom would be a great asset." Caileen smiled at Orri.

Tya nodded.

"Orri is building a council filled with his friends and family." Croston's normally calm voice sounded angry. "I heard that Yirseva's energy skills were fading."

Noor's supporters were not his supporters. Orri leaned back in his chair.

"Grief affects all of us. Yirseva has healed since her daughter's disappearance and would make an excellent addition to the council," said Alima.

His chest ached at the mention of his mother. Orri shifted in his chair, his mother's disappearance had touched many people in the small community.

Rute stood up. "I vote for Yirseva to return to council."

The only skulls to remain dark were Croston's and Thuan's.

"Yirseva has been approved to take a seat on the council," said Orri.

"I would like to nominate Slonnech..." said Raine.

Orri had to stop his mouth from falling open. Slonnech played on his popollama team. He had amazing skills on the field, but did he have energy skills?

We need younger blood, and he would do well on council. Noor's thought was clear in Orri's mind.

Orri pressed his lips together and considered Noor's advice. I hope you're right, he answered silently.

Crosten lowered his eyebrows and stared at Raine. "Who is that?"

"You cannot pick random people." Thuan shook his head. "What is this council coming to?"

"If you would let me finish, I will tell you." Raine's tone was more reasonable than Orri was used to. Raine continued, "Noor saw the boy playing popollama and recognized his energy skills. Noor trained him to take a place on council when the time came. That time is now. The boy has all the skills required to be a part of the council."

"Do we have any other choices for the council?" asked Caileen.

Orri watched everyone seated around the table. One corner of Tya's mouth lifted, and Orri recognized Caileen had asked the question because she knew the answer. Alima, Rute, and Vannen shook their heads. The rest of the council offered nothing.

"I trust Noor's judgment, and I vote for Slonnech to join the council," stated Orri.

When all the skull pendants lit up, Orri let out a slow breath.

"Raine, can you bring Slonnech here?" Orri asked.

Raine nodded and left the council room.

Orri turned to Alima. "Can you bring Yirseva?"

"Don't you want to tell her?" Alima asked.

"I have already talked to her. Your visit will not be a surprise."

Alima left the chamber.

Orri stood up. "We can take a small break and return in one time segment."

✧✧✧

Orri sat at the council table and watched everyone return and take their places. Slonnech and Yirseva sat on either side of Raine. He had never watched the council assemble before, but it seemed to be a natural thing to do.

Just as Orri was about to resume the meeting Alima stood up. "I propose that Orri, son of Sky, be the leader of the council."

Birds beat their wings inside Orri's stomach. Alima had always supported him but this was too much.

"You are ready to become a leader."

Noor's statement wasn't helping either.

"You are not alone. You have support," he continued.

The fluttering in Orri's stomach disagreed.

"Orri is young, and although Noor mentored him, he is not ready to assume the responsibilities." Crosten's reasonable statement gained nods around the table.

"Without Orri's leadership we wouldn't have the crystal artifacts to move Atlantis to safety." Caileen smiled at him.

"He only listens to opinions that agree with him."

Orri wasn't surprised at Thuan's statement or Vannen nodding.

"We still have a leader." Madhuri raised her arms and stared at the opening in the roof. "Noor is here."

No one will believe that nutty woman. Orri could hear the smile in Noor's thought.

Rute stood as she usually did to compensate for her short stature. "We shouldn't be too hasty to elect a new leader. If our history is anything to go by, our leader guides the council for a very long time."

Sweat ran down Orri's back at the thought of that.

"We need a leader to join our energies and move Atlantis to safety." Raine nodded at Orri.

The room went quiet.

"If there is no further discussion, I call a vote," said Raine.

Thuan, Vannen, and Crosten all had dark crystal pendants. Next was Madhuri and her skull remained dark too. Adam,

Caileen, Tya, and Alima lit their skulls in favor of the vote. Slonnech stared at the table and did nothing.

Orri's heart skipped a beat. The vote was against him becoming the leader.

Hold your head up. Atlantis will be safe when you become the leader, Noor coached.

Orri raised his head to see Rute, Raine, Yirseva's skulls glowing. He wanted to cheer, run around the table hugging his supporters, and show the doubters what a great leader he would be.

He didn't need Noor cautioning him to be careful to know he couldn't do that. He lifted his chin. "The council has decided, and I accept your decision. I will do my best to lead you wisely."

His first decision as leader might divide the council, but that wasn't going to stop him. Orri rose to his feet. "We have gathered in private to move Atlantis many times. It is time to have all the people in our city witness this new start for Atlantis." He rolled his shoulders back. "We will gather at the Plaza of Athena."

Raine stood up and smiled. "It has been a long time since we shared these moments. I agree with Orri."

One by one the council stood and added their agreement to Raine's. Most smiled, only Thuan and Madhuri agreed with solemn faces.

As the council members left the chamber, Orri gestured for Caileen and Tya to stay.

Alima stopped in front of him. "Noor knew you were ready for this. If you believe in yourself the people will too." Alima's eyes twinkled and the corners of her mouth lifted. She laid her hand on his arm, and a warm wave of support flowed into his arm and throughout his body.

Orri smiled down at her and squeezed her hand. A familiar feeling of appreciation filled his heart.

"Can you two bring the crystal hand with you?" Orri asked the two girls.

Chapter Forty-Two

Adam and Orri were striding down the main boulevard toward the plaza when Adam heard Tya yell, "Wait for us." He turned to see Tya and Caileen rushing to catch up with them. Tya carried the crystal hand. She hooked her free arm through his, and Caileen reached for Orri's hand.

"I'm glad we caught up to you," Tya said in a breathless voice. "I wanted to say goodbye before you left."

Tya's wide blue eyes gazed up at him and warmth spread through his body. "We don't need to say goodbye, I hope I can come back," said Adam.

"That's not what the archives in the library say."

"My time here isn't done." Adam didn't know how to explain it. If he had believed in destiny, he would say fate had told him to come back. "Do you ever have a feeling deep inside that doesn't make sense, but you know it's true?"

Tya closed her eyes and turned away. "I have, and I know one day I will find out what happened to my Nan."

Adam reached for her hand. "When I come back to Atlantis, we'll work on it together."

Tya squeezed his fingers. "I would like that."

They turned a corner and in front of them was the Plaza of Athena. Not the crumbling, broken plaza, but the plaza Adam remembered from his dream.

The tile patio had marble columns on all four sides, and in the center of the patio stood a waist-high, octagon shaped stone altar. The sides of the altar were covered with carvings of strange creatures. On the top sat the golden bowl filled with miniature skulls; this would be needed when Yirseva and Slonnech received their skull pendants. Circling the altar were twelve waist high pedestals. Adam hadn't seen them on his last visit to the plaza and wondered what they were for.

Alima stood by the altar with Raine, Yirseva, and Slonnech. The four of them joined the group, and Tya placed the crystal hand on the altar.

The rest of the council entered the square followed by hundreds of people. Each council member stood behind a pedestal. Adam followed Tya and Caileen to find his place in the circle.

Watching Orri standing at the altar reminded Adam of Noor. The new leader stood with his head held high and his gaze calmly watching the crowd. Adam recalled the angry teenager who met him at the gate when he first came to Atlantis, the responsible young man who helped him this time in Atlantis, and the friend he had discovered. His heart swelled as he watched Orri raise his hand.

When the crowd became quiet, he said, "I have been elected as the new leader of the council." The plaza filled with cheers and shouts of support. Orri smiled and let them continue for a minute before he raised his hand again. "I hope I will lead our beautiful city into peaceful and prosperous times." The crowd cheered again.

"Thank you!" Orri shouted and the noise subsided. "Today you will witness the forming of our new council and the relocation of Atlantis."

Orri moved to the side to give the people assembled in the square a view of the altar. He gestured for his grandmother to step forward. The grin on Orri's face showed how proud he was to invite Ya-ya back to the council. "Yirseva, please place your hand in the bowl." The tiny woman with grey hair flowing to her waist had to stand on her toes to reach into the bowl. A pink skull glowed. She took it out of the bowl and handed it to Orri.

He closed his fingers over the crystal and stared at his hand for a long moment before opening his fist again.

Noor had always made this look easy. Adam imagined Orri worried about living up to Noor's standard.

When the small skull hung from a silver chain, Orri smiled and put it over Ya-ya's head. She took her place beside Raine.

Next, Orri asked Slonnech to pick a skull. The tall boy pulled a dark green skull from the bowl. Orri picked up the small crystal and with a turn of his wrist it dangled from a silver chain. Orri placed the chain around Slonnech's neck and gestured for him to take the last open pedestal beside Adam.

Orri fixed his gaze on the golden bowl and it disappeared, leaving the crystal hand alone on the altar.

"Now we require the council's skulls." As soon as Orri finished speaking, twelve unique skulls materialized on the twelve pedestals.

Adam watched Slonnech reach a shaking hand to the cheek of his large, mottled orange skull. His tentative smile bloomed into a grin.

Yirseva stared at large blue crystal skull in front of her. It reminded Adam of Orri's old skull.

He stroked his teal blue skull, and warm energy tingled as it spread through his body. The connection hadn't changed. His heart swelled, and he took a deep breath. He knew he was born to take his place in this wondrous land. Adam removed his hand from the skull and heaviness replaced lightness. He couldn't stay here.

Adam heard Orri call his name. Looking up, he saw the thirteenth skull sitting on the altar in front of Orri.

"Adam, please join us at the altar." Orri repeated. Tya stood beside Orri and Adam took his place next to them. Tya moved the crystal hand to the middle of the altar, and Orri lifted his skull, the thirteenth skull, into place. It wriggled until it found a comfortable place on the hand. Orri pulled the keystone out of his pocket and gave it to Adam.

Adam watched the glow in the keystone deepen as he held it in his hand. He knew nothing would ever be the same after this. He bent down to find the slot for the keystone. He hesitated for a moment, feeling powerless to change the present or the future, then he slowly slid the keystone into place. Rainbows radiated from the crystals and a collective sigh moved through the crowd. He and Tya took their places in the circle.

The thirteen held hands in a ring around the altar. A small spark of light shone in each of the thirteen skulls. The embers in the skulls grew until a soft radiance embraced the plaza. The crowd and the council watched silently as the glow deepened. Adam looked around the circle feeling the energy grow within his body.

"The power has begun." The deep voice of the thirteenth skull resonated around the plaza.

"And with the power we will be," said Orri.

Adam saw Andros run down the street but didn't want to disturb the quietness. The energy built to a hurricane force as winds whipped through the plaza. Adam saw the temple on the hill crumble to the ground and a black hole opened underneath it.

They held hands and ignored the horror unfolding around them. An electric pulse of energy surged into Adam's hands from the people on either side of him.

The city shimmered and disappeared.

Chapter Forty-Three

Adam stared up at the Temple of Dendur in New York City's Metropolitan Museum of Art. His classmates chatted in groups while they waited for the tour to start.

He knew he'd lived these moments before. A strange feeling trickled through his mind. What would happen if he walked through the portal? Could he return to Atlantis?

He rubbed his hand down the leg of his blue jeans and felt a lump in his pocket. He reached in and pulled out the eye of Nethuns. How did that get here? Adam wondered. Rubbing his thumb across the golden orb he felt nothing. No warmth, no energy. He shoved it back into his pocket. It had given him energy when he needed it, and it had been with him through time loops and interdimensional travel, but something told him it wouldn't be able to help anymore.

Adam remembered seeing Andros running down the street near the canal, and then remembered the Temple of Nethuns crumbling to the ground before it was sucked into a black hole. The empty feeling in his chest told him Atlantis was gone. He stared at the massive pillars on either side of the doorway in the museum. Now a doorway to nowhere. He swallowed against the lump forming in his throat.

"Hey Adam, are you coming?"

He nodded at Shawn and trailed after the rest of his class. They entered another room and he saw James, his biological father, giving the green jade knife to a short man with round glasses. His actions must have changed the timeline on Earth as well. Adam pulled his hoodie over his head and turned his face away as he walked past them. He didn't want to take the risk of James seeing him.

They moved on to a room filled with South American artifacts. A golden face carved into a round platter reminded him of the lady in the burning door. Adam reached up to rub his chest and felt a crystal hanging on a chain underneath his shirt. His skull pendant.

Why did he still have his crystal skull? That hadn't happened last time. Was he supposed to use the skull?

Adam stepped away from his classmates. He gripped the tiny crystal, centered the energy in his body, and directed it into the pendant. The skull held the energy for a moment, but not long enough to do anything.

The empty feeling returned. He had witnessed Atlantis being pulled into a black hole. Nothing could survive that. "Why?" he whispered. "Why can't I save Atlantis?

The skull on his chest sent an answer to his mind. You will save Atlantis one day.

He wasn't sure he believed the little skull, but it didn't matter. He would always remember his time in Atlantis. The fabled city held a special place in his heart. It had taught him so much. He knew he couldn't always do things his way, and co-operation was important. Sometimes he needed help and that was okay too.

Adam's heart hurt when he thought about the friends and mentors he'd left behind and would probably never see again. But if his sacrifice moved Atlantis before the black hole sucked everything into it, then it was worth it.

Adam's his fingers brushed against the tiny skull on his chest.

You will save Atlantis one day, it repeated.

THANK YOU FOR READING THIS BOOK

Without the support of readers like you, writers like me would not be able to write more books.

Buying books is the best way to support an author, but there are several other things you can do to help an author without spending any money:

1. Review the book on Amazon, Goodreads or anywhere the book is sold. Writing a review, especially if you have never written one, can be a difficult task. Most importantly, be honest. Then write a meaningful review, beyond "I loved it!" or "I didn't like it.", explain why the book caught your attention. If you are not sure how to phrase your comments look at other reviews for ideas.
2. Follow the author on social media.
3. Post about the book online.
4. Tell a friend (or 20) about the book. Don't lend them the book, tell them to buy it.
5. Ask your local library to add the book to their collection.

ABOUT THE AUTHOR

J.M. Dover loves using both sides of her brain. Her past careers as a social worker, a fashion designer and an accountant prove she can be both creative and logical—sometimes strangely at the same time. Being a writer gives her a way where the two sides of her mind can play happily together.

She lives with her husband and requisite writers' pet (in this case, a loudly opinionated sheltie) in Calgary, Alberta.

Other Evil Alter Ego Press Books

The Atlantis Series by J.M. Dover

Finding Atlantis

The Fountain Series by Suzy Vadori

The Fountain

The West Woods

Mik Murdoch: Boy Superhero Series by Michell Plested

Mik Murdoch, Boy Superhero

Mik Murdoch: The Power Within

Mik Murdoch: Crisis of Conscience

Mik Murdoch: Identity Troubles

Scouts of the Apocalypse Series by Michell Plested

Scouts of the Apocalypse: Zombie Plague

Scouts of the Apocalypse: Zombie War

Scouts of the Apocalypse: Zombie Masters.

Anthologies

Dimensional Abscesses
(edited by Jeffrey Hite & Michell Plested)